Praise for the authors of

SHOTGUN GROOMS

SUSAN MALLERY

"Susan Mallery is warmth and wit personified.
Always a fabulous read."
—*New York Times* bestselling author Christina Dodd

"Ms. Mallery's unique writing style shines via vivid
characters, layered disharmony and plenty of spice."
—*Romantic Times Magazine*

MAUREEN CHILD

"Maureen Child is one of the foremost names
in Americana romance."
—*Romantic Times Magazine*

"…unique, endearing characters grab hold
of your heartstrings and never let go…"
—*Rendezvous*

* * *

Shotgun Grooms
Susan Mallery & Maureen Child
Harlequin Historical #575—September 2001

Join the fun
with

Susan Mallery
and
Maureen Child

as they bring you

SHOTGUN GROOMS

** an exciting Western historical featuring 2 stories in 1 **

Lucas and Jackson MacIntyre are forced to marry
in order to claim their inheritance!
But will these brothers find everlasting love?

SUSAN MALLERY

MAUREEN CHILD

SHOTGUN GROOMS

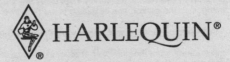

HARLEQUIN®

TORONTO • NEW YORK • LONDON
AMSTERDAM • PARIS • SYDNEY • HAMBURG
STOCKHOLM • ATHENS • TOKYO • MILAN • MADRID
PRAGUE • WARSAW • BUDAPEST • AUCKLAND

ISBN 0-373-29175-2

SHOTGUN GROOMS

Copyright © 2001 by Harlequin Books S.A.

The publisher acknowledges the copyright holders of the individual works as follows:

LUCAS'S CONVENIENT BRIDE
Copyright © 2001 by Susan Macias Redmond
JACKSON'S MAIL-ORDER BRIDE
Copyright © 2001 by Maureen Child

This edition published by arrangement with Harlequin Books S.A.

Visit us at www.eHarlequin.com

Printed in U.S.A.

CONTENTS

LUCAS'S CONVENIENT BRIDE

Susan Mallery

Please address questions and book requests to:
Harlequin Reader Service
U.S.: 3010 Walden Ave., P.O. Box 1325, Buffalo, NY 14269
Canadian: P.O. Box 609, Fort Erie, Ont. L2A 5X3

Chapter One

Defiance, Colorado, 1875

Emily Smythe was more than ready to dance with the devil—if only he weren't so large. Still, walking away now would be nigh on to shirking and she'd never once shirked in her life. She squared her thin shoulders, raised her chin and told herself that she had righteousness on her side. Righteousness and a plan. With the right plan, a person could take on the devil himself and win.

Ignoring the trembling of her limbs and the way her stomach seemed to be jumping around inside her, she pushed through the swinging doors of the Silver Slipper saloon and stepped into a smoky world.

She had a brief impression of a much larger crowd than she'd expected for a midweek afternoon. There were at least two dozen tables spread out around the main part of the room, nearly all of them occupied. On the far side of the saloon, men sat playing cards. Gambling, she thought with both distaste and shock. Gambling in the middle of the day. Who could imagine such a thing?

Her gaze drifted right and she saw the long, wide bar that stretched the length of the room. It was polished wood, nearly chest high and crowded with men. Behind the bar she saw mirrors, dozens of bottles of liquor and a big bear of man. Lucas MacIntyre, the devil himself.

Emily pursed her lips together in disapproval as she took in the tall, muscular man dressed in black trousers, a white shirt and fancy red vest. Lucas MacIntyre didn't wear a coat like a respectable man, but considering he operated a saloon, allowed gambling and sold spirits, she doubted the lack of formal attire would be noticed on his very long, very serious list of transgressions.

A voice in her head screamed at her to turn around and leave before anyone noticed her. She didn't belong here—she couldn't possibly do this. Yet she knew she didn't have a choice. Lucas MacIntyre was her only hope for success and she didn't allow herself to think of failure. She had right on her side. She was a hard worker and she had her plan. She would make him listen, then she would make him agree. All without giving in to the very real temptation to turn on her heel and run.

Emily raised her chin one more notch, sucked in a breath and made her way to the bar. She knew the exact moment that the men in the saloon noticed her presence. There was a heartbeat of excruciating silence followed by an explosion of voices. The crowd in front of the bar parted to allow her access. She marched directly forward, looking neither left nor right, until she could press her hands against the arm rail, then cleared her throat.

"Mr. MacIntyre, may I have a word with you?"

At the sound of her voice, the crowd grew quiet again. Lucas MacIntyre stood with his back to the room, polishing a freshly washed glass. In the time it took him to turn to look at her, she was able to surreptitiously glance about, noticing that while the smell of liquor and cigars was most unpleasant, the saloon was much tidier than she had imagined. The floor appeared to be freshly swept and the glasses were clean. Perhaps Mr. MacIntyre was a man with whom she could reason.

He turned slowly, first putting down the glass then taking the two steps to the bar. It was only when he reached the polished wood that he settled his gaze on her.

She knew the man by reputation but wasn't sure she'd ever actually seen him around town. Or if she had, she'd never really *looked* at him. He was tall and broad shouldered, which she already knew, but he was also handsome. Sinfully so. He had strong features with large, dark blue eyes and a full-lipped mouth topped by a silky brown moustache.

He looked her up and down, as if she was some kind of horse for sale, then he smiled.

"I'm going to guess you're lost, ma'am. Because you don't look like you're from Miss Cherry's and no other female would dare set foot in a saloon. Maybe you're looking for the Ladies Social Club. They meet on the first and third Wednesday of the month, over at the church."

Emily heard the sounds of male laughter. She felt her face grow hot and her limbs begin to tremble more. But she couldn't speak, nor could she move from her spot on the wood floor. It wasn't his words that kept her firmly in place; it was his smile.

Lucas MacIntyre's smile had transformed his face from just handsome to impossibly attractive. Tiny lines fanned out from the corners of his eyes and there was a hint of a dimple in both his cheeks. He looked teasing and irreverent at the same time. Emily knew she should be outraged and insulted, but all she could think was that she'd never seen a man smile quite like Mr. MacIntyre.

"I..." Her voice trailed off as she struggled to remember what she'd wanted to say. In all her twenty-six years she'd never been as affected by a man. Her heart was pounding so hard she was afraid it was going to jump right out of her chest.

"Mr. MacIntyre, I assure you I am not lost. I wish to speak with you for a moment."

Lucas gave her another smile, this one not quite so bright. "No offense, ma'am, but you don't look like the type to be bringing a man good news, so I'd rather say good-afternoon and suggest you go on your way." Then he turned and walked to the far end of the bar.

Emily practically sputtered. How rude! How ungentlemanly of him, although she shouldn't be surprised. Manners were a rare commodity in the West, as she'd learned in the nearly two years she'd been in Colorado. She was also used to being dismissed and ignored by men, although that unpleasant activity had begun long before she'd left Ohio. Emily was a realist. She knew she wasn't a pretty woman, nor was her appearance the kind to command attention or respect. She'd had to struggle to make herself heard more times than she liked to remember. Most of the time she no longer even bothered. But this was different. This was her future and her dream and she wasn't about to let this bear of a saloon owner upset her perfect plan.

"Mr. MacIntyre," she said in as loud a voice as she could manage, then headed for the far end of the bar.

The crowd was thicker there, and the men less likely to let her through. She found herself in the uncomfortable position of having to push between people when her polite "Excuse me" was ignored.

Conversation spilled over her. She ignored the swear-words, the calls of the gamblers on the far side of the room and the odor of too many unwashed bodies. Fortunately Mr. MacIntyre was tall enough that she could easily see him over the heads of his patrons. She moved steadily toward him, only to have him suddenly move back the way she'd come. She was forced to stop and turn herself.

"Excuse me," she said, trying to squeeze past two miners drinking beer.

Before she knew what was happening, they'd trapped her neatly between them, their heavy bodies pressing against hers. One of them put down his drink and grabbed both her arms.

"Not so fast, little lady," he said, his voice slurred from the alcohol. "Seems to me if you want to keep brushing against a man the way you are, you have to be ready to accept the consequences." The last word broke on a hiccup.

Emily turned her head from the horrible stench of his breath. "Unhand me, sir," she demanded, not exactly afraid but not comfortable, either. She didn't like the way the man's fingers seemed to be squeezing her arm, or his nearness, not to mention the closeness of his friend behind her.

"Don't you sound real uppity," the man said, his narrow eyes squinting at her. "What'd you think, Bill? She's got a mouth on her, which I ain't fond of with any woman. And she's skinny and ugly."

Emily gasped as a hand settled on that part of her she didn't even like to think the name of. That place where she sat. She tried to speak, but all that came out of her mouth was a high-pitched squeal.

"You know," the one named Bill said, "if we wait

until dark, we won't have to see her face anymore, and if we're drunk enough, we won't care that she's as bony as an old mule.''

Emily didn't have time to think or react. Suddenly a large hand settled on the shoulder of the man in front of her. The man looked startled, then he was flying through the air, landing on a table and crashing into the ground. She caught a glimpse of Mr. MacIntyre turning toward the one called Bill. That miner went sailing across the room, as well.

Emily couldn't catch her breath. She wasn't sure what to say as she started to thank her rescuer. But before she could speak, a different man threw a punch toward Mr. MacIntyre and the fight was on.

Fists flew, bodies tumbled, men grunted, yelled and cursed. And Emily was trapped in the middle of the fray. She told herself she needed to get out of the saloon as quickly as possible, but the swinging doors seemed so far away. She huddled close to the bar, trying to stay out of the way. But when a strange man reached for her, she reacted instinctively. She grabbed a bottle from the bar and crashed it over the man's head.

At that same instant, she saw a flash of movement. Something hard and horribly painful connected with her eye. She yelped in pain. Stars appeared in her head. She felt her lower limbs starting to give way when she suddenly recognized the man she'd assaulted with the bottle. Her last thought before the blackness reached up to grab her was that she'd accidentally cracked a bottle over the head of the local deputy.

Lucas didn't remember ever visiting a woman in jail. He wasn't sure why he was bothering now. Miss Emily Smythe—former schoolteacher and spinster—had gotten herself in plenty of trouble without any help from him. It wasn't his fault she'd hit Deputy Wilson over the head with a bottle of Lucas's most expensive Scotch. Hell, he wasn't even going to make her pay for the liquor. And he was sure that Wilson would get over his temper soon enough and release the woman from jail. So Lucas should just mind his own business and head back to the Silver Slipper.

Except he couldn't. He paced outside the sheriff's office that also housed Defiance's small jail and swore under his breath. So what if that skinny, pinched-mouth miss had wanted to speak with him? He didn't owe her his time. He doubted she could have looked more disapproving of him or his place of business. Like he'd thought before—he didn't owe her anything.

Lucas walked back and forth on the wooden plank sidewalk, hating himself for being curious about what she wanted and wishing he wasn't thinking what he was thinking. That she might just be the answer to his problem. Yes, he needed an answer and fast, but Emily Smythe? He couldn't really be considering *her* could he? He shuddered.

But time was passing quickly and he'd run out of options with last week's post. Grumbling under his breath, he pushed into the sheriff's office and asked to see the pinched-faced spinster.

Emily Smythe sat on the edge of the thin mattress in her jail cell. Her back was straight, her expression haughty. Even her black eye looked almost regal. She was the kind of woman who made a man feel he hadn't washed good enough and that he was going to put every foot wrong. She was cold enough to freeze off a man's privates. He shuddered again, wishing he could bring himself to ask one of Miss Cherry's lovelies to help him out. There he'd find a warm, willing woman with plenty of curves and the skill to keep a man purring long into the night.

At least the sheriff kept a clean jail, and it was nearly warm in the spring late afternoon. No doubt Wilson would see reason within an hour or so and let the lady go free, despite her unfortunate aim.

"Miss Smythe," he said, nodding his head.

He'd remembered to slip on a jacket before leaving the saloon, but he hadn't grabbed a hat. So when he reached up to tip it, he found his fingers gasping for air. He had to think quick and instead smoothed back his hair, as if he'd planned that gesture all along.

Emily regarded him with as much pleasure as she would an infestation in her flour. "Mr. MacIntyre. What are you doing here?"

Lucas cleared his throat. "Yes, well, ma'am, you mentioned wanting to talk to me."

"You weren't interested before."

He wasn't now, either, but he felt guilty. Why the hell couldn't he have lost his conscience when he'd lost his soul? He'd had more use for the former than the latter these past years.

"I was trying to be polite," he said. "I can see my effort is not welcome. Good day, Miss Smythe."

But before he could leave, she sprang to her feet and approached the bars. "No, wait." She grasped the metal with both hands and squared her shoulders. "I would very much like to speak with you, sir. I have a business proposition."

He was too startled to give her any reaction. In the space of time it took him to absorb her words and wonder if she really meant what she said, he noticed that she'd seemed to brace herself. As if she was expecting him to be angry…or perhaps laugh. There was pride in the haughty angle of her chin, but there was something else in her blue eyes. Apprehension? Fear? Embarrassment?

"What sort of business proposition?" he asked warily, thinking of only one way a woman could have business with a saloon. He doubted that was what someone as proper as Miss Smythe would have in mind.

She glanced left and then right, obviously aware of the men in the other cells unabashedly listening to their conversation. She leaned a little closer to the cell door and lowered her voice.

"I wish to speak with you about your saloon, Mr. MacIntyre. Or more precisely, the rooms upstairs."

"What about them?"

"I understand they are empty. I wish to change that." She cleared her throat. "I wish to use them to open a hotel."

Lucas didn't know what to say. There were plenty of empty rooms upstairs. In fact the Silver Slipper had been built to have a saloon on the ground floor and rooms to rent above, but he'd never wanted the trouble of running two businesses. The saloon was enough.

"Why?" he asked.

She sighed. "I believe a hotel will be successful. I'm a competent businesswoman—"

"You weren't much of a schoolteacher," he said.

She caught her breath and glared at him. She was a little thing, coming to his shoulder. But then he was tall, so most women were little things to him. She was as scrawny as a plucked chicken and she wore the ugliest gray dresses he'd ever seen. Her blond hair was a decent color and he'd noticed it turned nearly gold in the lamplight of the saloon, but she wore it all scraped back, with not a single curl to soften the effect.

"I was an excellent schoolteacher," she informed him in a voice sharp with that cold he'd been worried about before. "I taught those children more in the nearly eighteen months they were my students than they learned in the previous three years with the other teacher."

"But they left."

"The families returned to their homes in Maryland. That decision had nothing to do with my teaching skills." She removed her hands from the bars and pressed her fingertips together. "Unfortunately, those eight children were the only ones in town at the time, which left me without a position. I cannot wait for another family with school-age children to appear, which means I have to find other means of employment. A hotel is the perfect solution."

"Uh-huh."

Lucas eyed her doubtfully. He didn't know anything about Emily Smythe save that she'd once been the schoolteacher in town and that she hadn't been born out West. He would bet that her trip to Defiance had been her first journey west of the Mississippi. So why didn't she just go home?

"You don't have any family?" he asked.

"They have nothing to do with this."

So she did have relatives somewhere. Then why wouldn't she return to them? He doubted anyone as straitlaced as she could have done something to disgrace herself. Emily Smythe wasn't the type to cause a scandal.

"You're a teacher," he said. "What makes you think you know anything about keeping a bunch of miners, ranchers and who knows what kind of riffraff happy in bed?"

Color flared on her cheeks, but she didn't otherwise respond to his gibe.

"Mr. MacIntyre, I have traveled extensively along the Eastern Seaboard and abroad. I have stayed in exquisite hotels in dozens of cities. In addition, I have a head for figures and I'm not afraid of hard work. I know I can make the hotel a success. I also understand your reticence in allowing me to open my business above your saloon. Let me assure you that in addition to a modest rent, I would be willing to pay you a percentage of the profits."

"Generous," he muttered, taking a step back from her.

She wasn't ugly, he told himself, despite what the miners at his saloon had said earlier. She was a bit on the plain side, but she had big blue eyes he kind of liked. Her skin was pretty—all soft looking and smooth, with a hint of color at her cheeks. Her mouth was a tad pinched, but maybe if she didn't stand so stiff all the time, the rest of her would relax.

His gaze moved to her body, and what he saw there made him shake his head. She was skinny and didn't have even one decent curve. No breasts, no hips and he would bet a ten-dollar gold piece that she had bony knees. Lucas was more enamored with plump knees. He liked to kiss the crease in the back, then nibble around to the front, all the while listening to the lady giggle and feeling her squirm. Emily Smythe didn't strike him as the giggling, squirming type.

But she was a single woman, and that was what he needed right now.

"Stay right there," he said, then realized it was a stupid thing to say. Where was she going to go?

Ten minutes later he'd talked Wilson into springing

her. He led the proper Miss Smythe onto the sidewalk in front of the jail.

"Let's go talk in my office," he said. "It's around back of the saloon. We won't be disturbed there."

Excitement glinted in her blue eyes. "So you'll consider my proposition? How wonderful, Mr. MacIntyre. I'm sure you won't regret it for a minute. I've done the calculations and I expect the hotel to be turning a profit within the month."

He held up a hand to stop the flow of words, then led the way onto the muddy street.

It was spring in Defiance, which meant plenty of rain, flash floods and mud. Fortunately the Silver Slipper was only a couple of blocks away. The single horse and wagon in the street in the late afternoon was on the far side of the river of mud and they barely got splashed at all.

When they arrived at his saloon, he walked around to the rear of the building. The small door to his office was set under the stairs leading to the second floor that so interested her. Lucas wondered how crazy she was going to make him and how much he would regret what he was about to say. He thought about his current carefree existence and wished it could be different. But it couldn't. Damn Uncle Simon and his meddling.

He unlocked the door to his office and motioned for her to precede him. She did so, moving with a regal grace completely out of place in this mining town. Despite the fight and her time in jail, she looked as crisp and fresh as she had first thing that morning. Of course the black eye added a rakish touch to her otherwise perfect appearance. If only her gray dress weren't so ugly.

She paused in the center of the small room until he pulled out a chair for her. Then she settled stiffly on the wooden surface, her back as straight as it had been on that cot in jail. He wondered if she ever bent or relaxed. He had a feeling that if a man tried to have his way with her, she would snap in two, like a fragile twig.

"About the hotel," she said, as he came around to his chair behind the desk.

"Yeah, well, it's not that simple."

Despite owning a saloon, Lucas wasn't much of a drinking man. Still, he pulled a bottle of whiskey out of his bottom drawer and poured two fingers' worth into a glass on his desk. He ignored Miss Smythe's start of disapproval and downed the whole thing in one swallow. Heat burned to his belly, giving him a false sense of warmth and courage. He was an idiot. But he didn't have a choice. Uncle Simon had trapped him good and tight.

"I can show you my figures," she said, leaning toward him. "I have them in my room."

"I'm sure you're prepared to do things real proper like."

He leaned back in his chair and glanced around the small office, at the crates of liquor stacked in the corner and the barrels of ale. The bare wood walls weren't much, but they were his. He'd taken the Silver Slipper from a run-down place with a reputation for watered drinks and trouble to a successful, honest saloon. He ran clean tables, served decent liquor and never cheated anyone. If he lost the saloon, he lost the ranch. Without the ranch, he lost everything.

He returned his attention to Emily. She wasn't who he would have picked, but then he hadn't planned on this at all.

"I'll let you open your hotel," he began.

"Oh, Mr. MacIntyre, you won't be sorry," she assured him.

"You might be," he said dryly. "Because there are a couple of complications. You can open your hotel, if you cut me in for fifty percent of the profit. And if you agree to marry me, I won't even charge you rent."

Chapter Two

Emily stared at the man sitting in front of her and had the most unreasonable urge to cry. Since they'd left the sheriff's office, she'd allowed herself to hope that Lucas MacIntyre was going to listen to her plan, understand and let her open the hotel. She'd thought she'd convinced him of her abilities, her business sense and her sincerity.

She'd been wrong. He had no interest in her plan. Instead he was humiliating her for the humor it brought him. She was disappointed, hurt and determined that he would never know how her insides trembled and her throat felt all tight and sore.

"How interesting," she forced herself to say, keeping her voice low and even. "A proposal of marriage."

She wanted to stand and walk out, but she didn't yet have the strength. Was he doing this because she was a woman or because she was a plain woman?

Emily sighed. All her life she'd longed to be pretty, like other women. However the simple truth was that she was plain. Sometimes she wanted to scream out loud, proclaiming that her looks were not her fault. God had blessed her with many other fine qualities. She was intelligent, loyal, honest and caring. Why didn't people—men, mostly—care about that? Didn't they know that a pretty face aged with time, but that the heart and character of a person lasted forever?

Obviously not. She recalled what the miners in the saloon had said. How she was so skinny and unattractive, they couldn't possibly ravish her in the daylight. They would have to wait until it was dark. Probably they would have to be very drunk, as well.

Familiar pain filled her. The ache for a husband and children. She would never have either. She'd learned that lesson well over the years. Wishing for the impossible was a sign of weakness, and she'd always prided herself on being strong.

Remembering that, she stiffened her spine and drew in a deep breath. But before she could open her mouth, Lucas spoke.

"I don't know what you're thinking," he said, leaning toward her and resting his hands on the desk in front of him. "But I doubt it reflects well on me."

She rose to her feet. "I'm sorry to have taken up your time, sir. I can see I misjudged you and the situation completely. I apologize for that."

"Hold on there." He stood and moved toward her. "What's got your tail feathers in a twist?"

She blinked at the vulgarity of the question, then raised her chin. "I hadn't thought of you as a cruel man. I have provided you with an afternoon's entertainment. That should be enough. If you'll excuse me?"

"What are you talking about?"

She forced herself to meet his gaze. "You could have simply told me no. Instead you have chosen to mock me."

He muttered something under his breath that sounded

surprisingly like a swearword. Emily willed herself not to react. If she wasn't going to be conducting business with Mr. MacIntyre, there was no point in taking him to task on his language.

"I'm not mocking you," he said, then lightly touched her arm. "I'm completely serious. Please, don't go. Give me a chance to explain."

She wanted to tell him no. She wanted to jerk her arm free of his distasteful touch and stalk out of his office. But she couldn't. For one thing, she didn't find the light pressure of his fingers the least bit distasteful. Instead they were warm and caused a most disturbing tingling sensation that crept up to her shoulder. Her chest tightened a little, the way it had when she'd seen him smile in the saloon.

Unable to do more than keep breathing, she allowed him to lead her back to her chair where she settled onto the seat.

Once there Emily touched her temple to see if she had some kind of fever. Her skin felt cool as ever. Perhaps something at her noon meal had disagreed with her. Regardless of her brief physical ailment, she seemed to have regained her senses.

"What did you want to explain, Mr. MacIntyre?" she inquired, because trying to leave again would look foolish.

He grinned. "Considering what I'm about to say, you might want to call me Lucas."

Her mouth went dry and she could feel her eyes widening. She wasn't sure which shocked her more—his improper suggestion that she use his Christian name or the way his mouth had parted in that luscious, sinful smile.

Inside her sensible black shoes, her toes curled. Her

knees actually seemed to bounce off each other in a most peculiar way. The chest tightness returned. But before she could put a name to her condition, he was speaking again.

"It's all because of my Uncle Simon," he said, settling onto a corner of the desk.

His left...*limb*...swung back and forth, nearly brushing against the fullness of her skirt. She shifted slightly in her seat in an attempt to pull back from the contact.

"My parents died when Jackson and I were pretty little. Jackson's my brother. Uncle Simon raised us right here in Defiance." He shrugged. "It wasn't much of a town back then. Just a few mining shacks and an outpost that served as the general store."

She didn't think it was much of a town now, but if Mr. MacIntyre had grown up in the West, he couldn't possibly understand about the beauty of a large city.

"There's a mine up in the mountains," he continued. "Jackson sees to that. We bought this saloon about eight years ago and I run it. We also bought a ranch, just outside of town. We're going to catch wild horses, plus breed our own. For the army. We own the land free and clear, but we have to build corrals, barns, a house, plus pay for feed and stock. That's what the income from the saloon and mine are going for."

"That's all very interesting, Mr. MacIntyre," she said impatiently, "but I fail to see—"

"Lucas."

She pressed her lips together. "It wouldn't be proper for me to call you that."

He smiled at her again. His mustache twitched slightly. "I bet you can. Why don't you kinda roll your tongue around the word? Come on. Say it. Lucas."

She felt heat on her cheeks. Had he actually said that

word, the one naming that inner part of her mouth? Next he would probably name her limbs or something even more intimate. The man was impossible.

She thought about leaving, but she knew if she did she would never get a chance at the hotel. And then what choice would she have but to find another teaching position? At that rate of pay, it would take several lifetimes to save enough to open her establishment. She knew that she would never return home—at least not as a someone who had failed. She couldn't bear the humiliation.

Which meant she was going to have to humor Mr. MacIntyre.

"Fine," she said through only slightly gritted teeth. "Lucas."

He winked. "I knew you could do it. Now as I was saying, Jackson and I have this plan for the ranch. The money from my share of the profits of the hotel would really help. The problem is Uncle Simon died."

"Why is that a problem?"

"He left a will."

Emily frowned. "That sounds more responsible than problematic."

"You'd think. But there's the matter of what's in the will. You see he's the actual owner of the mine, the saloon and the ranch. According to the terms of his will, if Jackson and I haven't each married within three months of his death, we lose everything."

"That can't be right," she said without thinking. Why on earth would a family member put that kind of restriction on his only relatives?

It was as if Lucas read her mind. "I know what you're thinking, Em," he told her. "But Uncle Simon had his reasons. He wanted the family name to continue. For the past nine years he'd been waiting for Jackson and I to up and marry. I guess he finally figured that wasn't going to happen, so he decided to force our hands. The old coot.''

The last sentence came out as a grumble, but Emily—who couldn't believe the man sitting in front of her had had the audacity to call her ''Em''—heard the affection in his voice.

She wanted to ask why he and his brother had never married. She silently counted back nine years and realized Uncle Simon's expectations had started in 1866. The year the war ended. Of course, Lucas and his brother were of an age where they would have fought. When they returned safe, their uncle had wanted them to start a family. Why had they both resisted?

''So you can see that I'm rightly serious about my proposal, Em,'' Lucas said cheerfully. ''You get your hotel and I get to keep what's mine.''

''But why me?'' she blurted out before she could stop herself. ''There are other women you could marry.''

''Single ladies aren't that easy to find.''

''But there are those…'' She cleared her throat. ''What I mean is there are nearly a dozen attractive young women who would suit your purpose.''

She was speaking, of course, of the ladies of ill repute who lived in the great house across from her rented room. Emily would rather sleep on hot coals than ever admit that she might have, on one occasion or another, peeked out her window and seen men entering that building. She'd seen Lucas go in more than once. And she'd seen the beautiful women inside leaving. While her good Christian heart was appalled by their disregard for righteousness, her woman's soul envied their easy laughter and pretty clothes.

''Why, Em, you do me proud,'' Lucas said with a

grin. "I wouldn't have thought you'd even acknowledge Miss Cherry's existence, let alone that of her girls."

"I don't." She squared her shoulders and avoided his teasing gaze. Which helped her ignore the tingling brought on again by his smile. "I'm simply saying they might be more suited to your needs."

He nodded. "You know, I gave it a lot of thought, but there's a problem. I don't want a real marriage—I want one in name only. Then in a few months, I can get an annulment. One of Cherry's girls would undoubtedly tempt me into consummating the marriage and then where would I be?"

He stood up and paced the length of the small room. "I thought I'd solved the problem by sending for a mail-order bride. Actually I sent for two. One for me and one for Jackson. However, mine changed her mind. I received a letter a couple of days ago and now I find myself without a bride and not much time left until Jackson and I lose everything. Then you showed up today, wanting to rent the second floor of my saloon and I knew you were a gift from heaven."

Had Emily been the fainting kind, she would have found herself crumpled on the floor. His insult had been made so casually, she doubted he'd realized the import of his words. But she'd recognized the meaning and it burned. She clasped her hands together in an effort to hold in her pain and not let him know that she cared what he thought. Did it really matter that Lucas MacIntyre considered her charms so meager that she would be easy to resist in the marriage bed? With her he didn't have to worry about temptation. He could have his marriage of convenience and keep his inheritance, with almost no trouble.

She wanted to scream at the unfairness of it all, but

that wasn't her way. Instead she told herself she was going to refuse him.

Except the marriage would help her, too.

The thought came from nowhere. At first she wanted to dismiss it, but then she considered the meaning. If she married Lucas, she could write her family and tell them that she finally had a husband. A rancher would be considered respectable, even romantic, by her sisters and her mother. She wouldn't have to say anything about him owning a saloon or their marriage being one of convenience rather than affection. When she left Defiance to start her establishment, she could pass herself off as a widow. Again, respectable.

She glanced at the man sitting in front of her. He waited patiently. Yes, there was something in the situation for her, but he needed the marriage far more than she did. Which meant she was in the better bargaining position.

"I might be interested, however, I want to know what's in it for me."

Lucas knew he'd won. The prim Miss Smythe was going to agree to marry him, which meant he was halfway to his goal. "What do you want?" he asked. "I said if you married me, I wouldn't charge you rent."

"You suggested that before I knew all the facts. However, I know them now. Therefore, I'll pay you ten percent of the profits, no rent, and I want a cash settlement at the time of the annulment."

Had he been drinking, he would have choked. "Why?"

"Because you need to marry me more than I need to rent your hotel."

Lucas raised his eyebrows. Em might be a scrawny thing on the outside, but she had the heart of a lion. And she was a damn fine businesswoman. He was in trouble and she didn't hesitate to take advantage of that.

He stood and crossed to the door connecting his office to the main room of the saloon. He opened it and yelled for Perry to bring him a pot of tea and two cups. He glanced back at Emily.

"Bargaining is thirsty work."

Thirty minutes later Lucas knew he'd been had— cheated by a professional in spinster's clothing. In exchange for Emily's hand in marriage, he was getting a mere thirty percent of her profits, she wasn't paying rent and when the marriage was annulled he would pay her five hundred dollars. He should have been furious. Instead he was impressed.

"I think that's everything," she said, rising to her feet. "Thank you, Mr. MacIntyre."

He shook his head. "Lucas. Or the deal is off."

She pressed her lips together. "All right. Lucas. And I must tell you, I don't particularly care for you shortening my name. Emily is perfectly fine."

"I know, Em. I'll keep that in mind."

"When did you want to get married?"

"How about tomorrow morning? Say ten?"

"Fine. I trust you'll make all the arrangements?"

"Sure. Just meet me at the church."

"After the wedding I'll start moving my things in upstairs. I want to get the hotel open as soon as possible."

She nodded slightly, then turned to leave. Lucas watched her go. He had the oddest feeling that he should do something to seal the deal. But what? Shake hands? Kiss her?

That last thought came from nowhere and he quickly pushed it away. Kiss Emily Smythe? That would be about as exciting as kissing a block of ice. She might have a head for business, but she had the heart of a spinster. Her idea of warming her husband's bed would probably be to set the mattress on fire.

Chuckling at the thought, he watched her leave, then had the disquieting realization that by this time tomorrow, they would be married.

Curled up in a small chair just to the left of the window, Emily watched the men entering Miss Cherry's house. From across the street she could hear the music spilling out the open windows. There were faint sounds of laughter and occasional drifting bits of conversation. Bright lights illuminated the front of the house, as well as the well-kept wooden sidewalk.

Emily's room was at the top of the stairs, the third story of a building on the town's main street. The floor below housed the baker and his family and the ground floor held the bakery. When Emily had first arrived in Defiance, she'd been pleased with her narrow but private quarters. She'd spent many nights staring with fascination until she'd finally realized the purpose of the house across the street. The comments she'd heard around town had suddenly made sense. She'd been shocked and embarrassed, afraid someone might have seen her practically hanging out of her window, staring.

Unfortunately, her curiosity had never lessened, so she'd found a way to sit in her chair, out of sight of anyone on the street and yet still watch the goings-on.

Miss Cherry's girls were lovely in a way Emily could never be. They had large eyes and beautiful hair. Their bodies were full and womanly. They knew how to talk to men, to tease and laugh and flirt. Sometimes Emily's stomach hurt so much when she watched them.

She knew she wasn't pretty, but she also knew there had to be something else wrong with her. Other plain girls had managed to attract beaux and eventually husbands. Why couldn't she? Why didn't she know how to start a conversation with a man? She'd listened to her sisters flirting with their gentleman callers. Everything they said sounded so silly and the men had loved it. When she tried it though, men simply stared at her as if she were completely without sense.

A tall man turned in to the house. At first Emily's heart leaped into her throat. Lucas? But then the light caught the side of the man's face and she realized she didn't recognize him at all. No. Not Lucas. Not tonight. But he had visited Miss Cherry's before. Would he after they were married? She knew that some other husbands did, and theirs was to be a marriage in name only. Wasn't he marrying her because with her he wanted to be sure he wouldn't be tempted to consummate the marriage?

She continued to stare out into the night and ignored the single tear that trickled down her cheek. She told herself that she had made peace with her life a long time ago. A husband and children were not for her. She had other plans. Yes, of course it would have been lovely to fall in love, but she wasn't the kind of woman men responded to in that way. She had a greater purpose. She had a plan. And that was going to have to be enough.

Despite the fact that nothing about the marriage was going to be real, Lucas found himself surprisingly nervous the next morning as he waited for his bride-to-be and the minister to make an appearance in the wooden church on the west side of town. He'd come alone after making arrangements for Pastor Bird's wife and oldest boy to act as witnesses. He'd thought about sending a message to Jackson but figured his brother either wouldn't show or would make a scene. A brawl during the wedding wouldn't help anyone.

"Good morning."

He turned toward the sound of the voice and saw Emily had entered the rear of the church. She removed her dark cloak to reveal that she'd dressed for the occasion. Today's dress was *light* gray and edged in cream lace. At least she hadn't shown up in black. Not that he'd ever seen her in anything but gray.

Nothing else about her had changed in the night. She still wore her hair tightly pulled back in a knot at the nape of her neck. Her posture was straight, her thin shoulders square.

"Miss Smythe," he said, bowing slightly.

She raised her eyebrows at his formal address. He only did it to throw her off balance. While he hadn't spent much time in Emily Smythe's company, he'd learned several things about her. She was intelligent, determined, a damn fine negotiator and great fun to tease. If he *had* to be married, the last thing he wanted was some grim woman who didn't know how to laugh. He wasn't convinced Emily enjoyed humor, but he'd received a few hints that she might be tempted into a giggle now and again.

"I spent most of last evening packing my things," she said, walking up the center aisle of the small church. She placed her cloak and her gloves over the first pew. "I thought that after the ceremony I would begin to move in my belongings. I assume I may use the back stairs."

"Sure. There's a way up from the hallway behind the saloon, but I don't guess you'll want to walk through my place very much."

Her blue eyes widened at the thought. "No. Thank you."

He pretended to consider the idea. "In case you change your mind, seeing as we're going to be business partners as well as man and wife, I want you to know that any liquor you drink is on the house." He squinted at her. "I can't see you sipping whiskey, but you might enjoy a nice glass of apple brandy in the evening. To help you sleep."

Color flooded her face, but she didn't rise to the bait. "How considerate," she murmured. "I'll have to let you know later."

"Whenever. The offer stands. Oh, and I've put a couple of my men to work on cleaning the rooms. They haven't been used in years, so they're quite dusty. There's also more furniture up there than I'd remembered. Plenty of beds and dressers. All you'll have to do is provide mattresses, curtains and whatever other doodads you like."

"Thank you," she said, obviously pleased. "How very thoughtful and kind of you."

Her words and her smile made him slightly uncomfortable. "It wasn't anything."

"I disagree. It was a very nice something."

Light seemed to fill her blue eyes. That, along with the color still lingering in her cheeks, made her look...different. Not exactly pretty, but not quite so plain. But before he could figure out what, if anything, that meant, Pastor Bird, his wife and his oldest boy arrived. It was time for the ceremony.

Lucas and Emily stood together at the front of the church. Except for the exchange of vows, the large open space was quiet. Lucas tried to remember if he'd ever been to a wedding before, and, although he couldn't recall a time, the words he and Emily repeated sounded familiar.

As he promised to love and honor the stranger standing next to him, he felt a flare of resentment that he had to go through all this to keep something that was already rightfully his. Damn Uncle Simon. Did the old bastard really think he could force his nephews into marrying?

Obviously he had and it had worked. But he couldn't keep them married. Lucas had never planned on taking a wife and he didn't intend to keep this one for very long. He sure wasn't going to turn the marriage into a real one, so there weren't going to be any children. It was unlikely that Jackson would think any different, so the MacIntyre name would die out with them.

"You may kiss the bride."

The pastor's words brought Lucas back to the present. Apparently he and Emily were well and truly hitched. He leaned down to do his duty, but she shook her head and took a quick step back.

"A handshake will do, Lucas," she said primly as she extended her hand.

"Yes, ma'am," he murmured, taking her slender fingers in his and squeezing gently.

She seemed startled by the contact, or maybe she hadn't expected him to agree so quickly. She pulled away as fast as she could and busied herself thanking the pastor and his family for their assistance. As he watched her, Lucas had the crazy idea that it might be kind of fun to seduce Mrs. Emily MacIntyre, just to see what happened.

Then he reminded himself that he had enough troubles already, the main one being getting his brother married before the three-month deadline was up. He hoped Jackson's mail-order bride had plenty of backbone and didn't scare easy.

Chapter Three

"I heard you got hitched," Mangus Reeves said, then waved his beer in the air. "Say it ain't so, Lucas. Not you."

"I heard he married that schoolteacher lady." Barney Jefferson—a tall redhead with a temper to match his fiery looks—shook his shaggy head sadly. "It's a terrible day when one of our own gives in to a female. And that one in particular. It's not just that she's skinny. It's worse. She has a way of lookin' at a man as if she knows all the black secrets of his soul."

"And disapproves," another man added.

Lucas ignored the comments and kept pouring liquor. He'd known that he would get some ribbing about his sudden marriage, not to mention his choice of a bride. He could silence them all by telling them why he'd married, but strangely enough, he couldn't bring himself to do that. As if by telling the truth, he would embarrass Emily. Although why he cared about her delicate feelings was beyond him.

"She ain't so bad," Hep told the crowd collected around the bar.

The old miner was on the far side of sixty. Small and

wiry, he'd worked the mountain most of his life without ever once striking it rich. Now age and pain in his bones kept him from his chosen profession. Hep was honest and a hard worker, so Lucas gave him small jobs to tide him over through the cold Colorado winters.

"What do you know about the schoolteacher?" Mangus demanded.

Hep raised his chin and stared up at the man more than a foot taller and nearly two score younger. "She taught me some learning last winter. My letters and my numbers." The old man flushed slightly at the confession but kept on talking. "I'd tried before, but figured I didn't have a head for it. Miss Smythe—" he shot a look at Lucas and amended the title "—Mrs. MacIntyre was real patient and now I can read."

Lucas frowned. He hadn't known that prim Emily had ever bothered with the likes of old Hep. Maybe she wasn't as spinsterish as he'd thought. Damn. Until Hep had said something to defend her, Lucas had been content to let the men talk themselves out. Now he had to speak up.

"Emily MacIntyre is my wife," he said to the crowd. "I'm proud to have her as my bride. Anyone who says a word against her is going to answer to me."

He spoke the words easily, but their meaning was clear. He wasn't a man to go looking for a fight, but he wasn't afraid of one if it found him, and he generally left his opponent much the worse for wear.

Everyone got very quiet. Mangus and Barney avoided his gaze while Hep looked pleased.

"I'm sure she's very nice," Mangus muttered into his beer.

In the silence Lucas heard the sound of people climbing the steps leading to the second story. Emily had three men hauling trunks and boxes up to her new hotel. How many things could she have and how long was this going to take? He had a sudden sense of having gotten more than he'd bargained for when he married Emily that morning. Perhaps he'd better go see what she was up to.

An unexpected delivery, not to mention a brawl over a "friendly" card game, delayed Lucas's trip upstairs until nearly three that afternoon. He left Perry in charge and made his way up the rear stairs to the top story of his saloon.

The men Emily had hired had finished a couple of hours before. He found the rear door propped wide and dozens of boxes and trunks open in the large foyer area. Curtains, sheets, blankets and lace things that looked unfamiliar were stacked together in foot-high bundles. A stiff breeze attested to the open windows in all the rooms and he could hear banging from a far room.

He followed the sound, taking in the swept-and-washed floor and relatively clean walls. Lucas had never paid much attention to the upstairs of his saloon, but obviously this section of the building had been intended as a hotel all along. In addition to the foyer, he counted fifteen bedrooms, two linen closets and a small office just off the built-in reception desk.

Most of the rooms had at least a bed frame and a dresser. Some even had wallpaper. As he came to the end of the hall, he heard a sneeze, followed by a ladylike sniff.

"Em?" he called.

"In here."

He turned to his right and found himself in a large bedroom overlooking the main road. The bed was large and, unlike the others in the hotel, covered with a feather mattress thick enough to make Miss Cherry's girls envious. Emily had already hung crisp white lace curtains at the windows. She was in the process of hanging blue velvet drapes over the curtains. On the high dresser stood a basin and pitcher sitting on a lace table runner. A gilded-edged mirror hung opposite the window. There was a rocker in the corner and two table lamps, pillows on the bed, along with sheets, blankets and a coverlet in deep blue.

"I just can't…" Emily's voice trailed off as she tried to reach the last hook of the drapes.

"Allow me."

He motioned for her to step off the stool, then he reached up and slid the hook into place. When he was finished, he glanced around the room again because it was much easier than looking at the woman he'd just married.

"It's very nice," he told her.

Emily gave him a tight smile. "Thank you for both the assistance and the compliment." She picked up the stool and surveyed her handiwork. "I have enough linens for fifteen beds, although only mattresses for five. I've ordered the rest. I've also ordered more lamps, towels." She paused, then shrugged. "By the end of the day I'll have at least five rooms for rent. More tomorrow."

She led the way into the hall. "And speaking of customers, I want to talk with you about getting a sign. Something elegant. I thought I would put it on the side of the building, pointing to the rear stairs. Is that all right with you?"

"Order as many signs as you'd like."

"One should be sufficient," she said, moving into the bedroom next door. He followed.

Twenty-four hours ago he'd barely known that Emily

Smythe was alive. Now she was his wife. He'd also learned that she was a tough negotiator, a hard worker and that she'd taught old Hep how to read, although he couldn't for the life of him imagine where the two of them had ever met up long enough for her to offer assistance and Hep to accept.

Lucas glanced around and saw a feather mattress placed neatly in the bed frame. Folded linens sat on top. Two open boxes stood on the floor, one containing curtains and drapes while the other held a basin and two lanterns. Afternoon sunlight sparkled through a clean glass window.

He'd ordered his men upstairs the previous day. They'd swept out the place and had washed it down, but it never would have occurred to them to clean a window. Emily must have done that herself.

"You've been busy," he said, pointing to the glass.

"I didn't do them all," she told him. "Just the ones in the rooms I can get ready tonight. It's going to take me a few days to get things in order."

He tapped his toe against one of the open boxes. "Where'd you get all this? You have enough to fill a couple of houses."

She set down her stool, bent over the box with the drapes and pulled out the lace curtains. "Or one very large one."

He didn't understand. "Did you cart all this west with you?"

"Some of it. The rest my parents shipped to me."

When she reached for the stool, he grabbed it and the curtains from her. "I'll do that," he grumbled. "No sense in you breaking your neck on the first day we're married." Although he couldn't believe he'd just volunteered to hang drapes. Hell, he had a business to run.

He didn't have time to stay up here with Emily. Yet he didn't seem to be in any hurry to leave.

She pulled out a lace table runner from the box with the basin and put it onto the long, low dresser in this slightly small room. While Lucas fumbled with the curtains, she put the bowl and basin in place and assembled the lamps. He inhaled the scent of oil as she filled them, then something floral. He glanced over her shoulder and saw her tucking lace sachets into each drawer.

"The businessmen won't appreciate that smell," he said.

"They'll like bugs even less. When I'm sure the drawers are pest-free, I'll take out the sachets."

He reached for the length of velvet drapes. These were a deep burgundy. He noticed the coverlet matched. "Come on, Emily, tell me the truth. Why do you have all this? Was a hotel your plan from the beginning? And if that's the case, why'd you come to town as a teacher?"

She busied herself with making the bed. "I didn't plan on a hotel from the beginning. I really wanted to be a teacher. I liked the idea of starting a new life in Colorado. It's so beautiful here. I've never seen anything like the mountains in winter."

"Uh-huh."

He finished with the drapes and leaned against the wall, folding his arms over his chest. "Just say you're not going to answer the question. Don't avoid it like a preacher avoiding sin."

She glanced at him, a smile teasing the corners of her mouth. "Is that what I'm doing?"

"Absolutely."

She had a nice smile, he thought, wondering why he hadn't noticed it the day before. And while she was still a skinny thing, when she bent over the bed like she was doing now, he could see that she wasn't quite as lacking in curves as he'd thought. Her bosoms were small enough that she could never get a job at Miss Cherry's, but they were a mouthful and sometimes that was plenty.

Lucas realized the dangerous trail his thoughts had taken and quickly jerked them back into safety. No sir, he did *not* plan to find his wife anything but convenient.

Her smile faded. She sat on the edge of the unmade bed and for the first time her back wasn't stiff and straight. In fact, her shoulders seemed a mite slumped.

"My family sent me these things," she said, motioning to the contents of the trunk. "They're to help me get settled. You see, this is the West and everyone knows there's a shortage of women. My parents assumed that even I could find a husband."

Except she hadn't, he thought. He didn't count.

"Did you want to get married?" he asked.

"I thought I might, but it's not really important to me. I have other plans. My establishment."

"Your what?"

Light entered her blue eyes. They were a lovely color, he thought absently. The color of a summer sky.

"I want to open a school to train women so they're not so dependent on men."

He frowned. "I thought women liked being dependent on men. You want them to learn a trade?"

"That's part of it, but not all of it. I want them to learn to count on themselves. To be strong. I'm fortunate. I knew early I wasn't going to get married and I didn't want to stay in my father's house forever. Coming west solved many problems for me. But not everyone can do that. What about the women who don't have the education, or who don't know how to make their way in the world? What about women who are widows, or whose fathers or husbands are cruel?''

''Who was cruel to you?'' he asked softly.

She sprang to her feet and busied herself with the sheets on the bed. ''I don't know what you're talking about. My family is ever so kind. My father especially. He was proud of me. When I was little, he used to take me into the office with him and teach me the business. He had a shipping company. Quite successful.''

She smoothed the sheets across the bed. He thought about helping her but figured she would get nervous if the two of them were too close to a bed. After all, she hadn't even been willing to kiss him at the end of their wedding ceremony. He wondered if Emily had ever been kissed and if she had, who'd been the man brave enough to scale her resolve.

''So why'd you leave?''

''I told you, I…'' She pressed her lips together. After giving the sheets one last flick with her hand, she crossed to the window, pushed aside the drapes and stared out at the street.

''I have two younger sisters,'' she said quietly. ''They're not very smart, but that isn't important. They're both lovely, very accomplished.''

''But your father never took them to the office with him.''

''No.'' As she spoke, she continued to gaze out the window. ''My mother was thrilled with their social success all the while she despaired of ever finding me a husband. I didn't really mind.'' She gave a small shrug. ''My father and I were very close. As long as he adored me, I knew everything would be fine. As silly as it sounds, I used to dream about joining the family business.'' She touched the glass. ''It would have been better if I'd been born a boy.''

''Not for me,'' Lucas told her. ''Uncle Simon was real specific about us taking wives.''

She managed to give him a slight smile. ''It doesn't matter. I wasn't born a boy and one night, at a musical, I met a young man who seemed more interested in talking to me than staring at my beautiful sisters. David was kind and intelligent. He worked for my father.''

Lucas stiffened slightly. He had a bad feeling he knew where the story was going. He doubted it ended well for Emily.

''David and I grew close and then he proposed.''

''Did you accept?''

''I thought about it. I didn't really love him, but we got along and I doubted I would do better. Then I made the mistake of asking him to tell me the truth. Did his proposal have anything to do with my father's business?''

She paused. ''I have to respect David for being honest. David told me that my father had offered him a percentage of the company if he married me and we had children.'' She tilted her head to the side. ''My father was a good businessman. He wanted to make sure that David intended to make our marriage a real one.''

Unlike theirs, Lucas thought. ''So you get your negotiating abilities from him.''

She flashed him a quick smile that nearly hid the pain in her eyes. ''Yes, I did.'' She returned her attention to the window. ''After I learned the truth, I knew I couldn't possibly accept David's proposal. He tried to change my mind, to tell me that we were good friends and wasn't that enough. But it wasn't. I was still young and foolish enough to believe there was more available to me.''

Lucas felt awkward hearing about her past. He didn't want to know that she'd been wounded by the people most charged with loving her. He didn't want to know that their short marriage of convenience was something similar to what she'd been offered before.

"Once David and I broke things off, I knew I had to leave," she said. "There aren't many options open to an unmarried woman, so I took a teaching position to allow me time to think about my future. Over the past year or so, I've come to the conclusion that I want to open an establishment for women, as we've already discussed. And that, Mr. MacIntyre, is my entire history."

He didn't know what to say about her past, so he chose something more simple to comment upon. "So you won't keep the hotel once you have the funds you require?"

"No. Depending on how successful I am, I'm planning to stay here two years, three at most. In the meantime, I'm sure I'll enjoy my work. There is the appeal of my future plans, not to mention the fact that this floor is entirely mine to do with as I please."

"I'd prefer you didn't burn down the place."

She turned to face him. "I will do my best to avoid that circumstance. But you are missing the point. As a man, you've had many homes that are entirely yours. But as a woman I first lived with my family, then rented a room in an attic. I could never come and go as I wished. People watched, judged, offered opinions. Now I am entirely an independent woman."

He considered her words. "I've never thought that women don't have the same freedoms as men."

"Why would you? Your life is not one of restriction and rules." She waved a hand. "There are laws, of course, but I'm not speaking of the freedom to commit a crime. I simply want to be in control of my life to the extent my abilities will allow. I do not want to be controlled or dictated to because I am a woman.''

Lucas had known from the moment he'd become aware of her existence that Emily was a spinster. She was probably twenty-five or twenty-six, which wasn't so old that she had to give up the possibility of marriage, but old enough for everyone to know that she'd been passed over. He'd known other spinsters in his life, but he'd never once thought about their fate. Society didn't care if a man waited to marry, but he could see that it was particularly cruel to plain, unmarried women. Without skills and resources, those women had to rely on the whims of fate and the goodness of their families for their very livelihoods.

Emily had the advantage of brains, education and determination. Many others would not be so fortunate.

He nodded slightly. "I'm proud to be a part of your plan, Em. If I can help make the hotel a success, I'll do what I can."

This time her smile was genuine. She pressed her fingers together. "You've already done so much, sending your men to help me get the rooms ready, agreeing to let me be here in the first place. I do appreciate that."

Sunlight drifted through a crack in the drapes. It caught the side of her head and added a golden luster to her tightly drawn back hair. He had a sudden desire to know how far her hair tumbled down her back and what it would feel like in his hands. Would it be thick and heavy? Was there any kind of curl or wave?

Her skin was very lovely, he thought, moving his gaze to her face. Her eyes were wide, her mouth full. When she wasn't standing all stiff and looking disapproving, she was nearly attractive. Almost pretty, in a stern sort of way.

He noticed that she had delicate bones more suited to soft fabrics and feminine styles, not the thick wools and serviceable dresses she favored. If she would try a different color of clothes, or loosen her hair a little.

"Lucas, what on earth are you thinking? You have the most peculiar expression on your face."

"You don't want to know," he said, compelled to take a step toward her.

He was going to kiss her. He didn't know why and he thought he should probably stop himself before he got started. Yet he didn't *want* to stop himself. He wondered what her lips would taste like and how she would feel in his arms. It was idiocy. Worse, it was stupid and, with Emily's spinster sensibilities, potentially dangerous. However they *were* married and this *was* his wedding day. Was it so wrong to expect his bride to be willing to offer him a kiss?

Before he halted himself with a dose of good sense, he stepped toward her and placed his hands on her waist. Her eyes widened and her mouth parted. She was as still as a carving. Before she could change her mind and dart away, he drew her body against his, lowered his mouth and pressed his lips to hers.

Had Emily known what Lucas was about she would have stopped him. At least that's what she told herself in the single heartbeat of conscious thought she had between the time he put his hands on her person and when he, well, kissed her.

Then his lips were on hers and she was too confused to think or speak or even breathe. His mustache tickled…in the most charming way. He was touching her waist. Despite her layers of clothing, she could feel the heat of his fingers clear to her skin. His thumb slipped up and down, sending the oddest skittering sensation rippling through her torso. But even more strange than that was the feel of his kiss.

It was more gentle than she would have imagined, had she been the kind of woman who thought of such things. Like his hands, his lips were warm and almost—she struggled to find a word, which was difficult because her brain was so fuzzy—almost tender. Soft and lovely, yet firm as he moved against her, brushing back and forth.

She supposed she should have been horrified and insulted. She should have stepped back, and she would in a moment or two. But as this was her first kiss, she thought she should understand the entire act before deciding that she didn't like it.

She could feel the heat of his body and inhale the masculine scent of him. There were fragrances of different liquors and a bit of smoke, plus something spicy and intriguing, quite unlike any smell she'd inhaled before.

His hands moved around to her back and slid up toward her shoulder blades. His action forced her more firmly against him and suddenly they were pressing from shoulder to...to limb! Her arms, which had been resting at her sides, suddenly stiffened. All of her stiffened. A chaste kiss was one thing, but such intimacies as these were completely unacceptable.

She was about to tell him so when he did the most extraordinary thing. He touched the tip of his tongue to her lower lip.

Had anyone described such a thing to Emily, she would have been horrified and disgusted. The thought of it should have made her stomach turn. It was just too...

Warm, she thought, feeling herself melting. The sensation was most peculiar, but there was no other way to describe her body bending and leaning toward him as if she'd lost all her strength. Her limbs felt very heavy and she couldn't have moved if God himself had requested the action.

Lucas continued to stroke her in that strange way and she found herself liking it more. Tingling began in her arms and moved through her, making her—dared she think it?—chest ache as if her insides were suddenly pushing against her skin. Her limbs and that part of her she didn't even like to acknowledge, the female part of her, felt heavy and thick, which made no sense.

But what did sense have to do with anything? Nothing made sense. She didn't even protest when Lucas ran his hands down her arms until their fingers entwined. She let him raise her arms until her palms rested on his shoulders.

She couldn't believe it. They were touching and kissing and pressing and her hands were squeezing his powerful shoulders and she found herself wanting to run her fingers through his hair and have this never ever stop. Except they had to stop and she would tell him so—in another minute or two.

His tongue swept across the seam of her lips.

''Come on, Em, let me in. You'll like it.''

She had no idea what he was talking about and opened her mouth to tell him so. But instead of allowing her to speak, he pushed his tongue inside until it was touching hers.

She felt as if someone had lit her on fire. Heat filled her body. The trembling and tingling increased and she knew she was going to perish from all the different feelings in her person.

Aroused and more than a little scared, Emily managed to press her hands against his chest and push him away.

"Stop," she demanded, except her voice sounded breathless and far too weak.

Instead of looking mortified, Lucas MacIntyre actually smiled at her. A look of male satisfaction crossed his too-handsome features.

He took a step back and looked her up and down. "You are something of a surprise, Em. I didn't expect you to be quite that tempting."

His compliment both embarrassed and pleased her. She forced herself up to her full height and squared her shoulders. "I'll thank you to remember that this is a business relationship. You are not welcome to intrude upon my person again."

He had the audacity to wink at her. "And here I was thinking there are plenty more intrusions to be had, and I'm just the man to do every one of them."

At that, he touched her check with the back of his hand, turned on his heel and walked from the room. He left her sputtering and flustered and very, very pleased by her first ever kiss.

Chapter Four

Emily was determined to ignore "the incident," which was how she thought of the kiss she and Lucas had shared the previous day. Memories of the feel of him pressing against her, the sweet taste of him and the way he'd been so bold as to touch her tongue with his had kept her up most of the night. But she'd risen as early as ever, determined to get her hotel ready for business as soon as possible.

Now, as she worked in the fifth bedroom, she fought against the tingling in her body by instead thinking about how good it had felt to have her own room in her own hotel. When the business was a success, it would be because of her hard work and vision. She was responsible. Which meant it was her fault if the hotel failed, but she wasn't going to let that happen.

She spread the sheets over the feather mattress and smoothed down the material. As she worked, she half listened for the sound of the bell she'd left at the front desk, along with a note to ring for her if someone wanted a room. Bart Miller had already started work on the sign for the hotel, so maybe that would send some business her way. Although the sign was only for folks new to town. Anyone familiar with Defiance would have already heard the gossip about her marriage to Lucas and the new hotel.

As she turned to lift the blankets from the dresser to the bed, she remembered how Lucas's hands had felt on her back and the way his lips had—

"Stop it," she said aloud. "Don't think about that anymore."

Emily shook herself in an effort to dislodge the memories that seemed firmly stuck in her head. But while her brain was willing to listen, her body wasn't cooperating at all. Even when she didn't see Lucas in her mind, she could *feel* the strength and heat of him when they'd touched.

"What's wrong with me?" she asked herself.

Was this all because Lucas had been the first man to kiss her? Or was it because she wanted to know why he'd bothered?

Emily paused in her work and turned to face the mirror hung over the narrow dresser. She saw her familiar face. A plain face whose only hope of beauty came from a pair of large, blue eyes. But as she didn't know how to draw attention to that particular feature, it got lost in the rest of her.

Had he felt sorry for her? The question made her shiver, and not in a pleasant way. She shouldn't have told Lucas the truth about her past, except she never lied. So she should have stayed silent. Instead, the words had fallen out of her mouth before she could stop them. As she returned her attention to the covers on the bed, she suddenly realized why.

She was lonely. She'd been lonely for a long time. Certainly, when she'd first moved to Defiance, she'd missed her family. With time, her work at the school and the few acquaintances she'd made had eased the pain of being in a strange place. But then the children had left with their families and she found that her few acquaintances weren't enough. She could go several days without exchanging more than just pleasant greetings. There was no one she could really talk to or confide in. Still, telling Lucas about her past and her humiliation with David hadn't been very sensible. Obviously she would need to make more of an effort to develop friends in town. She would see to that as soon as she'd finished getting the hotel ready.

Emily tucked in the blankets, then drew the green coverlet over the made bed. She should have the rest of the rooms finished by the end of next week. Then all she would need was—

The sound of a bell cut through her musings. Emily froze as excitement gripped her. Someone—perhaps a customer—had rung the bell at the front desk. This could be the beginning of her success, she thought happily as she walked down the length of the hallway and turned left by the reception desk.

She slipped smoothly behind the counter, cleared her throat and glanced up at the person waiting to speak with her. Her greeting lodged in the back of her throat.

The woman standing in front of her was tall, several inches taller than herself. Her thick brown hair coiled around her head in an intricate arrangement of curls and knots, decorated with sprays of silk flowers, and was topped by a huge red hat. A dark smudgy line above her lashes emphasized her big, beautiful brown eyes and there was no denying the color staining her full lips.

Emily blinked, then swallowed. The woman in front of her did not disappear into a dream, as Emily had hoped. She remained firmly in place. Everything about the woman overwhelmed her. The stylish hair, her full bosom expertly displayed by a low-cut red velvet gown. Swags of fabric settled over rounded hips. Everything about the woman was excessively feminine. She was as lush as a ripe peach and, from the knowing look in her large eyes, she understood the impact she had on those she met.

Emily had never been so close to a woman like the one standing in front of her. Society dictated that she didn't even acknowledge her existence. Although with the woman leaning toward her reception desk, she wasn't sure how she was supposed to ignore her.

"I'm Dixie," the woman said in a low voice that was surprisingly cultured. She might be living in Defiance now, but she'd been born somewhere else. "I heard you were opening a hotel. I'd like to rent a room."

"A—a room?"

Emily bit her lower lip. This was not a situation she could have foreseen. While she wanted to fill the hotel as quickly as possible, she wasn't interested in offering a location for expansion for the likes of Miss Cherry and her girls.

"I'm not sure what you were told," Emily said formally. "This is a private hotel. My guests—" or the guests she would soon have "—are honest people who keep to themselves."

"That's just what I want, honey," Dixie drawled, and set a handful of gold coins on the desk. "I'm paying a month in advance. I'd like your most private room in this private hotel. And you can stop biting your lip. I'm not here to work. I'm here for some quiet."

The tall, beautiful woman offered a smile. "Over at Miss Cherry's there's never a moment's peace. Men are in and out of the place at all hours. They're forever knocking on my door. I don't mind working hard, which I do, but when I'm finished for the night, I want to be left alone.''

Emily didn't know what to say. She glanced from the money to the woman standing in front of her. She knew what Dixie did to earn that money. Well, she didn't know exactly, but she had an idea. It had something to do with men and women being together.

''Are you frightened of me?'' Dixie asked bluntly. ''Do you think I'll corrupt you or try to seduce your other guests?''

Emily felt herself blush. From the heat on her face, she could imagine her cheeks were bright red. Still, she kept her head high. ''Not at all,'' she lied.

''I won't do either,'' Dixie promised. ''Although I can't speak for the ladies in town. They might not approve of you catering to the likes of me. However, I'm paying in advance, I pay in gold and I won't make any trouble.''

Emily reached for the blank registration book, turned it toward the woman and pointed to the first line. ''If you would be so kind as to sign here,'' she said. ''Then I'll show you to your room, Miss, ah…''

''Just Dixie. If we're going to be passing in the hall every day, I don't see any point in being formal, do you?''

''No. Of course not.''

She glanced at Dixie's signature, then put her money into the strongbox at the bottom of the desk. When she straightened, she studied the keys hanging on the hooks attached to the wall behind her.

''The front bedroom is a little larger,'' she said, more to herself than her guest. ''But you'll have street noise. If you're interested in quiet more than space, I have a lovely room at the back." She looked at Dixie. "Let me show you these two rooms and you pick the one you like best."

"Good idea."

Dixie crossed to the stairs and called down. Instantly there were the sounds of footsteps on the stairs. Three young men appeared, each carrying a trunk, followed by two boys with large carpetbags.

Emily knew that the luggage contained more lovely dresses like the red one Dixie wore this afternoon. So much finery, she thought as she led the way down the hall. Beautiful clothes in soft, elegant fabrics. She fingered her own gray wool skirt and remembered a time when she'd worn pretty things. Nothing as spectacular as Dixie's dress, to be sure, but still nicer than her current garb.

But once Emily had decided to go west, she'd decided it was more important to be sensible than fashionable. She'd had her gray dresses made up. Lighter for spring and summer, darker for winter. The color didn't show the dirt and the fabrics lasted forever. Sensible, she thought again as she opened the door to the front bedroom. Now she was left to wonder if being too sensible had stolen her soul.

Dixie examined the first bedroom, then the second. She chose the latter saying, "You're right, it's smaller, but I prefer to be at the back, and that armoire is much bigger so I'll be able to store my clothes." Then she glanced at her trunks and bags and laughed. "Maybe I should take a second room for them."

Before Emily could answer, she heard the bell ring. She excused herself and hurried toward the reception desk. Two businessmen stood there. They were, they said, from Baltimore and needed two rooms for two nights.

Excitement filled Emily as she had the men sign her register. She only had five rooms to let and already three of them were full. The hotel was going to be a success, she thought happily. She was going to realize her dream.

"I understand you're full for the night," Lucas said as he walked into the reception area.

It was nearly six that evening and Emily hadn't seen him all day. In fact, she hadn't seen him since the "incident" the previous afternoon. She was instantly embarrassed and determined not to show it.

"Yes, we're full," she said. "I have two businessmen, two miners and—" This time she couldn't stop the blush from climbing her cheeks. "And someone else."

Lucas, so tall and handsome in his dark trousers, white shirt and bottle green vest, leaned against her registration desk and raised his eyebrows.

"I heard about Dixie," he said. "I was surprised."

"I don't care if you don't approve," she told him. "This is my business, not yours. I pay you a percentage of the money I make, however you are not my partner. You don't get to express your opinion on the day-to-day handling of things."

"I think you've got yourself a runaway horse." Lucas leaned toward her and gave her a smile. The one that turned her knees to jelly. "I said I was surprised. That's different from not approving. Dixie is a fine lady, despite her occupation."

Emily didn't want to think about how the man she'd married had come to know whether or not Dixie was a fine lady or a harpy. Nor did she feel comfortable with a conversation that might detail Dixie's "occupation."

"All right," she murmured. "The point is, until I get the rest of the rooms ready, I'm full. We need to discuss how often you wish to look at my ledgers. I thought perhaps weekly would be acceptable. Once you approve of the totals, I will deposit your share into the bank. Or would you prefer me to give it to you directly?"

"The bank is fine." He leaned a little closer. "As to looking at your ledgers, that's not necessary. I trust you, Em. We're married."

She did *not* want to think about that. "You don't know me. I could be dishonest."

He laughed. "No, you couldn't. Dishonest women don't kiss the way you did yesterday."

She opened her mouth to reply, but there weren't any words. How could he speak of the incident? How could he tease her and…and…

"I'm about to have supper," he said. "Would you care to join me?"

The change in subject made her head spin. She was still reeling from his mention of the incident and he was inviting her to a meal?

Of course she was going to tell him no, but before she could she found she really wanted to dine with him. She wanted to talk to him and listen to him talk to her. She wanted to put on a pretty dress—not that she had any—and have him compliment her. She wanted—

"I can't," she said flatly, knowing her disappointment showed.

"Why not? Do you have a secret sweetheart? We're married. I won't tolerate you sparking with other men."

She dismissed him with a flick of her hand, and had to blink back a burning sensation in her eyes. Tears? Over not being able to join Lucas for dinner? Impossible!

"I can't leave the desk," she said. "I don't have any employees."

He glanced around at the reception area. "Well, I'll be. For someone who prides herself on making a plan, it looks like you forgot one important thing."

"I know. It just slipped my mind."

He straightened. "You going to sit at that desk, day and night?"

"No. I'll think of something. But in the meantime, I can't join you for supper."

He reached forward and lightly touched the tip of her nose. "That's where you're wrong. You can't join me for supper, but I can bring supper to you." He gave her a wink. "Don't you go anywhere."

Emily stared after him as he walked downstairs. Lucas was being nice to her and she wanted to know why. Not that she expected him to ignore her or to be rude, but somehow she hadn't thought he would go out of his way to spend an evening meal with her. Perhaps she would ask him.

When Lucas returned with a basket of fried chicken, biscuits and several other dishes, she had cleared her desk and stretched a crisp white tablecloth across the surface. He poured them each a glass of what he claimed was "apple cider, not apple brandy" then settled on the straight-backed chair she'd found for him.

The hotel was quiet, with all her guests having gone out for the evening. The businessmen were dining at the restaurant three doors down, while the miners were in the saloon. Emily didn't want to think about where Dixie had disappeared to or what she was doing there. Because thinking about Dixie being with men made Emily wonder if Lucas had ever been with her in that way? It also reminded her of the incident, which she was trying to forget, although that was difficult, what with him sitting so close and smiling at her as she served up his chicken.

"This is very kind of you," she said, motioning to the food. "I didn't think we would be seeing each other like this."

He took a drink of his cider. "We're married, Em. Don't you think we should share a meal?"

"Is that why you're here? Because you want people to think we have a regular marriage?"

He grinned. "You've spent the last two nights alone. I don't think anyone believes we have a regular marriage."

"Oh."

Emily hadn't considered that. She'd spent her wedding night in her narrow room above the bakery, and he'd spent his in the small house he had shared with his uncle. Last night she'd been alone in the hotel.

He bit into his chicken and chewed. After he'd swallowed, he wiped his fingers on his napkin. "Were you shocked when Dixie appeared and asked for a room?"

Emily ducked her head. "Yes, of course. I didn't know her name, but I knew..." She cleared her throat. "At first I thought she wanted a room for her, um—"

"Activities," he offered helpfully.

She ignored that. "However she explained she wanted peace and privacy, both of which I can offer."

"Dixie's not so bad. I don't guess you two can be friends, but she's not an evil person."

Emily thought about her impression of the beautiful woman. "How long has she been in Defiance? With her voice and her manners, I thought she might be from somewhere back East."

"She arrived about five years ago." Lucas hesitated. "As for her past, you'll have to ask her."

Emily wondered if he didn't know about Dixie or if he was respecting a confidence. She looked at the man sitting across from her. Even seated, he was tall. His white shirt emphasized the breadth of his shoulders. She found her attention lingering on his silky mustache and remembered the feel of it yesterday when he'd kissed her.

Had she thought about being kissed by a man with a mustache, she would have assumed the experience would be unpleasant, but it hadn't been at all. She'd liked the way the surprisingly soft hairs had tickled her skin. For one frightening moment, she imagined him kissing other parts of her, such as her neck, and shivered at the thought of the teasing caress.

Emily stiffened. She would not allow herself to continue to think of the incident, nor would she imagine other familiarities. What was wrong with her? She was not the kind of woman who wasted her time daydreaming about a man.

She drew her attention back to the dinner and tried to remember what they'd been talking about. Ah, yes. Dixie and how long she'd lived in Defiance. Not a subject for polite conversation.

"Before, you had mentioned you've lived here nearly all your life," she said.

He nodded. "Yeah. I guess I was about five when Uncle Simon brought us here. Back then there wasn't a town, just a couple of miner's shacks and a big tent where an old man sold supplies."

"Your brother lives outside of town, doesn't he? I don't recall seeing him more than once or twice."

"He keeps to himself. He's got a house up by the mine."

"That's right. I remember you telling me about the mine when you explained your current predicament."

He grinned at her. "Why use a two-bit word when a dollar one works as well, right, Emily?"

She sipped her cider. "I'm sure I have no idea what you're talking about."

"I don't have a 'predicament,' I have a problem. Or a barrel full of trouble."

She felt awkward and foolish. "I'm sorry if my vocabulary discomforts you."

"It doesn't, but I think you should start loosening up. This isn't the schoolroom and you're not my teacher. Although if you wanted to tell me I was bad and give me a good paddling, I might be interested."

She had no idea what he was talking about and a complete certainty that he was teasing her, but she was too embarrassed to speak. Paddle Lucas? Why would he suggest such a thing? And why did the idea of even getting close to touching that part of him make her feel strange inside?

"We were discussing your brother," she said coolly, and hoped he wouldn't notice how difficult it was for her to speak normally when all she wanted to do was cover her face and run from the room. "You mentioned you'd sent for a mail-order bride for him."

"That's right." Lucas smiled at her in such a way that she knew he was letting her off easy.

"I never had a brother. It must be very pleasant to have that sort of familial relationship."

Lucas looked as if he was going to tease her about her word choices again, but he didn't. Instead he said, "It was. We got into trouble all the time while we were growing up."

"Sounds like fun."

"It was."

When he didn't volunteer any more information, they ate in silence.

Lucas finished the last of his meal, then wiped his hands on his napkin.

"How interested are you in helping downtrodden women?" he asked.

"I'm not sure what you're asking."

"You're going to need help around this place, with the cleaning, running errands and the like. I know a couple of young women looking for a job."

"What young women?"

His dark eyes turned angry. "Alice and Mary. I don't know how old they are. Alice might be fifteen and her sister is a couple of years younger. They don't have any family and they need jobs."

Emily wanted to protest that they were children—far too young to be working for a living. But then she remembered that some children were forced into the world by circumstances. If they had no one to support them, they would soon starve. At least by working for her, the girls would be safe. Their duties around the hotel wouldn't tax them overly much and she could teach them if they hadn't had much education.

"I'd like to meet them," she told Lucas.

"I'll bring them by later." He rose. "Thank you for supper."

"Don't thank me. You're the one who brought the food."

"Yes, but you provided the company."

With that he was gone and Emily was left to stare after him. She didn't begin to understand her handsome husband. Not his words, his actions or how he made her feel just by being in the same room. But she liked him.

He made her laugh. He seemed to enjoy teasing her and she enjoyed his attentions.

She thought about the "incident" and wondered if it was on his mind as well. As he'd been leaving, she'd half hoped he would do that again. He hadn't. Just as well, she told herself. She was not the kind of woman to dally with a man...although if she found herself in need of a dalliance, Lucas MacIntyre would be the man she chose.

Lucas returned shortly after nine. Trailing behind him were two overly slender girls in worn cloaks. Their eyes were large, their skin pale and Emily read the fear in their expressions.

"Alice and Mary, meet Emily MacIntyre."

The older of the two tried to smile. "Ma'am."

Like her younger sister, Alice had bright red hair and green eyes. The two girls held hands, clinging to each other as if they had no one else in the world.

Emily moved around the desk and approached the girls. "How old are you?" she asked.

Alice spoke for them both. "I'm fifteen. Mary is thirteen. We're hard workers, ma'am," she added. "We're both stronger than we look. I can scrub and clean. Mary's real patient when it comes to ironing and she knows some cooking."

"Good." Emily glanced at her husband. "Have they eaten recently?"

"About an hour ago."

She returned her attention to the girls. "I think we should talk about work in the morning. Right now you two need some sleep."

She showed them to a small room next to her own. She'd made it up quickly after dinner. The fresh mattress had been delivered just that afternoon. Emily had added a pretty pink coverlet and drapes, along with a pansy-covered basin.

Alice and Mary stared at the small room, then Alice shook her head. ''Ma'am, this is too nice for us.''

Emily took in the plain walls, the stains she'd been unable to scrub out on the floor and the skinny dresser. She'd been hesitant about renting out the room because it was so small and the window didn't offer a view of anything nicer than the building across the street.

Emily touched Alice's thin shoulder. ''I was about to apologize because it wasn't nice enough. You and Mary are safe here. Get ready for bed. We'll talk in the morning.''

With that, she left the sisters alone and shut the door behind herself.

She found Lucas waiting by the reception desk. ''Where did you find them?''

The anger she'd noticed before returned to his eyes. ''Their father tried to sell them to Cherry earlier in the week. She took the girls in because it was obvious he was going to get rid of them one way or the other. She's been trying to find a place for them ever since.''

Emily didn't know what to say. She'd never heard of such a thing. Did fathers really sell their daughters into service to men? Was it possible?

''That can't be legal,'' she insisted.

He shrugged. ''But it happens. Cherry thought they might be able to clean at her place, but Alice is too pretty to go unnoticed and Cherry was afraid someone would get drunk and hurt the girl. She mentioned the problem to me and I thought you might be willing to help.''

Emily wanted to know what Lucas had been doing talking to that woman. Had he been at her place of business, and if so, why? She reminded herself that theirs was simply a marriage of convenience and she shouldn't care if her husband took his person elsewhere. But the words didn't ease the ache she felt in her stomach or the way her throat started to hurt.

"I'm sure the girls and I can come to some kind of agreement about employment," she said stiffly. "I need assistance here and I think they'll enjoy the work. I'll pay them a fair wage. If they save, they can leave Defiance and start over elsewhere in time."

He stepped closer to her. "You surprise me," he told her.

"Why?"

"I thought you might be shocked and insulted to have those girls here."

"You forget I rented a room to Dixie. Mary and Alice are hardly more shocking than that."

"I know. When I heard what you'd done for Dixie, I figured I might have misjudged you." His dark eyes seemed to stare into her soul. "You're not at all what I imagined."

"You mean I'm not a prim schoolteacher who uses dollar words when two-bit ones will do?"

"Oh, you're all that, but you're also growing on me." He looked thoughtful. "Who would have thought." Then he leaned close and brushed his lips against her cheek. "You're not a bad kisser, either, Mrs. MacIntyre. One of these days we'll have to do it again."

Chapter Five

Alice and Mary were waiting for Emily when she walked out into the reception area the next morning. They had been seated on the worn red sofa she'd rescued from a back bedroom—one that desperately needed recovering but was the only one she had. The two girls, looking just as young, thin and frightened as they had the night before, sprang to their feet and gave her awkward little bobs of their heads.

"Good morning," Emily said cheerfully. "You two are up early."

Alice, the older and taller of the two, cleared her throat. "Yes, ma'am. We didn't know what time you wanted us to start."

Emily glanced at the small watch she'd pinned to the bodice of her serviceable gray gown. It was barely after seven.

"Not as early as this," she told them. She motioned the girls back to the sofa, then settled into the chair opposite them.

"I would like you both to start at eight," she said, speaking as kindly as she knew how. "You're to have Sundays and a half day on Wednesday for yourselves.

I'll provide the meals.'' She paused and smiled. ''Actually, Mrs. Martin will provide the meals at her restaurant, but I'll pay for them. You may dine there or have your food delivered here, as I do. Oh, and there's a small kitchen in the office. I'll show it to you. Please use that for tea or snacks.''

Emily could see both girls listening attentively. She longed to ask how they'd survived so far and what had happened to their mother. But she wasn't going to pry. With time and luck, the girls would begin to trust her. Until then, she could only offer a safe haven and hope they would begin to lose some of their fear.

''What I would like from you both is simple cleaning of the guest rooms.'' She went on to detail the things to be done, then named a salary. ''I'll pay you twice a month, on the first and the fifteenth. When you receive your first pay, we'll go to the bank and I'll show you how to begin an account.''

She turned her attention to Alice. The older girl wore her long red hair pulled back into a thick braid. Her green eyes were wide as she listened and nodded. Emily noticed that Alice's blue dress had been carefully patched. She made a note to talk to Mrs. Bird, the pastor's wife, about clothing the church might have to give to those in need.

She thought about mentioning that she was a teacher and would be happy to give the girls' lessons, but perhaps there had been enough changes in their lives for one morning. They could discuss that at another time.

She also decided that she would clean Dixie's room personally, and not ask the girls to have anything to do with it. The sight of all of Dixie's finery might bring back unpleasant memories from their time at Miss Cherry's.

"Do you have any questions?" she asked at the conclusion of her comments.

Mary, small and pale, bit her lower lip. "Ma'am, are you going to beat us?"

Emily's heart tightened at the words. She'd never considered herself overly maternal, but she found herself wanting to pull both sisters into her arms and hold them tight. Instead she forced a smile.

"No. I promise I won't. Not even if you break a pitcher or a basin." She hesitated. "Did anyone at Miss Cherry's beat you?"

Alice shook her head. "No, ma'am. It was our pa. Just with his belt," she added hastily, as if that made it all right. "When we was real bad. But he didn't mean anything by it."

"Of course not," Emily murmured, wishing she had the man in front of her right now. She would tell him exactly what she thought of his character. How dare he raise a belt to his daughters and then try to sell them to a brothel owner! He was not fit to be a father. Why if she were a man, she would hunt him down and—

Footsteps on the stairs interrupted her thoughts. She watched as Bertie, the lad who delivered meals for the restaurant, appeared with a large basket hanging from one arm.

"Mrs. Martin said you wanted breakfast for three," he announced as he set the basket on the desk.

Emily rose, then ushered the girls toward her office. Before going to bed, she'd set up a small table in the far corner. It was big enough for them to eat together. By the looks of things, the sisters hadn't been having regular meals. But now they were in her care and all that was about to change.

* * *

Emily spent the morning showing Alice and Mary how to clean the guest rooms. When the rest of the new mattresses were delivered, she started working on preparing the remaining rooms for guests. As she worked, she found herself thinking about her conversation with Lucas the previous night—specifically his assertion that she was a good kisser and that they would have to kiss again sometime.

Just thinking the words made her chest flutter in the most peculiar way. She suspected he was teasing her. Lucas did enjoy making her squirm. And yet there was a part of her that wanted to believe he meant his words. That he had been pleased by the incident and that he too was thinking about it. She wanted him to do that to her again, which should have scandalized her but didn't. She reminded herself that they were married and therefore those kind of familiarities were acceptable, even expected. Except theirs wasn't a regular sort of marriage.

He'd married her because of his uncle's will. Emily paused in the act of dusting a dresser. She couldn't let herself forget that. For Lucas, this situation was to be endured until he could claim that which he obviously cared about. And for her, the marriage was a means to an end. By marrying Lucas, she obtained the use of the hotel at a very reasonable price, along with a cash bonus when the marriage was annulled.

Emily sat on the edge of the bed. A spark of truth flared inside of her. She wanted to ignore the brightness and the accompanying revelation, but she'd always been painfully honest with herself. She didn't pretend everything was fine when it wasn't and she didn't ignore either her assets or her faults. So now she stared right into the light of the truth and allowed it to illuminate the pitiful state of her heart.

She liked being married to Lucas. Yes, it had only been two days and he hadn't spent much time with her, but she enjoyed his company. She liked dining with him in the evening and the way he teased her. She liked how his smile made her limbs tremble and the fact that he'd brought her Alice and Mary. She and Lucas had... possibilities.

"No," she murmured aloud. "We don't."

Because this was a marriage of convenience, nothing more. At least nothing more to him.

Emily shook off the thoughts. So Lucas was charming. She'd only known him a short time. He would be easily forgotten when he was gone from her life.

She winced as she felt a sharp pain deep in her chest. While she was being honest with herself, she might as well admit she didn't look forward to the day when he would want to end their marriage. She'd never thought about the marital state because she'd long assumed it would not happen to her. But now that it had, she saw it was as desirable as she'd imagined when she'd been a younger woman.

Without quite being aware of what she was doing, Emily left the bedroom, walked through the reception area, down the back stairs and into Lucas's office. From there she made her way to the door leading to the rear of the saloon.

She cracked open the door and waited for Lucas to glance up and see her. From her position, half-hidden from the patrons of the saloon, she had a clear view of the bar and the gambling tables beyond. It was still morning and only a half dozen or so men were scattered about the room. One of the gaming tables held four players and they looked as if they'd been at it all night. She didn't understand men's need to gamble. The idea of wasting money on the turn of a card didn't make sense to her. But then much of the world was beyond her comprehension. She also didn't know why men would spend money to be with a woman. Yet they obviously did, going in and out of Miss Cherry's at all hours.

Emily was about to change her mind and head back upstairs when Lucas turned in her direction. Any doubts she might have had about speaking with him were completely erased when he smiled and started walking toward her. At the sight of his smile, her limbs began their obligatory quivering. She felt her own lips tug in response. A light feeling seemed to flow through her, making her want to laugh.

"Good morning," he said when he'd entered the office and closed the door behind him. "How are you this morning?"

"Well, thank you. The girls were up early. They've been fed and have started their work." She found herself suddenly nervous. Coming down to see Lucas had been an impulse. Her question could have waited.

But Lucas didn't seem inclined to leave. He simply continued to smile at her and waited for her to continue.

She found her gaze drawn to his silky mustache. She liked the way he kept it neatly trimmed. She wanted to run her fingers over the short hairs and feel the contrast between the smooth length of the hairs and the stubby ends.

Shocked by her brazen thoughts, she took a step back and forced herself to speak.

"Last night, when you invited me to dine with you, I realized I had forgotten an important aspect of running a hotel. People. Alice and Mary will take care of cleaning the rooms on a daily basis. I know who to hire for heavy cleaning, but I'm less sure about who I might employ to watch the desk at night. I thought you might have a suggestion.''

Lucas's dark eyes crinkled slightly at the corners as his smile broadened. ''What about Hep?''

Emily knew instantly who he meant. Hep was an old miner. The pain in his joints kept him from working his stake. He supported himself with odd jobs.

''I understand you two are already acquainted,'' Lucas said. ''When he found out we'd married, he mentioned that you'd taught him to read.''

''Yes. Last year. He'd replaced a broken window in the schoolhouse. I discovered him attempting to read what I'd written on the blackboard. When he admitted he couldn't read at all, I offered to teach him.''

''Why?''

She didn't understand the question. ''It was my job.''

''Your job was to instruct the students. No one paid you to teach Hep to read.''

''I know, but I wasn't going to send him away. So many people aren't interested in learning. He seemed intelligent enough. Actually it didn't take but a few months. We met every day after I dismissed the regular students.'' She laced her fingers together in front of her waist. ''You're right, Lucas. He's an excellent choice for a night desk clerk. When you next see him, would you please send him upstairs so that I may speak with him?''

He surprised her by pulling her close for a quick hug. Emily went easily into his embrace, enjoying the strength and hardness of his body against hers. She felt something brush against her hair.

''I'll send Hep your way,'' Lucas promised when he released her. ''Perry doesn't start until this afternoon. I need to get back to the saloon.''

With that, he was gone, and Emily was left staring at the spot where he'd stood just moments before. Every part of her body felt warm and alive. All that just from Lucas's hug. Imagine how she would feel if he kissed her again? She must think of a way to make that happen, she thought happily.

"So you're really married?" Jackson MacIntyre asked incredulously before downing a shot of whiskey.

"Nearly a week now," Lucas told his brother. "And it's time for you to start thinking about doing the same."

Jackson, just as tall, big and stubborn as his brother, shook his head. "I ain't gonna take a wife. If some lawyer wants to think the mine don't belong to me, let him come and try to take it." Jackson grinned. "Or better yet, let him try to move me off the land."

With his too-long hair and untrimmed beard, Jackson looked as wild as a bear. Lucas knew his brother was also as strong as the ornery critter. Damn. Lucas was willing to take on just about any man in a fight, but with Jackson, he knew the match was nearly dead even. Which meant neither one was going to win and both of them would end up sore in the morning. He didn't mind the pain as long as it accomplished something.

"There's more at stake than the mine," Lucas reminded him. "What about the saloon and the ranch?"

Jackson looked uncomfortable. "They belong to us. It's wrong to say otherwise."

"It might be wrong, but the terms of Uncle Simon's will state things real clear." Lucas tried to swallow his frustration. He leaned across the table and stared at his brother. "I'm not asking you to marry for real, just take a temporary bride for a few weeks."

Jackson grunted. "Is that what you did? I heard you

married that schoolteacher. What happened to your fancy mail-order bride?''

''She wasn't fancy and she changed her mind.''

Jackson chuckled with amusement. ''She get a look at you and turn tail?''

''She never got on the train.''

''Someone must have told her you were an ugly cuss.'' He flicked his fingers toward Lucas's bright purple vest and grinned. ''She was probably worried about her husband dressing better than her. What does your bride think about you, Lucas?''

''I have no idea,'' Lucas said honestly. Not that he spent much time thinking about Emily's opinion of him. ''We get along.''

Which was a surprise. He hadn't thought about her one way or the other until he'd realized she was the answer to his problem. He still considered their marriage one of convenience. However, he found himself enjoying her company more than he would have thought possible.

''She's a bit on the skinny side,'' Jackson said, pouring himself another drink. Then he leaned back in his chair. Unlike Lucas, who always dressed in a clean white shirt, dark trousers and a colorful vest, Jackson preferred denim jeans and wool shirts. ''Not real pretty and she walks like she's got some kind of stick—''

Lucas moved with the swiftness of a rattler. One second he was sitting in his chair, the next he'd reached across the table and grabbed his brother's shirt in his hand.

''Apologize,'' he growled. ''Apologize or we'll take it outside.''

Jackson glanced around at the bar. ''You always did hate a fight in your place.''

"I don't like paying for the damage." Lucas didn't allow himself to be distracted. "Which is it to be?"

Jackson raised both beefy hands. "I apologize. I didn't mean to disrespect your wife. I also didn't know that you had a soft spot for her."

Lucas released him and slowly settled back into his chair. Anger still raced through him and he had to take deep breaths in an attempt to calm himself down.

"I don't have a soft spot, but I won't tolerate you speaking about her that way."

Jackson frowned. "Tolerate? Why're you talking like that, Lucas?" Then his smile returned. "I suppose it comes from spending so much time in the company of a schoolteacher."

Lucas ignored his brother and took a drink of the whiskey.

"Maybe when all this is over, you'll find yourself wanting to stay hitched," Jackson teased.

"Not likely."

Not ever was the real answer, he thought grimly. His marriage to Emily was strictly about the will. He would admit that he liked her a whole lot more than he'd thought he would. She was kind, taking in both Alice and Mary, and giving Hep a job. She was smart as a whip and as fervent as a preacher when it came to her plans. And she kissed finer than a skinny, spinster schoolteacher had the right to kiss. Lucas would have bet a hundred dollars in gold that he'd been the first man to taste her lips and yet she'd left him shaken and aroused. Which was why, despite how much he wanted to, he hadn't done it again.

But, even ignoring his attraction and the fact that she was someone very special, their marriage couldn't last.

He looked at his brother. "She doesn't know," he said quietly. "About what happened."

Jackson didn't say anything. He didn't have to. They'd never kept secrets from each other and their war experiences were no exception.

Jackson raised his glass. "To my little brother. And his bride."

Before Lucas could respond, Jackson was scrambling to his feet and running his free hand through his messy hair. Lucas turned around and saw that Emily had entered the saloon. She rarely came into his place of business, preferring to wave to him from the open door of the office or send in one of the boys always lurking about.

But it was relatively early in the day and there weren't very many customers.

Lucas motioned her forward, then put his arm around her. "Emily, this is my brother, Jackson MacIntyre. Jackson, my wife."

Jackson shifted uncomfortably. He reached for his hat, then realized he wasn't wearing one. "Ma'am. It's a real pleasure, I'm sure."

Emily smiled. "The pleasure is mine, Mr. MacIntyre." She glanced at Lucas, then back at Jackson. "I've never had a brother and I'm quite pleased to be able to claim that familial relationship at last."

Jackson blinked as if he hadn't exactly understood what she was saying. "Ma'am. Ah, me too." With that, he mumbled an excuse, grabbed his jacket and hurried from the saloon.

Emily turned to stare after him. "Will he be back? I wanted to invite him to join us for dinner."

Lucas thought about his brother's weekly visit to Miss Cherry's. "I think he already has plans."

"Oh, maybe next time."

"I'm sure he'd really enjoy that."

Since moving into the hotel, Emily had unpacked more of her treasures from home. The evening meal had become progressively more formal as she put those treasures into use. Lucas tried to imagine his brother carefully placing a starched linen napkin over his lap and picking the right fork. Oddly enough, Lucas found her ways didn't bother him. He enjoyed the contrast between proper manners and the wildness of Defiance. In some ways, that contrast existed within Emily herself. He'd never known anyone as proper, well-spoken or well mannered. Yet she hired orphaned children, rented a room to a lady of questionable reputation and had married a man who ran a saloon. He wondered what other surprises Emily had in store for him.

That evening Lucas surveyed the table in front of him. Three days before, he'd cleared out a storeroom and had found an unused table upon which they now dined. Silver and crystal sparkled in the light of the glowing candles. Emily carefully served a slice of apple pie, then set the dessert next to his fork.

"I want to take some up to Hep," she said when she'd served herself. "He has a real sweet tooth."

She smiled as she spoke and Lucas realized that in the forgiving light of the candles, she looked very pretty.

"How are things going with him?" he asked.

"Perfect." She picked up her fork and smiled. "He grumbles all the time about wearing a suit, but I think he likes it. I catch him preening in the mirror when I walk by the desk."

"You did a nice thing, hiring him. Without him finding some kind of indoor work, I didn't think he'd make it through another winter.''

"I wasn't being nice," Emily protested. "I needed someone to stay by the desk all night. Hep's willing to do that. I certainly wasn't interested."

He thought about the cot Emily had tucked behind the desk, in case Hep got too tired to stay awake. That soft heart of hers really touched him.

"Did you and Jackson discuss his mail-order bride?" she asked.

He frowned. "Some. Jackson's so stubborn. I'd like to pound some sense into him, but he'd just pound me back."

"You're both big men. I can't imagine who would win."

"It's usually a painful draw, which is why I don't bother." He chewed a bite of pie. "But when the woman arrives, he's going to have to marry her. Jackson talks about the mine being his and he dares any lawyer type to take him away from it. But it's not that simple."

"That's right. You have to worry about the saloon and the ranch, as well." She looked at him. "I, for one, do not want anyone taking the saloon away from you. I have a contract allowing me to rent the upstairs for three years."

She was teasing him and he couldn't help smiling at her. As he looked at her he noticed a single strand of blond hair had come loose from her tight bun. The bit of hair had a slight curl to it as it drifted past her cheek. As he had before, he wondered what her hair would look like loose, and how it would feel against his bare chest when they—

Lucas nearly dropped his fork. What the hell was wrong with him? He'd thought about Emily's hair being loose, but he'd never thought about them being naked together. He swore again and vowed to get his wayward thoughts under control. No way was he interested in keeping her around on a permanent basis. Consummating the marriage would only complicate things. Apparently it was time to make a visit to Miss Cherry's and get his needs taken care of.

"Why doesn't Jackson want to get married?" Emily asked.

Her question was so different from what he'd been thinking that it took him a bit to figure out an answer.

"My brother isn't very social."

"Has he always been like that? Was he quiet as a child?"

Lucas thought about his brother as a boy. Jackson had always been a prankster, like himself. Uncle Simon used to say they'd been born to trouble.

"He changed," Lucas admitted. "The war changed him."

"Wouldn't a wife help him change back?"

Lucas shook his head. "Some things can't be fixed."

Emily knew that was true, yet she couldn't help wishing it were different. She'd been sixteen when the War Between the States had ended. She'd seen many boys return as very different men.

"Were you in the war?" she asked.

Lucas nodded.

She wanted to ask what it had been like. She'd heard whispers, but no one had ever explained it to her. She knew there had been fighting and that men had died. But what had it been like? Had he been afraid? Or was that a silly question? Did men feel fear?

"Jackson saw more fighting," Lucas continued. "He has a bad scar on his face. That's why he wears the beard.'' He looked at her and smiled. ''He's jealous because I stayed handsome and he didn't.''

He spoke lightly, but Emily heard the pain behind the words. Lucas might not have any scars that she could see, but she knew there had to be plenty inside him. There was an unfamiliar darkness in his eyes; the coldness there frightened her. For the first time she wondered if his friendly teasing ways hid something very different in his heart.

''Lucas, I—''

''No. Let's talk about something else. Why don't I teach you how to play poker? With your head for figures, I'll bet you'd be good at it.''

''Lucas, I do not play card games!''

''Are you afraid you'll lose?''

Though she allowed him to change the subject, she still wondered about his ghosts from the war. Did they visit often? Could she help? Would he let her?

As she silently asked the questions, she realized that, despite the fact that their marriage was only to be one of convenience, she'd come to care for her husband. He was important to her and, when he told her their marriage was over, he was going to break her heart.

Chapter Six

"Em?"

Emily straightened from the box she'd been sorting. Lucas leaned against her reception desk and winked.

"I've been looking for you all over. I thought maybe you'd left town," he teased.

"Now why would I do that?"

"We're coming up on three weeks of marriage. I thought maybe you were having second thoughts."

If only that were true, she told herself. If only she could find Lucas physically unappealing, or annoying or anything worse than he was. Instead she considered her husband charming, handsome, caring and irresistible. Thoughts of him haunted her sleep and she desperately longed for him to repeat the kiss they'd shared. All to no avail. He remained friendly yet distant, and she didn't know how to make that change.

"I'm very content with our arrangement," she told him, hoping the small lie wouldn't count against her. "Did you wish to make a change?"

"No, but I would like to make a reservation. Miss Molly Malone is due in on the Wednesday stage and I want her to have the best room in the house."

Emily consulted her reservation list. "Number seven," she said, more to herself than him. "It has a view of the town, the window is large, which adds light, and it doesn't get too warm in the afternoon. I'll make a notation."

"You do that. I'm guessing she'll be here no more than two nights. We'll have the wedding a day or two after she arrives."

"How gracious of you to allow her to rest from her journey," she teased.

He ignored her humor. "After the ceremony I'm going to drive her up the mountain. Will you come with us?"

Emily blinked in surprise. "Why are you driving her up the mountain? Won't your brother do that?"

Lucas cleared his throat, then stepped back from the desk and shoved his hands into his pockets. Emily had never seen her husband act this way before. If she didn't know better, she would think that he was nervous.

"Jackson won't be here for the ceremony."

"What?" She didn't even try to keep the outrage from her voice. "How can he not be here?"

"Simple enough. We're holding a proxy ceremony." Lucas wouldn't meet her gaze. "Look, Em, I saw my brother a couple of days ago and he was pretty sick."

Her gaze narrowed. "He looked fine when I saw him."

"That was over a week ago. I've seen him since and he was feeling so poorly he didn't even make his weekly visit to Miss Cherry's."

Emily was momentarily distracted by the need not to blush at the mention of that woman and her business. "Then postpone the wedding."

"I can't. We don't have that much time. I'm going to

marry Molly by proxy. I've already checked and it's legal. Then you and I can drive her up the mountain."

Emily didn't like the sound of this one bit. "I've heard that he's not much interested in getting married, despite the terms of the will. Will he welcome her?"

Lucas laughed. "Jackson won't be mad at her. I'm the one he's going to want to kill."

"How comforting," she murmured dryly.

"Look, all that matters is meeting the terms of the will. Once Jackson is married, whether it's by proxy or not, we get our inheritance. We need to keep what's rightly ours."

"I know."

Emily understood Lucas's frustration at having to answer to the whims of a dead man. She even understood why the saloon and the ranch on the outskirts of town were so important to him. But she couldn't help feeling a little sad that their marriage was simply a convenience to him. She found herself wishing that she could matter a little, too.

Still, there was no point in pining for the moon. All it did was make one unhappy.

"I will be happy to accompany you and Miss Malone up the mountain," she said formally. "I wish to assure myself that she's satisfied with your brother's company."

Lucas looked relieved. "For all we know he might *like* having a woman around."

He didn't look very convinced of his statement and Emily thought it best to change the subject.

"While you're here," she said, pulling out a ledger and opening it to the first page, "this might be a good opportunity for you to go over my books. I've offered them to you several times, but you're never interested."

He settled on the corner of her desk. "Em, I trust you. You're making regular deposits into my account."

"I know. Every week. It seemed the easiest way to handle things. But I would feel better if you would check my figures."

He raised his dark eyebrows. "Are you cheating me?"

She stiffened. "Sir, I resent the implication."

"I wasn't implying anything, I was flat out asking. Like I said, Em, I trust you. You're honest. So why do I need to waste my time going over your books?"

He was frustrating her, but that was nothing new. Lucas made her squirm, he made her tingle, he made her long for impossible things, all the while remaining completely unmoved by her presence. She'd long ago decided that life was not going to go the way she wanted, but she found this situation even more vexing than most.

"Fine," she said, slapping the book closed. "I suppose it is your decision to trust me. I assure you I am not cheating you by even one penny." She drew in a deep breath to calm herself. "While you might be sorry that your mail-order bride changed her mind before arriving, you can console yourself with the thought that the woman you did marry is providing you with a good income."

Lucas stepped around the desk, moving until he was right in front of her. "Em, is that what you imagine me thinking? That all I want you for is my share of the profits?"

He was so close that it was difficult for her to form words. And why had the temperature in the room just risen several degrees?

"Not at all," she managed to say between suddenly dry lips. "I know you married me because of the terms of the will."

"There is that," he said and reached up to stroke her face. "It's midmorning, so I'm going to guess that most of your guests are already out."

Her throat felt tight, as did her torso. Trembling seemed to fill her limbs. "Yes."

He moved closer still, which she hadn't thought was possible. "Where are Mary and Alice?"

"Cleaning the, ah, bedrooms."

"So we're practically alone."

"Uh, yes."

"Good." He bent slightly and brushed his mouth against hers. "You have more to offer than your income or the terms of the will, Em. Did I mention you're a damn fine kisser?"

Her heart was pounding so loudly she had trouble hearing him speak. "You mentioned it before."

"Good. Because it's true."

He might have said something else, but she didn't care, nor was she listening. Instead she was *feeling*. Feeling the tender caress of his lips against her. She sighed against his mouth, savoring the sensation she'd been longing to experience again. It was as wonderful as she'd remembered. She loved the heat of his body and his strength.

He put his hands on her waist. Without thinking she responded by placing her hands on his shoulders. The nearness of him was nearly as delightful as the pressure of his mouth against hers and the tickling of his mustache. She found herself needing to strain forward, to rest her weight against his. She gave in to the need and shocked herself by leaning closer still, until her... her...chest was against his.

No one had ever touched her there, she thought, dazed from her boldness. While her curves were slight, she found they were exquisitely sensitive. She felt a heaviness in her chest, and a sensation of swelling. As if that part of her was somehow a little bit bigger. Low in her torso, she felt a similar heaviness, an almost aching. It was—

He swept his tongue across the seam of her mouth. All thoughts fled her mind as she parted to admit him. This was what she'd recalled the most, she thought dreamily. The sensation of him inside of her. Touching, teasing, exploring, discovering. He was bold, but not overly so. His tongue brushed against hers, making her want to sigh his name.

He tilted his head slightly and she moved in the opposite direction. It was easier to kiss now, and she found herself wanting to never stop. This moment could go on for eternity and she would be content. Heat filled her, starting at her curling toes and moving to the very top of her head. In between, all those places that defined her as a woman reacted as if touched by fever. In fact that same malady invaded her brain, making her think crazy thoughts.

She'd heard vague whispers about what went on between a man and a woman. She knew nothing specific and what she did know didn't make sense. Yet she wanted to ask Lucas to explain it all to her and perhaps even do some of those things. But only if they were as delightful as kissing.

As if he read her mind, he began to move his hands up and down her back. He stroked her like a cat, and like that same creature, she arched into his touch and wished she could purr her pleasure. On a return trip, his hands slipped lower still until he cupped her...the...that place upon which she sat.

Emily's eyes shot open in shock as he pulled her

closer to him. She planned on protesting, yet found herself assisting the contact by tilting that part of her forward until her, well, until they were touching most intimately.

The layers of her petticoats and skirt were too thick to allow her to feel anything, which was most frustrating. She knew that men were different from women, but no one had been clear on the specifics. How unfair. Her one experience for knowing and she had no way to find out the truth.

Lucas pulled away slightly. She thought he was going to say something, but instead he kissed her cheek, her jaw, then that spot behind her ear. When he nibbled on her earlobe, she both laughed and shuddered.

"Emily," he breathed softly. "Who would have thought you'd be like this?"

"Like what?"

He raised his head and gazed into her eyes. His expression was different from any she'd ever seen before. A muscle twitched in his jaw and there was a smoldering darkness in his eyes.

He groaned. "You really don't know, do you? Which is why I shouldn't be here."

He kissed her quickly and fiercely, then walked away without a backward glance. Emily stared after him, confused, still tingling and not sure if their situation had been improved or made worse.

Lucas stalked into his office and slammed the door shut. He headed for his desk and yanked open the bottom drawer. But after staring at the bottle of whiskey there, he kicked the drawer closed and sank into his chair.

Damn, he thought grimly. What the hell was he doing? He couldn't go around kissing Emily like that. It would only lead to trouble. She was too innocent. Worse, she was his wife. If he didn't control himself, he couldn't get the marriage annulled. Consummating the marriage would complicate everything. And complications were the last thing he needed.

But the speech wasn't working. His arousal throbbed painfully and he found himself wanting Emily with a desperation he couldn't recall experiencing before. She wasn't like the women he generally chose to warm his bed. For that he liked charming and willing. For a while there had been Rose, a widow traveling through the West as a way to ease her suffering. They'd spent a long summer together, helping each other. When she'd moved on, he'd missed the pleasures of her body, but little else.

There were the girls at Miss Cherry's, and other women in other places. Women he could laugh with and share a bed with, all without having to worry about anything more than walking away.

Emily wasn't like that. He supposed the problem with Emily was that he cared about her. She'd begun to matter. Maybe it was because she was so smart and prim. Those dresses and her formal manner of speech all cried out *spinster*. Yet she had a big heart. She did what she thought was right without caring about the town's opinion. And she kissed as if she'd been born for pleasure.

He rubbed his hands across his face and tried to think about something other than the way Emily had felt in his arms. He couldn't be with her in that way. He knew that. She would make some man a damn fine wife, just not him. He couldn't risk it. Loving someone, being loved, was not allowed. He'd been spared, but he hadn't paid for his sins.

He dropped his hands to the desk and drew in a deep breath. That's what he had to remember. He'd been sentenced to hell, and he refused to make Emily live there with him.

She needed a plan, Emily decided two days later. Despite the way Lucas had kissed her, he now seemed determined to avoid her. He'd even made excuses not to dine with her for the past two nights. Men were most confusing creatures, but she was going to figure them out. Or if not all of them, at least the man she'd married. She was stubborn enough and smart enough to be able to look at the problem from many directions. What she didn't have was information.

Which explained why she was lurking in the hallway of her hotel a little after midnight, a time when she would have normally been in bed. She was waiting up for the one person who might be able to help her.

Dixie entertained men, so she must know many things about them. Emily was reasonably confident she didn't need quite that much information, but whom better to ask? She'd tried to speak with Dixie that morning, but Mary had been dusting the stairs and within earshot. Which meant Emily was now forced to lurk like a common criminal.

Fifteen minutes later she heard steps on the stairs. Hep greeted their permanent guest with an ''Evening, Dixie.''

''Hello, Hep. You look especially fine tonight.''

Emily smiled as she imagined the bent old miner blushing and ducking his gray head. Hep mumbled something she couldn't hear, then Dixie appeared at the end of the corridor.

If the tall woman was surprised to see her landlord hovering in the hallway, she didn't show it. Instead she nodded slightly and opened her door, then ushered Emily inside. Emily went quickly and shut the door behind her.

"I take it you wish to speak with me," Dixie said in the darkness of the room. "Should I be concerned?"

"What? Oh, no."

Emily laced her fingers together in front of her waist and paced to the window. While Dixie lit the lantern, Emily busied herself with closing the drapes. She turned back to her guest and forced a smile as the lantern caught, illuminating the small room.

"You look very lovely," she said, taking in the green silk dress.

The garment shimmered in the light. Tiny sleeves hugged to Dixie's shoulders while the bodice of the dress clung in a way that made Emily blush. So much of her, ah, chest was exposed, it seemed she might fall out at any moment. The bodice was fitted to the waist, where it flared out over petticoats, falling in graceful swags to the floor.

Dixie wore her hair in an intricate style of sweeping curls. Matching green flowers decorated her hair. Her arms were bare except for several gold bracelets. Her face—a perfect oval defined by large eyes and full lips— looked slightly flushed. Emily wondered if the color came from cosmetics. She'd heard of such things but had never used any herself.

Dixie settled in the room's only chair to wait for Emily to speak. Emily drew in a deep breath.

"This is most difficult for me," she admitted. After all, she was married and should, by now, understand the workings of a man. Pride made her want to leave, but the need to know was stronger.

"Take your time," Dixie said. "I'm not going anywhere." She nodded to the bed. "Maybe you'd feel better if you sat."

Emily glanced at the bed, then at the woman. She

suddenly thought of Lucas and wondered if he'd ever...if he and Dixie had...well, if, when he'd visited Miss Cherry's place, he'd ever chosen her.

"I—"

The thought made her limbs go weak. She sank onto the bed rather than fall onto the floor. All the breath seemed to leave her and she suddenly wanted to cry.

"It's about Lucas," she forced herself to say.

Dixie surprised her by leaning forward and taking her hands. "Is that what has you so upset? Were you wondering if he and I were ever together?"

Emily didn't answer. She only stared at the long, pale fingers touching her own.

"Let me set your mind to rest," Dixie told her. "Lucas and I have known each other a long time. A few years back, he paid for my services a time or two, but we found we enjoyed talking more. We're friends, Emily. That's all. Besides, Lucas hasn't come calling at Miss Cherry's since the wedding, so you have nothing to worry about."

Dixie squeezed her hands, then released them. "Does that help?"

Emily nodded. "Some. I mean I'm happy to know that he's not going there to do that." Whatever "that" was. "But I need to speak with you about something else. And you must promise to be completely honest with me."

Dixie raised her eyebrows. "I've found that being completely honest often leads to trouble, but if you insist."

"I do." Emily straightened. "I would very much appreciate it if you help me be more attractive. I would like to have Lucas notice me." She felt heat flaring on her cheeks, but she forced herself to go on. "I understand that, given my appearance, you may think the task impossible. If so, please tell me.''

Dixie studied her. ''That would be the completely honest part.''

''Yes.''

Humiliation filled her, but Emily forced herself to keep her chin high.

Dixie pressed her lips together. ''I'm trying to figure out what it is you're not telling me. Is this about seducing Lucas?''

Emily's shoulders slumped and she covered her face with her hands. ''Is it so obvious that he finds me easy to ignore? It is impossible, isn't it?''

''Honey, no.'' Dixie moved to the bed and put her arm around Emily. ''I can help you look very pretty. You have lovely hair and beautiful eyes.''

Emily dropped her hands to her lap and looked at the other woman. ''Really?''

''I swear.''

''And you'll help me?''

''I would be happy to.'' She glanced around her room. ''You're not going to like this, Emily, but we really need to go to Miss Cherry's. She has lots of dresses and lingerie. You'll have to sneak in the back, though. Still, it will be worth it.''

Emily wasn't sure she could do that, but she didn't have a choice. ''Thank you,'' she said, then swallowed. ''Do you know why he married me?''

''Because of Uncle Simon's will.''

''So you really are friends.''

''Yes.''

She took a deep breath. ''Am I a fool for trying to capture his attention?''

Dixie smiled. ''Actually I think you're very smart and

very brave. Lucas won't make it easy, but I suspect he's one of the few men who are worth the trouble.''

Emily couldn't believe she was sneaking into the rear of a house of ill repute. Her! Emily MacIntyre, scurrying around in broad daylight. But here she was, checking both ways before scuttling up the rear steps and following Dixie through the open doorway.

"You need smelling salts?" Dixie asked in a teasing voice. "Is your heart going to give out from the shame?"

"I'll just be extra fervent in my prayers," Emily told her, and was surprised to find herself smiling.

Dixie laughed. "You do that. And mention my name." She motioned for Emily to follow her. "We'll use the back stairs. There's less chance of discovery that way."

Emily trailed after her hostess. They left the plain mudroom and entered a busy kitchen. A woman stood at the stove, removing a tray of biscuits from the oven. Two boys were peeling vegetables. Emily glanced around in interest.

"I didn't know that meals were served here," she said.

Dixie shook her head. "They're not for the customers. It's for the girls. We have to keep up our strength."

Emily opened her mouth, then closed it. She didn't know what to say. Dixie chuckled and kept walking.

Keeping up their strength? Emily was both shocked and intrigued. So it took effort, to do those things with men. She still didn't know what it was exactly that they did. Maybe if she asked Dixie, she could—

Emily stepped into the hallway leading to the rear stairs and came to a stunned halt. To her left was the front room of the house. She could hear a male voice but couldn't see anyone. But what was within view was enough to make her gape.

The walls were covered with deep red fabric. The wood trim and ceiling were cream and there were flecks of gold in the paint. All the occasional tables were gilded, as were the legs of the sofa she saw. The sofa itself was red, as was the carpet.

Something tugged on her arm. She saw Dixie had returned to her side and was urging her toward the stairs. "Stop staring," the other woman said. "You want to get caught?"

"No. Of course not. I just didn't know there was that much red and gold in the world."

"Now you know. Hurry."

Emily picked up her skirts and ran lightly toward the second floor. Dixie waved her forward and they eased into the second door on the right.

"This is my room," Dixie said, "when I'm working. Stay here while I go get Cherry and some clothes."

Emily barely heard her leave. She was too busy looking around at the magnificent bedroom. It was easily twice the size of the room Dixie rented at the hotel. In the center was a large four-poster bed so high that there was a step stool to help one up to the mattress. The coverlet was a patchwork of red velvet, lace and satin. Across from the bed was a huge mirror, with a low sofa in front of it. A dresser stood in the corner. Leather straps slipped from a drawer onto the floor.

Emily glanced at herself in the mirror and saw that her mouth was open. She forced her lips together and tried to imagine what went on in this room. She recalled Dixie saying that she and Lucas had been intimate a few times, years before. Her chest tightened at the thought of someone else knowing her husband in a way she didn't.

Before she had a chance to get comfortable in the room, Dixie reappeared, bringing with her a petite blond woman in a red dress.

"Emily, this is Cherry."

Cherry was older, perhaps close to forty, with beautiful pale skin and light blue eyes. She wore her blond hair piled high on her head and had a beauty patch on her right cheek. But her most impressive feature was her bosom. Around her even Dixie looked small. Emily knew she looked as flat as a ten-year-old.

She folded her arms over her chest and tried to smile. "Ma'am. It's a pleasure to meet you."

Cherry offered a wide smile. "Don't you dare call me ma'am, like I'm an old woman. We don't stand on ceremony here, honey. Come on. Let me welcome you proper."

Cherry advanced and caught Emily in a hug. She barely came to Emily's shoulder but she was plenty strong and about squeezed the life out of her. Then Cherry reached up and patted Emily's cheek.

"I owe you for taking those poor girls in. I couldn't believe it when their bastard of a father wanted to sell them to me. I took 'em because if I didn't, someone else would. But I had no use for 'em. Alice was practically of an age to make a decision about working for me and she wasn't interested. Mary was too young and too pretty to stay around here. I tell you, I was mighty worried. So you saved me from that."

She clapped her hands together and turned to Dixie, who had several dresses over one arm. "Now Dixie tells me you want us to fix you up so your new husband pays attention to you." Cherry grinned. "I don't guess you want to know the secrets of keeping him happy in bed."

Emily blinked but didn't know what to say.

"We can teach her that later," Dixie said, setting the dresses on the bed. She walked to the armoire on the far side of the room and pulled it open. "Right now let's get him to notice her. Once she's had him in her bed for a year or two, we'll worry about keeping him there."

She glanced at Emily over her shoulder. "Take off your clothes."

Emily hesitated. Dixie pointed to the dresses on the bed. "You need to take off what you're wearing if you want to try on those."

"Yes," Emily said with a cheer she didn't feel. "Of course."

She forced herself to reach for the buttons running down the front of her gray dress. Cherry moved behind her and began pulling the pins from her knot of hair.

"Let's see what this looks like, too," Cherry said. "It's a real pretty color. Does it go to your waist?"

There was a tug, then her hair tumbled free. Before Emily could answer, Cherry sighed. "Beautiful. And there's a wave in it. Honey, why are you wearing your hair all caught back like that? It's not particularly flattering. You gotta let it be a little loose. Kinda like me."

She chuckled at her own humor. Emily tried to smile, but she was also dealing with the embarrassment of undressing in front of these two women.

Finally she got her dress unbuttoned and slid it off her shoulder. After stepping out of it, she set it on the bed. Dixie walked over and stared at her.

"She's skinny," Cherry said bluntly. "Not much on top. Still, we can make the most of what God gave her and lie about the rest."

Dixie smiled reassuringly. "The French have solved your problem. With a few tucks, some lace and tiny stitches, they have worked miracles. Take off your petticoats."

Emily began untying the layers of cotton. When she was down to her chemise, she was humiliated to discover that they expected her to take that off, too.

Heat flared on her cheeks as she bared herself to the waist. But neither woman took any time to stare at her. Instead they slipped a new lacy garment over her head. It fit tightly under her bosom, pushing up her meager curves and barely covering the puckered tips.

"Better," Cherry pronounced. "You have a tiny waist. You need to show that off. And gray. Emily, what were you thinking? You need to wear blue or rose. Colors that bring out your eyes."

A sound of laughter came from downstairs. Cherry shook her head. "I have to return to my guests. Dixie will take care of you, honey. The dress and the undergarments are my gift. If you want to order any more, tell Dixie and she'll write it all down." Cherry paused at the door and winked. "You'd be surprised how many good women have me order things for them from France. Those French know how to keep a woman beautiful and a man happy."

With that, she was gone. Emily stared after her. "She's so different from anyone I've ever known."

"It's part of her charm. Cherry might live an unconventional life, but she's a good woman."

Emily glanced at Dixie. "So are you. I appreciate you taking the time with me."

Dixie secured another petticoat around her waist. "I like you, Emily. You don't put on airs."

"I like you, too."

They both smiled. Emily realized that she hadn't had a real friend since coming to Defiance. It felt good to have one now.

"Cherry's right about the colors you should wear," Dixie told her, reaching for a blue dress and pulling it over her head. "Throw away those ugly gray clothes and start over."

When the dress was smoothed over Emily, Dixie walked behind her and fastened the buttons. Emily glanced at herself in the mirror and was shocked to see actual curves thrusting up above the low-cut bodice.

"Is that all me?" she asked in amazement.

"See. Those tucks and lace can push you right up. Lucas won't know what to think."

Emily didn't know what to think, either. She loved the deep blue of the gown and the way the soft fabric felt against her skin. It wasn't practical and she wouldn't be able to wear it very much, but for the first time in her life, she saw that she had possibilities. Maybe she could order some wool dresses in blue or even rose. While she had to be practical when she was working, there was no reason she had to be unattractive.

"Now sit," Dixie told her, pushing her toward the low, backless sofa facing the mirror. "Let's see what we can do with your hair."

Thirty minutes later, Emily barely recognized herself. Dixie had secured her hair at the nape of her neck, but unlike her usual tight bun, this style allowed her hair to wave slightly. There was a row of curls across her crown, and two loose curls by her ears.

Between the feminine hairstyle and the beautiful new dress, she was transformed. Her cheeks glowed with color and her eyes were huge.

"I love it," she said fervently. "You've made me pretty."

"You always were," Dixie told her. "You just didn't know it."

A moan came from the next room, followed by a rhythmic thumping against the wall. Emily frowned.

"What's that?"

Dixie laughed. "Catherine is working."

"But—" Emily caught her breath. "Oh."

Dixie smiled at her in the mirror. "You're a virgin, aren't you, Emily?"

"I, um, yes." Emily ducked her head.

"I thought so. Lucas married you because of the will. You married him for a different reason."

Emily kept her eyes tightly closed. "I wanted to turn the upstairs into a hotel."

"I see. So it was strictly a business arrangement. Except now you want it to be a real marriage."

Emily risked looking into the mirror. She studied her new friend. "Do you think that's wrong?"

"No. I think it's very right. Lucas needs someone like you in his life. The problem is he doesn't know it and, even if he did, he would resist. Although looking at you now, I'd say he's going to have a little more trouble."

Emily smiled. "Really? I didn't know much about him when we married, but now that I've spent more time with him, I quite like him. He's very kind and he teases me. No one has ever done that before. I'm not really the teasing kind."

"That's all going to change. Once Lucas sees you in that dress, he won't be able to think about anything else."

Emily regarded her finery. "I can't wear this for everyday."

"True, but you can still keep your hair like this and you can get more sensible dresses in flattering colors."

"That's what I thought, too." She rose and turned to Dixie. "How can I thank you?"

"Go see your husband and try not to laugh when his jaw hits the floor."

Chapter Seven

Lucas looked up when a woman entered his office. She was at once both familiar and a stranger. Tall, slender yet with a delightful expanse of bosom displayed. The blue of her gown matched her eyes and she—

"Emily?" he asked in disbelief. He rose to his feet and came around the desk. "Emily?"

"Hello, Lucas. I just stopped by to say good-afternoon. I haven't seen you yet today." She looked past him and raised her eyebrows. "I didn't realize you had company."

"Huh?" He followed her gaze to the young woman sitting in front of his desk. "Oh. Emily, this is Molly Malone. Miss Malone, my wife."

Emily smiled. "Welcome to Defiance. Did you just arrive?"

"Yes. On the stage. Your husband was kind enough to meet me."

They continued talking, but Lucas wasn't listening. How could he with Emily standing there looking so *different?* He told himself it was just that the dress was much prettier than the usual gray garments she wore and that her suddenly fuller appearing bosom was more because of padding and stitching than due to any increase in her feminine gifts, but none of it seemed to matter. His brain wasn't listening, and neither was the sudden throbbing in his groin.

He wanted her.

That wasn't anything new. He'd wanted her from their first kiss and his attempts to stay clear of her had only increased his longing. Now she'd gone and gotten herself all fussied up. He studied her softer hairstyle and the long curls tickling her cheeks. His fingers itched to unfasten the row of curls and release her hair until it tumbled down her back. He wanted to bury his face in the golden length, inhaling the scent of her as he—

"Lucas?"

He shook his head and turned attention to his wife. "Yes?"

"I thought I'd show Molly to her room."

"Yes. I'll send her things upstairs." He thought of Molly's traveling companion and knew that Emily would enjoy the surprise. "The ceremony is at ten in the morning."

Molly glanced at him. "Are you sure Jackson is too ill to attend the ceremony?"

"He was when I saw him a couple of days ago. A fever, I think."

She didn't look convinced but didn't ask again. Emily glared at him. She thought she knew the truth about his brother. Lucas knew different. However if Emily understood all about Jackson's past, she would never let Molly Malone head up that mountain. He eased his own guilty conscience by reminding himself that as soon as he was able, Jackson would head down the mountain to beat the hell out of his brother. Lucas figured a beating would be worth it. As soon as Jackson and Molly were married—

by whatever means necessary—the terms of the will would be met.

Emily led the way up the stairs toward the hotel. Jackson's bride wasn't anything like she'd imagined. Emily supposed she'd expected a young timid woman afraid of her own shadow. Instead Molly Malone was at least twenty-five. Obviously she wasn't afraid of very much, because she'd just traveled across the country by herself to marry a man she'd never met.

"You must be tired," Emily said as they reached the reception area in the hotel. "It was a long journey."

"I'm fine." Molly turned in a slow circle, taking in the desk, the worn wallpaper and sitting area. "Well then, isn't this fancy." She glanced at Emily. "Your husband was tellin' me that you run the hotel yourself."

"Yes. We have an arrangement whereby I rent the space from him."

"A woman ownin' a business." Molly smiled. "I'm impressed. I thought I was being brave traipsin' all across the back of beyond to find a husband, and you've gone and made the kind of life that doesn't even need one."

Emily thought about the last time Lucas had kissed her. She was starting to think she needed her husband very much. "I have a head for business," she said, "but that doesn't mean I wouldn't want to be married."

"I suppose not. Most women want a family." Molly brushed at the front of her dress. "So I'm to spend the night in this fine establishment. It'll be far nicer than anywhere I stopped on the journey." She leaned close to Emily. "I thought fishermen smelled bad at the end of the day, but they're positively doused in perfume compared to some of the people on the train and stage."

Emily laughed. Molly was exceptionally pretty with copper-colored hair that tumbled down her back to her waist and beautiful green eyes. When she'd first seen her, she'd been a little put off by her beauty, but now she found herself warming to the other woman.

"We try to keep the smells down to a minimum," Emily assured her. "I can even arrange for you to have a bath in your room, if you'd like."

"That sounds like heaven. I can change my dress as well. I have a special one I've been saving for the ceremony." Molly's mouth straightened. "And a new hat, although from what I hear, my husband won't be there to see it."

Emily felt a flicker of guilt. She suspected there was more going on than either she or Molly was aware of. Jackson could very well be ill, but she wasn't sure that was the only reason he wouldn't be at the ceremony.

Before she could decide if she should say something or not, Perry appeared carrying a trunk. Perched on top of it was a very large, very brightly colored bird in a cage.

"What is it?" Emily asked in delight.

Beside her Molly laughed. "Captain Blood. He's a parrot. He's all that I have left of my family. Which, when you think on it, is a mighty sad statement to be makin'."

Perry set down the trunk and stepped back. "I don't think he likes me."

Molly sighed. "The captain isn't too fond of anyone."

"*Ahoy, maties,*" the parrot squawked. "*Abandon ship.*"

"Not just yet, Captain," Molly said, running a finger along his red, yellow and green back. "I'm thinkin' we might just find a home here in Colorado."

As Perry hurried down the stairs, Emily cautiously approached the bird. "I've never seen anything like him."

"He belonged to my uncle, God rest his soul. Now he's mine. He didn't much care for traveling, I can tell you, but I'm hoping he'll settle down now that we've arrived."

Emily thought about asking if she could hold the bird, then she studied his sturdy beak. Perhaps Captain Blood was best admired from a safe distance.

"Your room is in here," she said, motioning down the hallway. "You should have a quiet night. I don't have many guests this evening, and they're all at the other end of the hotel." She eyed the bird. "Does he need a perch? I have a coat rack. Would that work?"

Molly smiled. "How kind of you. The captain's too ungrateful to say thank ye, but I'll do it for him."

"Good. I'll bring it in shortly."

She opened the door to Molly's room and stepped back to let the woman enter. This room was done in greens, with thick drapes to block out the morning sun. The walls were plain and Emily rubbed them with her fingers.

"Maybe I should paint," she murmured more to herself than her guest.

Molly set Captain Blood on the footboard, where the bird slid back and forth, squawking softly. "It's pretty," she said, fingering the coverlet. "I like the green."

"It matches your eyes. They're a lovely color."

Molly ducked her head and smiled. "Thank you." She cleared her throat. "But I'm thinkin' a little paint on the walls might brighten up the place."

"Yes, I agree. I wanted to get the hotel open quickly so there was only time to clean, not decorate." She touched the walls again. "Maybe a soft yellow."

"That would be nice." Molly walked to the window and glanced out at the street, then she turned back to face the room. "Have you seen Jackson's house? Do you know what it's like?"

Emily realized her guest was nervous, and why not? She'd traveled more than halfway across the country to marry a stranger.

"Molly, why don't I have your trunk delivered to your room? You can freshen up and I'll make tea. You can join me in my office in a few minutes and we'll talk."

"I'd like that," Molly said.

Twenty minutes later Emily finished brewing a pot of tea. She set fresh tea cakes on a plate and put them and the pot onto the small table in her office. She'd also changed back into one of her gray dresses, not wanting to spoil the new blue one. She wanted to wear it tomorrow, to the wedding. She only wished she'd had it when she'd married Lucas.

She glanced at the clock and thought there might be time to go to the mercantile this afternoon. If not she would go first thing in the morning. Either way, she wanted to look over the ready-made dresses they had in stock, plus buy some length of cloth. She would get two or three dresses made up in a week or so. However much it cost, she didn't want to be wearing her gray gowns any longer than she had to.

A light knock on the open door caused her to look up. Molly stood in the doorway.

"Please come in," Emily said, pulling out a chair. "I have tea and cakes. Are you hungry for something more? We'll be dining at six and I thought the cakes would hold you, but if you'd like something more…"

"No. The cakes are plenty." Molly took the chair Emily offered.

Emily served them both, then returned to the conversation they'd been having in Molly's room.

"I've never seen Jackson's house," she said. "I know he lives in the mountains, some distance from town." She frowned. "It can't be all that far, because he comes to town at least once a week."

"I'm hopin' he's a good man," Molly said.

"I'm sure he is. He and Lucas were raised by their uncle. Lucas runs the saloon here in town and Jackson works the family mine. They have some land outside of town. Their goal is to start a ranch and sell horses to the army."

"Oh, a man with plans. That's encouraging." Molly sipped her tea. "Have you been married long?"

Emily laughed. "Less than a month." And she was still untouched by her husband, although she wasn't about to share that information with Molly.

"Are you happy?"

Emily considered the question. Was she happy? Her husband had married her for reasons that had nothing to do with affection and everything to do with the family inheritance. While he kissed her with great intensity, he didn't seem interested in consummating their marriage. The hotel was successful, which was good. She had a new friend and might eventually learn how to be pretty.

"I'm content," she said at last. "Some things are good, some things could be improved upon." She looked at the woman sitting across from her. "If you don't mind me asking, why did you agree to be a mail-order bride?"

"There wasn't anything left for me back home. So many men were lost during the war. Men became scarce." She shrugged. "I have a bit of a temper and

I've been known to be stubborn with good reason. However much I don't mind those qualities in myself, some men find them too difficult. I thought someone from out West would appreciate my spirit."

Molly set down her cup and placed her hands on the table. "I want a family. With my uncle gone, it's just me. I know that some would say that marryin' a stranger is crazy, but I disagree. I think happiness in marriage is a decision both people make and I intend to be happy."

"I admire your courage."

"It's not courage, it's having no other choice. I didn't want to die an old maid. Besides, if Jackson is honest and decent, I can fiddle with the rest and bend him to my will. And if he's as stubborn as me, then we'll never run out of things to argue about."

Molly bit into a cake. Emily didn't know what to say. She'd never met anyone like the woman sitting across from her. She almost mentioned the fact that when Molly married Jackson, she and Molly would be sisters. Except Lucas intended to get the marriage annulled. So there was no point in claiming a relationship that would only be temporary.

Molly glanced over her shoulder, as if to make sure they were alone. "I don't suppose you'd be tellin' me about the marriage bed? I don't know much and I'm thinkin' that Jackson will want to have his way with me when I get up the mountain."

Emily had been swallowing as Molly spoke. She choked on her tea and it was some time before she was able to speak.

"The marriage bed?" she repeated weakly.

"Yes. I don't know very much about what happens there."

Me, either, Emily thought sadly. If only that were different.

"I, ah, think it's best if you discuss this with your husband," she said by way of an excuse. She absolutely couldn't confess her ignorance to Molly. It was too humiliating.

Molly looked disappointed. "Maybe when I've been with my husband I'll understand why none of you want to talk about it."

Maybe when you've been with your husband you can tell *me* what happens, Emily thought with a sigh.

The wedding was delayed by Pastor Bird having to make a sick call to a nearby ranch and it was after three by the time Molly Malone had been legally wed—if only by proxy—to Jackson MacIntyre. Emily watched Molly recite her vows and felt more than a twinge of discomfort when Lucas replied in his brother's stead.

She consoled herself with the fact that while her husband might be saying the marriage vows to another woman, he kept stealing glances at her.

She smoothed down the front of her new blue dress and resisted the urge to pat her hair. While she hadn't been able to duplicate Dixie's style exactly, she'd come close. Now she wore her hair more loosely, allowing curls to drift across her forehead and along the back of her neck. She felt almost pretty and wished she'd looked better for her own wedding.

At least she knew what to do now. She'd gone to the mercantile that morning and had purchased two new simple dresses, one in dark blue and the other in a deep pink. She'd also purchased lengths of cloth and had taken them over to Mrs. Baker to have them made up into dresses. Just as soon as she had her new wardrobe assembled, she would offer her gray dresses to Alice and Mary to make over. Both girls had the right coloring to carry off the shade.

Pastor Bird pronounced Jackson and Molly married. Lucas shook hands with the bride, who smiled happily. He joined Emily.

"I'll be taking Molly up the mountain in the morning," he said.

"I'd like to accompany you," she told him.

He grinned. "You can even come with us, if you'd like."

She put her hands on her hips. "I refuse to believe that you think 'accompany' is a big word. It isn't."

"If you say so. But to my way of thinking, once a woman turns into a schoolteacher, she never turns back."

"And what exactly is wrong with being a schoolteacher?"

He leaned close. "I think that's something we need to discuss in private."

He was only teasing her, yet Emily couldn't help blushing and wishing that they were in private right now. She had a feeling that Lucas would kiss her. She'd seen him glancing at her low-cut dress when he'd thought she wasn't looking. Was he admiring her? Did he want to touch her there?

The thought was so incredibly shocking that she nearly choked. How could she have thought such a thing? Under other circumstances she would never consider thinking about a man touching her at all, let alone in such an intimate manner.

Except, a small voice in her head whispered, Lucas wasn't any man. He was her husband. And hadn't she been wishing that he wanted her the way most husbands wanted their wives?

Someone cleared her throat. Emily turned and saw Molly standing close by.

"I appreciate the hospitality and all, but I think it's time I headed up to greet my new husband."

Emily frowned. "We're going to take you in the morning."

"Why wait?" Molly asked brightly. "I can rent a buggy and take myself there tonight."

"No," Lucas said. "It will be dark soon. Jackson's place is too small for all of us to stay there the night."

"I'm not asking you to come with me." Molly raised her chin and met Lucas's gaze with a stubborn glance of her own. "I've managed to travel all the way from Massachusetts by myself. I've no doubt I can find the cabin. As for it getting dark, I'll have the stars to guide me. My uncle taught me well how to navigate."

Emily had been about to protest Molly making the journey on her own, but she had second thoughts. The woman had a point. She *had* come all the way to Defiance without any man to guide her, just as Emily had come from Ohio. If she were in Molly's place, she wouldn't want to wait until morning, either.

"Lucas, she's right," Emily told her husband. "Why can't Molly go tonight if she wants to? The road is safe and she can find the cabin as easily as any man."

"I never said she had to be a man to go."

"You want to take her."

"Because it's polite."

"Don't twist the truth. You think she needs an escort because she's a woman."

"Now you know what I'm thinking?"

"If there's a road, then there's no problem a'tall,"

Molly announced. "If you'll just be tellin' me where I can rent a buggy."

Lucas grumbled something under his breath. "This is all your fault," he told Emily.

"Really? I thought you were the one who wanted your brother married."

He glared at her. "We'll discuss this later."

It had now been three nights since they'd dined together. Molly's determination gave her a little courage of her own. "Over dinner?" she asked dryly. "Are you finished avoiding me?"

"I haven't been avoiding you."

Molly started moving down the center aisle of the small church. "I'll go find the blacksmith myself."

"No, wait. I'm coming with you." He glared at Emily. "Yes, I'll be there for dinner." He stalked away muttering something about "damn women."

The sight of her usually calm husband all flustered did much to bring a smile to Emily's lips.

"Molly departed all right?" Emily asked as she served baked chicken to her husband.

"She seemed to. At least she knows how to handle a horse. Good thing. That damn bird of hers kept squawking."

"I liked Captain Blood."

"Figures."

He was still in a temper, no doubt from their encounter earlier in the day. For some reason, that pleased Emily. Even if he didn't care about her the way she would like, the fact that she annoyed him meant he was unable to ignore her.

"You don't like it when I disagree with you, do you?" she asked.

He glared at her from across the table. "Of course not. You wouldn't like me disagreeing with you."

"I might not mind if you were right about something and I was not."

His glare turned into a scowl. "You're saying you were right and I was wrong?"

"Not at all. I was merely making an observation."

He grunted.

Emily smiled. He wore a red vest over his white shirt, along with a tailored black coat. Elegant as always, she thought, pleased with her husband's handsome face and fine manners. She wondered if he knew he looked like a little boy when he scowled and sulked. She thought he did not and assumed it would be wise to keep that information to herself.

"Molly is looking forward to being married. She said she's wanted a family all her life."

Lucas didn't reply. She wondered what secrets he was keeping from her about Jackson and his past.

"Molly said that happiness in a marriage is a decision, not a matter of luck. Do you agree with her?"

"I've never thought about it."

"Really." She leaned toward him. "You've never thought about marriage at all?"

His blue eyes darkened with temper. "Emily, what is the point of this conversation?"

"I didn't know you expected there to be one. I was simply sharing the things I learned during my visit with my new sister-in-law. I found her quite charming. Molly also said that if Jackson is an honest and good man, she'll be well pleased. She knows she can mold the rest of him into being whatever she'd like."

Lucas swore, but she chose to ignore the word.

"What is it about you women?" he demanded. "Why do you think you can change a man?"

"I'm sure I don't know. I've never thought such a thing."

"Pull the other leg."

She stiffened. "Lucas. I have never lied to you. I don't lie."

He frowned. "All right," he conceded. "Perhaps *lie* is too strong a word. I'll agree that you haven't deliberately set out to change me."

"Not even a little."

"Yet here I sit—a changed man."

She looked at him. "I don't see a change. Your clothes, your manner, everything about you is as it was when we met."

He glared. "I'm here."

She looked around at her office. Why was it men always talked about women being difficult? Personally, she had absolutely no understanding of her husband's complaints.

"All right," she said slowly. "You *are* dining in this office, which you would have not done before our marriage. I do not see how that is so great a change."

"There are other things."

"Such as?"

He threw his hands into the air. "There you go, demanding things. When did you become a shrewish wife?"

"Shrewish? Lucas, what's wrong with you this evening?"

"Nothing." He stared at his coffee. "I need a drink. And you shouldn't be wearing that dress."

She glanced down at the blue gown and had to bite her lip to keep from smiling. Was that the problem? Did he find her attractive? Perhaps the contrast in her appearance was great enough to make him nervous. If only she knew how to use her advantage to further their relationship.

"Why is it you and your brother have never married?" she asked when nothing more brilliant occurred to her.

"I can't speak for Jackson," he mumbled, avoiding her gaze. "For myself, I never wanted to."

"Why? You're married now and doing very well." She held in a smile. "For one married to such a shrewish wife."

"You're going to keep mentioning that until I apologize, aren't you?"

She toyed with her dinner so he wouldn't see the amusement in her eyes. "I'm sure I don't know what you mean."

"I'm sure you do." He sighed. "I never planned on getting married, because I'm not the marrying kind of man. This is only temporary, so it's easier."

His words burned away her humor and set up an aching in the region of her heart. She set her fork on the table.

"I remember," she said slowly. "You married me because of the will and because my hotel provides you with income, nothing more." She studied his face. "What else is there, Lucas? I don't believe your statement of being the kind of man who doesn't marry. What dark secret are you hiding from me?"

She waited for him to deny there was a secret. She waited for him to laugh, or perhaps even to confess. What she didn't expect was for him to toss his napkin onto the table, rise and walk away without saying a word.

Chapter Eight

It had rained until dawn. Emily knew, because she spent much of the night awake and pacing in her room. She'd tried to sleep, telling herself that her worries were silly. But she couldn't quite make herself believe the words.

Something had happened the previous evening at dinner. She could almost understand Lucas's confusion at the change in her appearance. She thought the transformation to be miraculous, so perhaps he did as well. She wasn't sure why the sight of her in a low-cut dress had muddled his thinking, but she was pleased to learn the fact. What she didn't know was why he'd stalked away from the table.

She'd tried to speak with him later, but he'd kept to the saloon. Her going to see him there during the day was one thing. But his place of business was very different at night and she did not venture past the door of his office. Which meant they had not talked again.

For perhaps the hundredth time she replayed their conversation over dinner. She still didn't understand what had upset him so. Was it because she'd asked about his secrets?

Emily twisted her hair up into a loose knot and secured it at the nape of her neck. She thought about fashioning some curls but didn't bother. She had a feeling that Lucas wouldn't notice anything about her today.

Did the man have secrets? She'd only been guessing, trying to figure out what would have kept him from marrying. Despite his claims to the contrary, he was a good husband. He seemed to enjoy her company; they got along well. So why would he so resist an institution designed to bring him happiness and children? What man wouldn't want both?

But Lucas didn't. Or he wouldn't let himself. Or there was a dark, mysterious secret from his past that haunted him. Was that the problem? Had she innocently touched an open wound?

She finished with her hair and reminded herself that no answers would be found in her room. If she wanted to know the truth, she needed to speak with her husband directly.

But it was midafternoon before she could confront Lucas. He'd been gone all morning. Perry had claimed he had business at several establishments in town, but Emily hadn't been so sure. Was Lucas avoiding her? He'd done it before, although not by going to all the trouble to leave the saloon. Then after lunch the rain had stopped and she'd made her way to the mercantile to buy paint.

By two she'd made her choices and had returned to the building housing both her business and her husband's. She hesitated before climbing the stairs leading to the second floor, then made her way into his office instead.

He was sitting behind his desk. When he looked up and saw her standing in front of him, something dark crossed his face. She couldn't read his expression, nor did she know what he was thinking, but deep inside, she knew he'd been avoiding her.

Sadness, disappointment and a bit of anger blended inside her, churning until she spoke without thinking.

"You may sulk if you wish," she announced. "It has stopped raining and I'm going up the mountain to check on Molly."

She turned on her heel and started to leave.

"Hold it right there, Emily," Lucas growled.

She froze. Not because of his instruction, but because he called her by name. Emily, not Em.

He rose and came around to stand in front of her. For the first time since they'd met, he seemed to loom above her—a powerful man capable of taking what he wanted by brute strength.

"Sulking?" He glared at her. "You think I'm sulking?"

She might not know much about the intimacies of a marriage, but she easily recognized when a man was trying to intimidate her. She raised her chin and squared her shoulders.

"Yes. You're acting like a small boy who hasn't gotten his way. You stalked away from our evening meal without a single word of explanation. You've also avoided me today. If you are upset about something, why can't you simply tell me?"

"I'm not upset. I don't get upset." He spoke through gritted teeth.

Emily didn't know how to respond. For the first time in her life, she could understand the appeal of punching someone. Were she a man, she would do that to Lucas right now. The thought of sending him flying across the room and landing on the floor, a surprised expression on his face, gave her great pleasure.

She shrugged. "There is obviously something wrong with you, but if you do not wish to discuss it, I can't force you to do so. However, I wanted to let you know that I'm leaving."

He glared at her. "It's going to rain."

"It rained all night. The skies are clear now. Do not worry yourself on my account. Or if I am wrong and I do get caught in a shower, console yourself with the fact that I may catch a chill and die, thereby relieving you of the trouble of annulling a marriage you obviously do not want."

Lucas reached for her arms. She had no idea if he was going to pull her into his embrace or shake her. But his fingers never touched her. Instead he stiffened then dropped his hands to his side.

"You don't know the way," he said at last. "I'll take you."

"That's not necessary. I am perfectly capable of renting a wagon or a buggy on my own."

"I know." He sighed then gently took her arm and propelled her out of the room. "I know I'm going to regret this, but I'm coming with you. But I have to tell you that if it starts to rain, I'm going to be damn annoyed."

"It seems to me you are anyway," she said with a sniff.

He grumbled something under his breath. She didn't catch the words and decided that it was better not to ask. She was willing to put up with a lot of things from Lucas, but she found she disliked being ignored. She vowed to never let him treat her like that again. The next time he walked out on her, she would go after him and demand the satisfaction of finishing the conversation.

* * *

They were halfway up the mountain when the heavens opened. Rain poured onto them as if God had dumped a large bucket on their heads. Lucas kept hold of the wagon's reins. He didn't say a word to Emily.

But she must have heard what he was thinking because she turned to face him. "This isn't my fault."

"I didn't say it was."

"You're thinking it."

He glared at her. "You don't know what I'm thinking."

Rain dampened her face and dripped off the brim of her hat. It looked as if she were crying. Lucas's gut tightened at the thought. He knew he could bear anything except Emily's tears.

To avoid looking at her face, he made the mistake of lowering his gaze. A groan caught in his throat as he took in the way her wet dress clung to her, outlining every inch of her.

Despite the cold drenching, he found himself heating from the inside as blood rushed south and he became aroused. Damn. Why hadn't he just stayed at the saloon? Why hadn't he let her head off on her own? Except he knew he couldn't have done that. Which made no sense, because he'd let Molly go up the mountain on her own the previous day.

"I'm sorry," he told her as he forced himself to face forward.

"I don't know what you're talking about."

Of course she didn't. He didn't even know why he'd apologized. Something was wrong with him. He knew he'd been acting different ever since he got married. He was both avoiding her and compelled to be with her.

Which didn't make sense. He hated her questions, but he hated the pain in her eyes even more.

She wanted to know about his secrets. She wanted to know why he'd walked away from her last night. What was he supposed to say? That if she knew the truth, she would despise him? That he could read her thoughts and knew that she'd become fond of him? That her feelings scared him to death because he knew exactly who and what he was—and she would never understand?

They rounded a bend in the muddy road. Lucas pulled on the reins as he stared ahead at the swollen stream.

"What is that?" Emily asked, pointing at the now raging river that lapped at the edge of the bank.

"Spring runoff always makes the waters rise. Because of the storm, the road's flooded."

"You mean we can't get up to your brother's cabin?"

Lucas shook his head. "Until the waters go down, there's no telling if we would make it across. We can't risk it."

She stared into the forest ahead. "How do we know if Molly is all right?"

"She would have made it up the mountain before it started raining. We're less than a mile from the cabin. We didn't pass her on the road, so if she got this far, she would have found her way there."

"I hope so."

Beside him, Emily shivered. She pulled a shawl over her shoulders, but the dripping length of wool wouldn't do much to warm her.

Lucas urged the horse forward, then turned the animal in a slow circle. "We need to get back to town," he said unnecessarily. "We're going to freeze out here in the rain."

Emily nodded but didn't speak. He could see she was shivering. He swore under his breath. This was not turning out to be his day. As soon as they got back and were warm, he and Emily were going to talk. He was going to have to explain to her how things were between them. Theirs was still a marriage of convenience. That's all he'd ever wanted and nothing had changed. He would be sorry if that reminder hurt her feelings, but better she remember the truth now than later.

They were both shaking with cold by the time they returned to town. Lucas yelled for Perry to return the horse and wagon to the blacksmith, then hustled her up the stairs. Alice met them in the reception area.

"Get hot water," he told the girl. "Plenty of it."

She nodded, gave Emily a reassuring smile, then hurried to do his bidding.

"I've never been so cold," Emily said between clattering teeth. Her skin was pale, except for the hint of blue around her lips. Lucas didn't like the looks of that.

Ignoring his own chill and the way they were dripping on her clean floor, he picked her up in his arms and headed for the hallway.

"Which way?" he asked.

"Lucas!" She was completely stiff in his arms. Her fists flailed against his chest and shoulders. "What are you doing?"

"Carrying you to your room. Which one is it?"

"You can't! Put me down at once. I insist."

"Yeah, I know. Which room?"

She squirmed a couple more times, then gave in and pointed to the right. He walked to the end of the hall and opened the door she indicated.

He had a brief impression of a small room decorated in shades of blue. There was a screen in the corner and plenty of room by the small fireplace for the tub. He walked behind the screen and set her on her feet.

"Take off your clothes." He pulled the coverlet from the bed and draped it over the screen. "Wrap yourself in this until the hot water arrives. I'll be right back."

He was already pulling off his dripping jacket as he walked back into the hallway. He saw Mary carrying an armful of coal.

"Mary, go tell Perry I need some dry clothes. He can send one of the boys to get them at my house. And bring us some towels."

Her eyes widened, but she nodded in agreement. Lucas returned to Emily's room. He agreed with her assessment that he didn't remember ever being this cold. His fingers weren't cooperating as he unfastened his vest. He was soaked to the skin, he thought as he closed the bedroom door behind himself.

"How are you doing?" he called.

"F-f-fine."

He pulled off his boots and socks, then shrugged out of his shirt. He thought about removing his trousers but figured that wasn't a good idea. He and Emily were alone in her bedroom and he might find out he wasn't all that cold after all.

Still shivering, he rubbed his hands up and down his arms. There was a light knock at the door. He opened it and saw Mary standing there with an armful of towels. Her mouth parted when she saw his bare chest. She blushed, thrust the towels at him and ran down the hall.

"I just embarrassed Mary," he said as he closed the door.

"How?"

"I opened the door and I'm not wearing a shirt."

"O-oh."

He hung a towel over the screen. "Here. This should

help." Then he dried himself off and hoped that his clothes arrived soon. His wet trousers were freezing.

He crouched by the fire and quickly lit the kindling. While it wasn't that cold in the room, the extra heat would help. As he watched the flames dance around the coals, he listened for the sound of Emily undressing. There was only silence from behind the screen.

"Em? Are you all right?"

"Y-yes."

Her teeth were still chattering.

He grimaced. "Are you taking off your clothes?"

There was a long silence. "I'm t-trying."

"What seems to be the problem?"

"M-my fingers are sh-shaking and I c-can't unfasten the b-buttons."

Damn. Just his luck. If Emily were any other woman, he would think she was teasing him. But not his Emily. She was too innocent by half and it would never occur to her to tempt a man by showing off her body.

He thought about calling for Alice. He thought about leaving Emily to take care of undressing herself. Then he sighed and straightened. He was her husband. Until the marriage was annulled, she was his responsibility. He was just going to get her out of her wet things. That was all. He could do that, he told himself. It wouldn't be difficult.

He shifted the screen so he could slip behind the protection. Emily looked up and gasped when he came around the corner. Her eyes widened and she folded her arms protectively over her chest. A particularly foolish gesture considering she'd only managed to unfasten the buttons on one cuff and had barely started on the other.

"What have you been doing?" he demanded. "Just standing here?"

"I've been trying to undo the buttons. The wool is wet, which makes the unfastening more difficult. Not that it's any business of yours. Go away."

He noticed that her face was bright red, which contrasted oddly with the blue around her mouth. She was shaking, but had managed her speech without once stuttering.

"You'll freeze to death before you finish," he grumbled, and reached for her left cuff.

She tried to step away from him, but the movement only settled her in the corner.

"Lucas, I'm warning you." She glared at him.

"I know. I'll consider myself warned. Now be quiet and let me help you."

He grabbed her arm and worked at the buttons. She glared at him but didn't pull back.

The buttons did not cooperate. Lucas had to push them through the wet wool with more force than he would have thought. He concentrated on his task and tried to ignore the fact that she was standing so close to him.

He also ignored the way her gaze had settled on his bare chest. He could feel her studying him, visually exploring him. Her attention made him realize that she'd probably never seen a man's chest before. Which reminded him that she'd never seen other parts of a man, either. Just as well. She was too ignorant to notice that certain parts of him were larger than they had been a few moments before, and continuing to grow.

He reached for the buttons trailing down the front of her dress. As his knuckles grazed her throat, they both caught their breath. Emily's eyes widened.

"Lucas?"

"It's fine," he lied. "Pretend I'm your brother."

"I don't have a brother and, if I did, I would never let him do this to me."

Yeah, well, that was the best he could come up with under the circumstances.

He worked as quickly as he could, concentrating on pushing the buttons through the thick fabric. He ignored the way her damp chemise left her small, perfectly shaped breasts nearly bare. He didn't think about what it would be like to slide his hand up from her narrow waist, along her ribs to those two breasts. He never let his gaze linger on the tight points of her nipples or notice the way her chest rose and fell with each breath.

When the last button was released, he shoved her dress over her shoulders and down her arms until it pooled at her feet. He crouched low and unfastened her boots, then eased them off her feet.

She still wore her undergarments, but there was no way in hell he could take those off her. He tried to think of himself as her brother, or even her father. But the familial thoughts wouldn't stick in his head and he found himself wanting her naked, on the bed, with him touching every inch of her. He wanted to taste her and discover her. He wanted to be inside her, changing her from a virgin to a wife in one slow thrust. He ached in a way he didn't recall ever aching before. The need was so powerful he didn't know how he would survive not having her.

A knock on the door made him jerk the coverlet off the screen. He wrapped it around her shoulders and hurried to the door. Perry held a change of clothes for him in one hand and a bucket of steaming water in the other. Behind him was a teenage boy with a tub. Alice and Mary each had buckets of water as well.

Lucas stepped back to let them enter. He would let

them fill the tub, then he would change his clothes and get the hell out of Emily's room before he did something they both regretted.

Five minutes later, he jerked off his wet trousers and reached for clean clothes.

"I'm nearly finished," he called to her. "When I'm gone you can take a bath and get warm."

She didn't answer. Lucas felt the hairs on the back of his neck prickle. Never a good sign, he thought. Something was wrong. He stood there, naked, not sure if he should ignore her silence or ask. He really didn't want to know. Every instinct warned him that he was inches away from the worst kind of trouble. The ache in his body threatened death if he didn't give in to his need. It hadn't been a very good day.

Then he heard it. A soft, muffled sob. His gut tightened and he dropped his head to his chest.

She was crying.

Not that, he insisted to himself. Anything but that. Tears. He hated tears. Why did women cry?

Cursing himself, his need, the world and, most of all, Uncle Simon, he pulled on his dry trousers and walked toward the screen.

"Em, what's wrong?"

He heard her sniff. "Nothing. I'm fine."

She was anything but, he thought grimly. He swore under his breath, then walked around behind the screen.

Emily crouched on the floor. She'd pulled the coverlet around her but she still shivered. Her hair dripped onto the floor, but it was her tears that captured his attention. They spilled out of her beautiful blue eyes and slipped down her cheeks.

He reached for her hand and carefully drew her to her feet. He grabbed one of the towels and placed it across her shoulders, then reached behind her and removed the pins from her hair. It tumbled down her back in soggy strands. Tears still trickled down her cheeks.

"Tell me what's wrong," he said quietly.

She shook her head.

He brushed his fingers across her cheeks. "Tell me."

She wouldn't meet his gaze. "I can't. It's not important."

"Of course it is. I don't want to make you cry."

She squeezed her eyes shut. A sob ripped through her. Not knowing what else to do, he pulled her close and wrapped his arms around her.

It was torture. Pure, gut-wrenching torture. While she was completely covered, he couldn't forget the fact that her dress was in a pile on the floor. She was practically naked, they were alone and there was a bed only a few feet away. That most male part of him wanted to know why they were waiting.

He risked his self-control by lightly kissing her cheek. "Why are you crying?"

"B-because I'm ugly."

He'd been expecting nearly a half dozen different answers, but not that one. Lucas set her away from him and stared into her face.

"I don't think you're ugly."

She wasn't. Even wet, her hair was nearly the color of gold, and her skin was lovely. He adored her big eyes and the way she looked when she smiled.

Emily stared at the floor. "You must. I don't know what happens between a husband and wife, but I remember hearing friends of my mother's talking once. They said that when a man undresses a woman, he loses control and becomes an a-animal." Tears filled her eyes and leaked down her cheeks. "They laughed about it. How they only had to let their husbands see their..." She hesitated and made a vague gesture toward her chest.

"Their bosoms?" he asked.

She nodded. "See that and they became wild." She squeezed her eyes shut. "You aren't acting wild or like an animal. So I must be more ugly than I thought."

It would have been easier if she'd cut out his heart, Lucas thought as he stood in front of her wondering what he was supposed to do now. He'd tried so hard to do the right thing. He'd married to keep his inheritance, but he'd told Emily the reasons why and he'd never once lied to her.

Maybe he shouldn't have kissed her, he thought grimly. Maybe he shouldn't have started dining with her in the evening. Maybe...

But the maybes didn't matter anymore. The past had already occurred. There was only this moment and Emily's tears. How could he possibly make her understand?

He knew he had to try. He owed her that and so much more.

He touched her chin and raised her head so that she could see his face. "It's not what you think," he told her. "I *do* have those feelings for you. If you knew more about men and their bodies, I could prove it, but for now you're going to have to trust me."

He read the doubt in her eyes.

"Not all men act like animals," he said. "I very much enjoyed looking at your bosoms. They're very pretty."

She grimaced. "They're too small."

"Not for me." His hands ached to show her all the possibilities, but he could not.

She frowned in confusion. "I don't understand."

"I know."

He took her hand and led her around the screen. When she was by the bed, he urged her to sit, then settled next to her on the mattress.

"Emily, my reasons for not taking you into my bed have nothing to do with you. Last night you asked me if I had ever considered marrying. The truth is that many years ago I assumed I would take a wife and have a family. Then something happened and now I can't."

"Why?"

He didn't want to tell her. He didn't want to see the scorn and loathing in her eyes. But he wanted to see the self-doubt and pain even less.

He took her hand in his, fully knowing that it was probably the last time he would be allowed to touch her.

"It happened during the war," he said at last.

And so he told her his deepest, darkest secret. The one that shamed him so that he could no longer worship in the house of the Lord. The one that kept him up nights, filled with questions and self-hatred.

"During the war, I killed a man," he said.

"Many men killed."

"I know, but this was different. Jonathan was a friend of mine. We'd served together for nearly three years. We were of an age. Although he was from Boston and I was from here, we found we had much in common."

He told her about the summer battle, and how many lay dying. He explained about the retreat of their army and how he and several men had been trapped behind Confederate lines.

"I knew we could escape in the dark," he said, not daring to look at her, but instead staring into his past, seeing the forest, smelling gunpowder, blood and death. "But we had to survive the rebel patrols."

He remembered the silence of the forest. And then he'd heard it. A low moan.

"I walked toward the sound and saw that Jonathan had been shot in the stomach. Blood seeped from the wound. There was no way to save him, and it's a slow way to die."

He remembered his horror and tasted the rising bile, just as he'd tasted it that long-ago summer day. He closed his eyes, but that didn't help block out the memories.

"He was in so much pain," Lucas said slowly. "He begged me to put him out of his misery. He knew that he could take several days to die, each hour more painful than the last."

Something settled on his arm. He glanced down and saw Emily had put her hand on him. "Lucas, you don't have to tell me this."

"Yes, I do. You need to know the truth about me." Staring into her bottomless blue eyes, he continued. "I heard several rebel soldiers in the distance. They were getting closer and I knew it was just a matter of time until they found us. So I killed him."

He waited. Emily stiffened but didn't pull her hand away, for which he was grateful.

"I covered his mouth and nose with my hand, and he let me." He remembered staring into his friend's gaze as Jonathan died.

"You were merciful," Emily said urgently.

"Was I? Or was I a cowardly bastard who didn't want to be captured?"

Emily read the doubt in her husband's expression. She felt his pain, his anger and his guilt. He blamed himself and every day he wondered why he'd taken his friend's life.

"That is why I never married. I don't know my measure as a man. Not anymore. I can't be a husband or a father. I can't be sure about myself."

She knew nothing of Lucas's experience with war or his pain, but she understood his guilt. He believed he didn't deserve happiness, because to accept life's bounty meant forgiving himself. And in his mind, that absolution was beyond even God's great powers. She knew then that he hadn't wanted to consummate their marriage today because of what he thought of himself, not what he thought of her.

His steady gaze reminded her that he awaited her judgment of what he'd done. She suspected he thought she would be repulsed by his confession.

She wanted to tell him that his past mattered only because it still had the power to wound him. She wanted to say that the fact that he questioned his actions meant that he was a good and honest man. She wanted him to know that saving his own life was not a sin, but the act of a man who had something to live for.

She wanted to tell him that she loved him. For the act of hearing his darkest secret had allowed her to see the truth about her own feelings for Lucas MacIntyre. She loved him from the very bottom of her heart.

Despite the feelings welling up inside of her, she somehow knew that he would not want to hear any of those words; that he wouldn't believe them. So instead of speaking, she shrugged off the coverlet and wrapped her arms around her husband.

He resisted, pushing her away and starting to stand. She didn't let him go. Instead she clung to him, silently begging him to stay with her. He hesitated. His gaze drifted down to her chest. She knew that her—she could barely think the word he'd spoken so casually—bosoms were clearly visible under the damp cloth.

His expression hardened. For a heartbeat she was afraid he was lost to her, but then she saw the fire in his eyes and knew that he was experiencing that animal desire she'd heard tell of.

Gathering every ounce of courage she had ever possessed, she reached for his hand and gently placed it on her chest.

Lucas jerked back as if he'd touched fire. Then he groaned low in his throat and gathered her close. His mouth came down on hers, stealing her breath and igniting her heart.

Chapter Nine

Never having been with a man, Emily didn't know what to expect. Lucas kissed her as he had before, but this time there were no gentle preparations. He plunged his tongue into her mouth, exploring her, tasting her, feasting on her as if she were his last meal.

While his actions didn't frighten her, she felt a small sense of trepidation, right until his tongue brushed against hers. Then she felt only heat and something aching inside her. Something that urged her to wrap her arms around him again and hold him close.

He shifted until they were both stretched out on the bed. Still kissing, he ran his hands up and down her bare arms. A thousand shivers rippled through her. A thousand places of heat burned on her skin. She felt both awkward and perfectly at home. She was in his arms; nothing could possibly go wrong.

At the same time a voice in her head screamed that she was lying on a bed with a man. She was barely covered by her undergarments, he wore only trousers and it was still the afternoon. Emily ignored the voice. Lucas was her husband and she loved him. Everything they would do together would be exactly right.

So she concentrated on the glorious feel of his kiss and the way his hands moving against her skin made her want to purr like a cat. She enjoyed gathering the courage to touch him back, to explore his arms and shoulders, noticing that his skin felt different from her own and that she could feel the twisting, rippling movement of his powerful muscles.

He shifted again and she found herself on her back. He continued to kiss her, but his hand moved at the same time, distracting her. He slid from the arm at her side to her waist. The layer of her chemise was thin enough that it was as if she weren't wearing clothing at all. She sucked in a breath. Anticipation and fear filled her in equal measure.

A short time ago, she'd brazenly put her husband's hand on her chest. She'd been so intent on staying brave that she'd barely registered his touch. Now her entire being focused on that hand moving closer and closer. She felt it pass over her ribs, then settle on her...bosom.

He covered her completely. She felt heat and pressure, then a wonderful aching sort of shivering pleasure that she'd never felt before. He moved his hand so that his fingers and thumb brushed against the tip. Fire shot through her. She broke their kiss and gasped, clutching him, barely able to breathe.

"Lucas!"

He chuckled and kissed her throat. "I thought you might like that."

Like? Like did not *begin* to explain what she was feeling. She started to tell him that, but he kept on touching her and speaking was impossible.

As his fingers continued to make her gasp, he kissed along her neck and onto the skin above her chemise. Warm, wet trails of kisses, she thought dreamily, and the tickling of his mustache. It was all better than she'd imagined. Not that she'd let herself think about such things. Lower and lower until he kissed her other bosom. Her eyes shot open and she nearly sat up in surprise. He took her in his mouth!

Emily wanted to protest. This couldn't be right or natural. It had to be some horrible…

She sank onto the mattress and breathed what she thought might be her last. If she were to die now, life would have been perfect. His fingers touching one tight peak, while his lips caressed the other. Liquid heat poured through her, making her limbs impossibly heavy and her head spin.

"Sweet Em," he breathed against her skin. "You shiver when I touch you."

"I know. Touch me more."

She was instantly shocked by what she'd said, but he only laughed. Before she knew what he was about, he'd slipped his hand down to the waistband of her pantaloons and had worked his way under them. He was touching bare skin and moving lower.

Her eyes popped open. Suddenly she knew he was going to touch her *there,* between her limbs, and it could not happen. She would not allow it. They might be married, but that didn't give him the right to…

"Relax," he murmured in her ear, then licked her lobe. "I'm not going to hurt you. If you think me touching your breasts is good, this is much, much better."

Her mind screamed silently. *Breasts?* Had he really said *breasts?* She'd never even allowed herself to think the word. Next thing she knew, he'd be calling her limbs *legs* and naming who knows what body parts. She simply couldn't allow it. They would have to stop right now.

She opened her mouth to tell him, but at that same

moment, his fingers parted her most private place and touched a tiny spot of exquisite sensation. She nearly screamed aloud. Amazing feelings shot through her, making her limbs tremble and her feet burn. She clutched at him, mystified and drowning.

"Lucas?"

"Hush, Emily. Trust me."

He kissed her mouth, then returned his attentions to her bosoms, all the while continuing to touch her down there. Over and over. He'd taken control of her body. She couldn't do anything but accept the amazing experience of being so completely out of control. It was as if he were drawing her up a hill. Higher and higher and yet...

"It's all right," he whispered in her ear. "Just let it happen."

She had no idea what he was talking about. None at all. But she wasn't about to tell him that. Not when she couldn't really think about anything but how his touch felt and why no one had ever explained this to her before.

And then it didn't matter. It was as if she'd shattered, much like a large glass window. She felt herself separating into dozens of pieces. Or maybe...

It didn't matter, she thought again hazily, losing her ability to do anything but get lost in the waves that rushed through her. She might have spoken, might have called out. And then she was falling and falling and Lucas was there to catch her and hold her close.

When she could finally breathe again, and open her eyes, she found him staring down at her. His handsome face, so familiar, so beloved.

"I want you," he told her.

The words made her shiver again. He wanted her. He

wanted to claim her as his own. At last she would know all the secrets. She smiled and held out her arms.

"Yes," she told him. "Want me and have me."

He was touching her again. Her breasts, her hips. He pulled off her chemise and her pantaloons, until she was naked. Then he rose and slipped off his trousers.

She stared at him, taking in the broad shoulders, the flat stomach, then moving her gaze lower, following the arrow of dark hair leading to his maleness. He was thick and swollen, jutting out from his body. She swallowed.

"It's not as big as a horse's," she blurted before she could bite back the words.

Lucas laughed. "Were you worried about that?"

"A little. I've never seen a man, but I've seen a stallion. I tried to consider the size difference between a horse and a man, assuming that part of him would be equally reduced. But I could never figure it out."

"Now you don't have to."

He slipped next to her on the bed and drew her close. She felt his arousal brushing her belly. He was velvety soft, yet hard and jutting.

"Are you afraid?" he asked.

She nodded.

He kissed her deeply, then drew away. "When you part your legs for me, I'll settle between them." He trailed his fingers across her belly and between her curls again. She felt the tingles return. "I'll enter you here."

A single finger demonstrated the journey.

"Will it hurt?"

"Yes. The first time. You'll probably bleed. But after that, it will get better. Soon you'll be experiencing the same reaction when I'm inside you as when I touched you."

She thought about how wonderful that had been and

wanted him to get started with her lessons. But more important than that, she wanted to hold his words close to her. Because they implied he would be sharing her bed for a long, long time.

Contentment filled her. She loved this man and she wanted to be his wife in every sense of the word.

Silently she parted her legs. Lucas moved between them. He kissed her slowly, deeply, nearly making her forget what they were about to do. Then she felt his hardness probing. Instinctively she drew back her knees. He pushed in, filling her.

The sensation was uncomfortable. She felt trapped by his weight. Before she could protest, he shifted so that he could reach between them. He stroked that one amazing spot again and made her gasp. She quickly found herself caught up in the same journey, rising higher and higher. But before she could reach her completion, he began to move into her.

There was a bit of pressure, followed by a sharp pain. Emily clung to him knowing that she had been irrevocably changed. She smiled.

"Make me yours," she whispered to the man she loved.

Lucas had intended to go slowly, to try to make Emily experience bliss again. But the combination of her tightness, her perfect body and her words made it impossible. Everything about her aroused him. Her pale skin, the taste of her sweet breasts, the way she'd responded to him, so naturally and easily, finding paradise on her first attempt. He suspected he could make her experience it again now, except he didn't have that kind of control. Not with her.

He thrust into her and felt the pressure building.

"I can't hold on," he breathed. "Em, I—"

"It's all right. I'll be here, holding you."

He gave in to the need, filling her again and again until he lost himself inside of her.

They must have both fallen asleep, because the next thing Lucas knew, he awakened in a darkened room. He recognized the scent and feel of the woman next to him. Emily.

He rolled onto his back and stared up into the darkness. In one single moment, he'd changed her forever. He'd taken away her innocence and made an annulment impossible. If he were a drinking man, this would be a fine time to get drunk. How could he have been with her?

How could he not?

Lucas exhaled slowly and knew that there was no way he could have resisted her. She was nothing like the practiced women at Miss Cherry's. She was innocent and untouched. Yet her eagerness, her responses had all reduced him to a man overwhelmed by desire. Even when he'd seen the light burning in her eyes and had known that she had come to care about him, he couldn't resist her. He couldn't have stopped their intimacies if the price had been his life.

And now he had to pay the price for that. He—with the dark stain upon his soul—had taken her greatest gift. He who knew what it all meant, had given in. Not being able to resist her wasn't an excuse. He wasn't worthy of her. Telling her the truth and having her still want him spoke of her greatness and her forgiving spirit, but did nothing to assuage his sins. If anything they were greater now.

He wanted to wake her by shaking her and demanding to know what she'd been thinking. Didn't she realize that he wasn't allowed to be happy? Did she know that he would never subject her to the horror that was his life as he lived out his punishment of having killed for reasons of cowardice?

But even as he longed to push her away, to turn his back on her, he needed as much to hold her close. To feel her body next to his, to taste all of her, to have her confess her feelings.

He was more of a bastard than he'd thought.

"Lucas?"

Her quiet voice filled the dark room. He turned and saw that she'd awakened and was studying him.

She was barely visible in the dimness, so he fumbled with the lantern on the small table next to the bed. As he held the match to the wick, he swore to himself that he would not destroy this for her. He could not take back their joining, so he would do whatever he could to make the memory a good one. Later, when she'd recovered, he would explain that he could never be with her again that way and, that for him, nothing had changed. They might not be able to annul the marriage, instead they would divorce.

But that was for another time. When he finished with the lamp, he smiled at her. "You're naked," he said in a teasing voice.

She blushed instantly and moved to cover herself. He grabbed her hands and drew them toward his mouth, then kissed her fingertips.

"Thank you," he said.

"Shouldn't I be the one thanking you?"

"We're married, Emily. I don't think thanks are required."

She squirmed, then turned toward him. One of her legs

slipped between his. "Was it all right? I don't know anything about, well, you know."

He wanted her again. His arousal jutted toward her, but he was careful to keep from getting too close. Instead he released her hand, then stroked her face.

"Couldn't you tell?" he asked. "Didn't you feel my pleasure in you?"

More color stained her cheek, but she nodded despite it. "I thought you were eager."

He chuckled. "Eager is a good word. I was very eager." He kissed her lightly. "And now I'll have to sneak back into my own room, like a man leaving his mistress."

"But you're not leaving your mistress. I'm your wife."

He knew that. He also knew what the soft light in her eyes meant.

"Emily…"

She leaned over and kissed his cheek. "Close your eyes."

"What?"

She smiled. "Close your eyes. I want to get up and pull on my nightgown."

"But I've already seen you naked."

"I'm sure I don't know what that has to do with anything."

He had a sudden desire to know if she was going to be prim for the rest of her life, or if she would get bold with time. Then he remembered he wasn't going to be married to her long enough to find out. Another man would learn that about her—not him.

He obliged her by closing his eyes and felt the bed move as she rose. He kept his eyes shut, as much to please her as to hold in the pain of imagining her with another man. Someone who could be worthy. Someone who wasn't him.

Emily had never danced much. While she'd had lessons as a girl, not many boys had offered to take her around the floor. But today that didn't matter, because Emily was dancing all on her own.

Yesterday she'd finally learned the secrets between a man and a woman. Her body ached in places that had never experienced pain, but even the slight discomfort was welcome because now she knew. She hugged the information to her chest and smiled as she remembered how glorious it had been. After she'd pulled on a nightgown, Lucas had insisted she join him again in her bed. They'd slept in each other's arms until he'd left her at dawn. She'd thought they might be together again, but he had not reached for her and she had not had the courage to suggest it herself.

Tonight, she thought dreamily as she tried to study her account books. Tonight he would touch her again and she would feel the heat and the desire. He would make her melt and she would then do the same to him. Even imagining what they would do was enough to make her body feel warmer than usual.

"You look happy about something."

Emily glanced up and saw Dixie standing by the desk. She wore a low-cut yellow gown and radiated a kind of beauty that Emily could never possess. Despite that, Emily smiled. Today it didn't matter that she wasn't beautiful. She was pretty enough to attract her husband and that was all she needed.

"I am very content," Emily said, trying to keep from smiling too broadly.

Dixie raised her eyebrows. "I know that look. So Lucas finally gave up trying to resist you. Congratulations.''

''Thank you.''

Dixie leaned forward and lowered her voice. ''Lucas and I have been friends for a long time, so let me give you some advice.''

Emily remembered Dixie telling her that she and Lucas hadn't been intimate in many years. She told herself the wise course would be to ignore the flare of jealousy and to simply listen.

''I would like that,'' she said.

''Don't let him go back to his own place tonight. Do whatever you have to so you keep him in your bed. Lucas has many ghosts from his past. The only way to defeat them is to show them for what they are. Just ghosts. Not living demons or anything that can hurt him.'' Dixie paused. ''You love him, don't you?''

Emily felt her eyes fill with tears. She nodded. ''Very much. I haven't told him.''

''You should. Hold him and love him and never let him go until you've finally convinced him that he has to make peace with the past.''

''Did he tell you what happened during the war?''

Dixie shook her head. ''He never speaks of it. I know that it's bad, but he won't tell me what happened.''

Oddly, that pleased Emily. Her husband had told *her* the truth.

Dixie looked her up and down. ''I suggest you invite him to dinner in your room tonight. But instead of that blue dress, wear a nightgown.''

Emily gasped. ''To dinner? I couldn't.''

Dixie laughed. ''Honey, if you show up in a nightgown, you're not going to be eating dinner. Trust me.''

* * *

Lucas barely saw the small table set up in Emily's room. The tempting aroma of dinner drifted toward him, but he wasn't interested in food. He had to tell her the truth. He had to explain that he couldn't be with her again, not the way he'd been with her the previous night. They weren't really man and wife, and pretending they were would only end up hurting her.

He might not want to be married to her, but he was willing to admit that he'd come to care about her. She was important to him, and a decent woman. By marrying him, she'd done him an important service. He didn't want to repay that by making her miserable.

He heard a noise from the corner of the room and for the first time, he realized he wasn't alone.

"Emily," he called.

"Yes. I'm here."

Her words came from behind the screen. He frowned. "What are you doing?"

"Thinking."

"Behind the dressing screen?"

He heard a soft laugh. "Actually, yes. I had much to consider."

"Like what?"

She stepped from behind the screen and walked toward him. "Such as whether or not I had the courage to appear before you dressed in this."

He couldn't speak, nor could he breathe, but he sure as hell didn't care about either. Emily stopped in front of him and tilted her head to one side.

"I don't think it's really appropriate for an evening meal, but Dixie assured me you would be pleased."

Dixie. He might have known she would meddle. Later he would be angry with her, but now...

He opened his mouth, but couldn't find any words. He remembered that he was supposed to talk to Emily about their marriage, and the fact that it was still ending. He knew he'd planned on telling her that he couldn't be with her again, not intimately.

But he also knew he had to have her tonight. Now.

She stood before him dressed in cream-colored lace and silk. The filmy nightgown skimmed over her body, slipping past curves, teasing at hollows. He thought the gown looked expensive, perhaps a gift from her parents—a part of her trousseau. Her arms were bare, and he thought there must be a robe to cover the gown, but she'd chosen not to wear it. Just as well. He enjoyed the view of her practically bare breasts and the way her long, wavy blond hair tumbled down her back.

He wanted her. The desperate need was as sudden as it was powerful. An aching filled him. All his vows and promises disappeared, like so much smoke in the wind.

"Emily," he growled, even as he moved toward her. "We can't do this."

She stepped into his embrace. Their mouths met. Her last words were, "Whyever not?"

Lucas spent the next three weeks with one foot in heaven and the other in hell. Every morning he left Emily's bed and promised himself it would be the last time. Each night he found his way to her side. She smiled at him, or kissed him or lightly brushed his hand and he was lost.

When he was with her, in her arms, tasting her, breathing her scent, he knew a contentment that had been missing from his life for the past ten years. But when they were apart, he knew that he had to end it, and quickly. Before the happiness in her eyes turned to something else. Before their time together was more than just amusing and assumed a deeper meaning.

But while it was easy to make the plans, it was more difficult for him to follow them through. She lit his world, much as the sun lit the sky. He lived for the sound of her laughter, of her gentle voice and the way she insisted on showing him her ledgers, when he knew she would cut out her own heart before cheating anyone of a single penny.

He sat in his office on that bright spring morning and stared at the telegram in front of him. It had been delivered just a few minutes before. He hadn't read it, but he knew what it would say. The telegram and all it represented were an act of cowardice that made him ashamed. But why was he surprised? He'd showed his true colors with Jonathan, during the war. His lack of character was the reason he couldn't keep Emily as his wife. Now he had to tell her the truth.

He rose slowly to his feet, feeling old and broken. Telling himself he was finally achieving his dream didn't help. There weren't any words to make himself feel better. He didn't deserve to feel better.

He walked out of his office and up the stairs toward Emily's hotel. She sat on a stool, behind the reception desk. A cup of tea rested beside her open ledger book. When she saw him, she smiled.

He marveled at the changes in her. Gone was the prim schoolteacher who had confronted him from behind the bars of her jail cell. While she still sat as erectly, she'd softened in other ways.

She wore her hair different. The looser style allowed her natural wave to add fullness and curl. Instead of drab gray gowns, she dressed in soft colors like blue and pink. Her eyes were brighter, her lips nearly always smiling.

An air of contentment cloaked her, giving her beauty. The same intelligence brightened her eyes, eyes that now glowed with some emotion he didn't dare identify.

"Lucas," she said, sounding delighted. "This is a surprise. I'm having tea. Would you like me to get you some coffee?"

"No. I can't stay long. I want to tell you…"

He hesitated, not sure what he was supposed to say. Perhaps it was finally time to speak the truth.

He crossed to the desk and set down his telegram. She stared at the sheet of paper but didn't try to read it or speak. Instead she waited for him.

"Now that both Jackson and I are married and have fulfilled the terms of Uncle Simon's will, the properties can be deeded to us."

Her expression didn't change but he saw wariness in her eyes. "You must be relieved. I know you have been concerned about losing your inheritance."

"Yes."

He cleared his throat. This was harder than he would have thought. He turned so that he could see down the stairs, telling himself he wanted to make sure they were alone rather than avoiding Emily's gaze.

"Once we have title of the properties, I want to move to the ranch. I have no need for the saloon."

He heard her sharp intake of air. "I see," she murmured, sounding stunned.

He still didn't look at her. "I've been in touch with a man in Boston. He'll be buying the saloon from me." He touched the telegram. "I'll stay until he arrives, then leave for the ranch."

Finally he forced himself to face her. All the color had drained from her face. Her eyes were wide and she looked as if she might faint at any moment.

"I've also told my lawyers to start preparing the papers for us," he told her.

"What do you mean?"

"Once the property is deeded to Jackson and me, you and I can get our divorce."

Chapter Ten

Emily waited for the world to stop spinning, or at the very least slow down enough so that she could understand what was happening. Her chest tightened so much it was impossible for her to breathe, and her stomach felt as if she'd been stabbed.

"Divorce?"

She could barely speak the word—didn't want to speak it—didn't want to make it real. No. No, this wasn't happening. The man standing in front of her, *her husband,* could not be saying these things to her.

"Lucas."

He wouldn't look at her. "Emily, it's time. You always knew we married because of the will."

"At first," she admitted. "But not now. Not after..." Not after he'd taken her into his arms, night after night. Not after... "Lucas, I love you."

He shuddered and clenched his hands into fists. "Don't say that. Don't ever say that."

Her eyes burned, but she refused to cry. She would not show weakness in front of him. Something inside told her that this was a time to be strong.

"I will say it. I'll tell you as many times as I need to

until you understand. I love you. You are my husband. I don't want a divorce and I don't want our marriage to be over. If you wish to sell the saloon, that's fine. I'll join you at the ranch.''

"Don't you understand?" He spun toward her and slapped his hands down on the desk. "I don't want you there. I don't want to be married to you. You can keep your hotel. I've made those arrangements with the new owner. You may stay here for the next three years, giving him the same percentage of profits. That should give you enough time to save the money you'll need to start your school for women.''

She stared at the man she thought she'd come to understand. His handsome face was familiar, yet she knew he was a stranger.

"So you have taken the time to secure my financial future," she said slowly, barely able to speak past the pain. "How kind. If only you'd been as concerned for the state of my heart.''

He flinched. "I'm sorry.''

All she wanted to do was curl up in a ball and sob. The pain inside grew and grew until she knew it was going to swallow her whole. She welcomed the thought of oblivion but doubted she would be that fortunate. In some deep part of her being, she sensed that she would love him forever.

"I'm sorry," he told her, still not looking at her. "I tried to warn you away.''

"You didn't try very hard." The bleeding wound sucked her strength, but she forced herself to stand straight and strong. "You once asked me who had been cruel in my life. I told you about my past and how I had come to realize that no man would want me for myself, just for what I could bring to the marriage. I married you understanding ours was a marriage of convenience.''

She had to swallow against the tightness in her throat, but she forced herself to continue. ''Over time, I began to trust you, Lucas. You were kind to me. I thought I had reason to hope. And then I began to love you. I did not think that love would be returned. I knew you had reasons for not wanting to take a wife. But when you told me about your past and then took me into your bed, I thought things had changed. You made me your own and now that you have finished with me, you are tossing me aside.''

He finally looked at her. ''I didn't mean for that to happen.''

''Do you think I care about that? Your intentions are of little consequence. When you told me about what happened during the war, I didn't question your courage. While I know you suffer greatly from that time, I did not think it lessened you as a man. However, I question your courage now. I believe you are acting in a cowardly fashion. You knew what would happen if we shared a bed. You knew that I would be changed forever and that I would most likely fall in love with you. You knew that I would assume that love was returned, or at least might be returned in the future. Even knowing you had no intention of making our marriage real, you still defiled me.''

She paused, hoping he would tell her that she was wrong and perhaps even get angry for thinking so ill of him. But he didn't. He simply nodded slowly, as if she'd finally voiced the truth.

She hadn't thought she could hurt more, but intense pain flooded her until she could only pray for the strength to continue. From somewhere it came, surging through her, giving her the ability to finish speaking the truth.

"You thought that when you told me about your past, I would turn away from you," she said. "You were wrong. I could love that man, because he was honest in his fears and his questions. But the stranger in front of me can have no place in my heart. I despise you now, Lucas MacIntyre. I have been nothing but good to you. You have repaid my kindness by treating me more cruelly than anyone of my acquaintance. I am sorry I met you, and having met you, I am sorry I married you."

Knowing that she was about to collapse, Emily turned on her heel and hurried toward her room. From the corner of her eye, she saw Dixie in the hallway and had the added humiliation of knowing her friend had heard every word.

Lucas stood alone in the reception area of the hotel. He felt battle weary, as tired as he'd been at the end of the war. She was right, of course. About everything. He'd taken her innocence, knowing what it would mean to her. He'd used her body, broken her spirit, acted with all the indifference of a supreme bastard. There weren't enough words to describe his horrible actions.

Without warning, something cracked across his face. He turned and saw Dixie glaring at him. "How dare you?" she demanded.

He rubbed his cheek. "Why'd you do that?"

"Because it's the least of what you deserve. If I were a man, I'd shoot you right now, you dog. How dare you?"

He stared down the hallway where Emily had disappeared. Despite the fact that she hated him, he wanted to go to her and pull her into his arms. He wanted to tell her he was sorry and that they would work it out. But he couldn't. Not ever.

"You don't understand," he said wearily.

"I understand perfectly. You're a self-indulgent idiot and I'm sorry you're my friend." Fire flashed in her brown eyes. "Damn you, Lucas. Damn you. Don't you realize Emily is the most amazing woman you're ever going to meet? How many others would have had the intelligence to open a hotel and make it successful in such a short period of time? She has a head for business and a heart bigger than the entire West. She's my friend. *Mine*. How many women would have welcomed me into their home?"

"You don't have to recite Emily's virtues to me. I'm intimately familiar with them all."

"I don't think you are. Otherwise, you wouldn't be so quick to let her go. She's the best person you'll ever know. She loves you. Why are you throwing her away?"

He grabbed her arms and shook her. "Don't you think I know that? Don't you think I'm aware that I'll miss her for the rest of my life? I don't have a choice."

She studied him, then narrowed her gaze. "I wish I'd hit you harder. You have a choice. We all have choices. Emily deserves better, but you're the one she wants. So be with her. Find the courage to claim her."

He walked to the sofa and sank down. "I can't. I don't know how. There are things from my past." He shook his head. "You wouldn't understand."

"You're wrong about that, too. I have plenty of secrets from my own past. Do you think I'm happy about what I do for a living? Do you think I'm proud?"

He raised his head and, for the first time since he'd met her, he saw ghosts in Dixie's eyes. Of course she had her own dark secrets. "I'm sorry."

"Don't apologize to me. I'm not the one you're destroying." She planted her hands on her hips. "You're being selfish, Lucas. Wallowing in the guilt and wishing you were dead is easy. It's living well that's hard. This is one time you're going to have to take the more difficult road. You owe her."

He shook his head. "I can't have her."

Dixie caught her breath. "Because you love her. You're paying for your sins of the past, and think you're not allowed to be happy."

He nodded.

"But what about what Emily deserves?"

"She'll have to find someone else."

His friend stared at him as if he were the stupidest man she'd ever met. "I have two things to say about that. First, you'll never survive without her. Second, you won't be able to stand seeing her with someone else."

She turned on her heel and flounced out of the room. He heard her head down the hall, then she knocked and opened a door. A muffled sob drifted to him and was cut off when Dixie closed Emily's door.

Dixie was right. He couldn't survive without Emily, nor could he stand to see her with someone else. Yet he had no right to her.

Without thinking, he pushed to his feet and hurried from the hotel. He took the stairs two at a time, and when he reached the sidewalk, he starting walking. He headed out of town, not sure where he was going or why, only hoping he would figure it out by the time he got there.

The sun moved across the sky. Lucas wrestled with his past and his present, not knowing which way to turn. He'd always thought he would be alone. Letting Emily go was the right thing to do. Then he heard Dixie's words, the ones that told him he owed Emily and the way to make her happy was to love her.

He rounded a bend in the road and saw a familiar vista stretching out in front of him. The south end of the ranch reached toward the horizon. His land. The land where he would live out the rest of his days. In his mind's eye he saw dozens of horses cantering across the open fields. Newborn colts racing beside their mothers, the stallions in corrals on the other side of the barn. He heard laughter. A woman's laughter.

Emily.

Lucas leaned against a tree and closed his eyes. The past blurred then came into focus. He heard Jonathan begging him to kill him. To make the pain go away. He heard the sound of the rebel patrol.

"Why did I do it?" he cried to the heavens.

Had he been compassionate or cowardly?

"I love you, Lucas."

Emily's words drifted to him, wrapping themselves around him, healing him. He would never know the truth, he realized. But she was the best person he'd ever met and she loved him.

He fell to his knees and prayed as he'd never prayed before. There was no burst of light, no answer from God. Not even peace. All he knew was that he couldn't live without her. Perhaps the kindest act would be to let her go, but he couldn't. He needed her. He wanted to spend his days and nights with her, have children with her, grow old with her. Selfishly, he wanted to die with her holding his hand.

He raised his head and saw that not only was the sun close to setting, but he was nearly eight miles from town and he didn't have a horse. Cursing himself for being as stupid as Dixie had said, he stood and started the long journey back.

"I don't understand," Emily said, trying to keep the tears from flowing once again. She felt as if she'd been crying all afternoon. Actually, she had been.

Dixie pulled her close. "I know, honey. I'm so sorry. Lucas surprised me on this one. I knew he'd have some trouble coming around, but I never thought he'd be such an idiot as to let you go."

Emily nodded but couldn't speak. The tears were too close to the surface. She'd thought the ache inside might ease some, but it had only gotten worse throughout the afternoon. Every time she thought about checking on Alice and Mary or returning to work, she began sobbing again.

How could this have happened? How could she have been so wrong about him?

"At least you told him off good," Dixie reminded her as she stroked her back. "I'm real proud of you for that."

"I guess I'll be proud of myself later." But the truth was, if Lucas walked through that door and told her he'd changed his mind, she would be in his arms in a heartbeat. "Right now it hurts too much."

"I know."

Dixie held her, as she had for the afternoon. Emily had protested, telling her friend that she had to go to Miss Cherry's. But Dixie had dismissed her concern saying that the men could survive without her for a day or two. Besides, the way she was feeling about men in general, she would definitely do more harm than good.

She drew in a deep breath. "I really need to—"

Her bedroom door flew open. Lucas stepped inside,

looking as if he'd been dragged by a horse. He was out of breath and sweaty. There were stains on his trousers and a tear in his shirt, not to mention an ugly red mark on his cheek.

"I ran the whole way," he said, barely able to speak. "Dammit, Em, I'm sorry. I'm so sorry. I can't let you go. I know it's the right thing to do and I'm wrong to keep you, but I can't make it without you."

She stared at him, not quite able to believe he was really here and speaking. "Lucas?"

He took a step toward her. "Em, please. Don't go. Please don't go. You're better than I deserve, but I can try to be a different man. I can improve. You'll see. Just don't leave."

She didn't dare hope. Not yet. Still she rose to her feet and approached him. "I never wanted to leave. You're the one who wanted a divorce."

"I know." He took her hands in his and stared deeply into her eyes. "I'm sorry. I'm just so damn scared. About the past, about not being the man you want me to be. I don't ever want to disappointment you. I love you."

Her heart stopped. Just plain stopped beating while Emily allowed those magical, wonderful words to sink into her being.

"If you don't want to disappointment me, then stop talking about getting a divorce."

He touched her face. "Can you ever forgive me? I love you, Em. For always. I'll keep the saloon if you like. Or we can move to the ranch. I don't care. I just want to be married to you for the rest of our lives."

She threw herself into his arms and kissed him. His lips clung to hers and she had the feeling that he might never let go. Some part of her sensed Dixie quietly leaving the room and closing the door behind her. Emily would thank her friend later. Not only for being discreet, but for talking some sense into the stubborn man she loved with all her being.

"I love you, too," she said, when he let her catch her breath.

"You swear?"

She laughed. "Yes. And despite my rather excellent speech before, I wasn't really going to let you get away so easily." She felt herself blushing. "It's early to tell, but I think I might be having a baby."

Lucas stared at his wife. "You're pregnant?"

She flushed even more. "I'm *increasing*."

He lifted her in his arms and laughed. "Whatever word you want to use, there's going to be a baby."

Lucas hugged his wife tightly to him, careful not to crush her. As she brushed his lips with hers, he felt the pure light of joy fill him. It was as if the hand of God had reached down and touched him.

A new life. A baby. It was, he knew, finally proof of forgiveness.

"Let go," a voice seemed to whisper in his ear. "Live well, love well. Accept my bounty."

Lucas had never felt God's grace on the battlefield with the dying or in his long nights of guilt and pain. But he felt it now, in the arms of his wife, as a tiny baby grew within her belly.

"Thank you," he whispered, then cupped Emily's face in his hands. "I will love you forever," he promised. "I will be a good husband and do everything within my power to make you happy."

"I believe you," she said with perfect trust.

True to his word, Lucas did as he promised and loved her well all the days of his long life.

* * *

JACKSON'S
MAIL-ORDER BRIDE

Maureen Child

Please address questions and book requests to:
Harlequin Reader Service
U.S.: 3010 Walden Ave., P.O. Box 1325, Buffalo, NY 14269
Canadian: P.O. Box 609, Fort Erie, Ont. L2A 5X3

Chapter One

"Jackson MacIntyre had *better* be sick," Molly Malone MacIntyre muttered to no one. She held the wagon reins in her left hand while trying to push her hair out of her eyes with the right. She'd so wanted to make a good impression on her new husband. She'd purchased a new hat for her journey from Rocky Point, Massachusetts, to Defiance, Colorado. But now the darn thing was covered in trail dust that was quickly turning to mud, thanks to the steady rain that had started twenty minutes ago.

Soaked to the skin, her long, copper-colored hair hung down on either side of her face, looking like molten pennies. Her green eyes narrowed against the pelting rain and she gritted her teeth as the wagon bounced over yet *another* canyonlike rut in the road. "If you could call it a road," she said tightly. The clearing through the trees was little more than a beaten path, barely wide enough to allow her rented wagon to pass. Pine branches seemed to reach out for her, snagging at her shirtwaist and tugging at her hair.

But the horse plodded on, no doubt dreaming of a warm stable and plenty to eat.

"Avast," a voice near her ear screeched, *"dangerous waters ahead!"*

Molly sighed and flicked a quick glance at the red, green and yellow parrot perched on her shoulder. The ancient bird dipped its head and rolled its little eyes as if in sympathy. And she could use a little sympathy at the moment.

This wasn't at all how she'd imagined her arrival in Defiance.

Six months ago, she'd been happily living in Massachusetts, a resigned spinster looking after her seafaring uncle's home. But then the old pirate had died and Molly was on her own. A few weeks of silence and loneliness had been more than enough. Surrendering to the adventurous streak she'd no doubt inherited from her late uncle, Molly had answered an ad for a mail-order bride.

After all, if she'd stayed in Rocky Point, she'd have died an old maid. The Civil War had claimed so many lives that women back East outnumbered the men almost four to one. And with those kinds of odds, a man could afford to be picky—and certainly wouldn't be choosing a twenty-six-year-old hardheaded spinster when he could have a dewy-fresh, biddable child.

So she'd accepted Jackson MacIntyre's long-distance proposal, packed up her belongings in her uncle's sea chest and set sail for adventure.

"Awwwkkk…" the parrot called, shaking raindrops off its head, *"Abandon ship!"*

"Safe harbor, Captain Blood," she said, hoping to high heaven she was right. The old bird was her last link with her past. Though he was annoying and often profane, Molly refused to part with him. Since her childhood, Captain Blood had been the one friend she always could count on.

And today, she'd needed him more than ever.

During the days spent traveling on a train and then a stagecoach, Molly had clung to a fantasy of what her first meeting with her betrothed would be like. And at no time had she imagined the man wouldn't even be there to meet her when she arrived!

His brother, Lucas, and Lucas's wife, Emily, newlyweds themselves, had met her stage and quickly scooted her off to the saloon where she'd spent the night in a small room upstairs. Then first thing this morning, she'd been whisked off to a tiny church where she was married by *proxy* of all things. Torn between fury and humiliation, Molly'd entertained herself with thoughts of what she would do to her new husband when—and *if*—he ever presented himself.

Until, of course, Lucas had explained that Jackson was too sick to attend the wedding. Somewhat mollified, she'd declined Emily and Lucas's offer to spend another night at their saloon-hotel before continuing up the mountain to her new home. She smiled to herself as she remembered Lucas trying to argue her out of her decision.

"You can't go up the mountain yourself, Molly," he'd said. "You'll never find Jackson's place."

She smiled and lifted her chin slightly. If he'd known her better, he would have recognized the gesture as an indication of her stubbornness. "I managed to travel here from Massachusetts on my own," she'd told him. "I've no doubt I can find the cabin. And if it gets dark, I'll have the stars to guide me. My uncle taught me well how to navigate."

He had looked as if he wanted to argue, but his wife joined in on Molly's side before he had a chance.

"Lucas," she said, "Molly is just as able to follow the path to Jackson's cabin as a man would be."

"I didn't say she wasn't," he argued, and it looked to Molly as though these newlyweds weren't having an easy start to their marriage.

"You implied it," Emily had told him.

"Now you read minds?" Lucas asked.

"There's a path?" Molly said, interrupting the flow of their argument. "Well then, there's no problem a'tall, is there?"

Lucas looked like a man caught between a rock and another rock. Clearly he and his wife had things to discuss, so Molly spoke up quickly. "If you'll just be tellin' me where to rent a buggy, I'll be going to my new home."

And so here she was, Molly thought, halfway up a mountain in the wilds of Colorado. But what other choice had she? If her husband was sick, he needed her. And truth be told, she was anxious to start her new life and not eager at all to spend the night with newlyweds who looked to be having their first argument. Besides, her place was with Jackson MacIntyre now. Even if he did live at the back of beyond.

She let her narrowed gaze drift across the rain-smeared countryside and couldn't help wondering if there were animals out there, crouched in the damp shrubbery. Big animals, with lots of hair and sharp teeth, just waiting to take a bite out of an unwary traveler.

She gripped the reins tighter, shook her sodden hair back behind her shoulders and urged the horse, "Hurry up then, let's be about our business, shall we?"

Rounding a curve in the muddy track, Molly spied a dim light in the surrounding gloom. A flicker of hope ignited in her heart. As the wagon rolled closer, jouncing and rocking along the pitted path, she kept her gaze fixed on that point of light and almost sighed with relief when she recognized it as lamplight shining through a window.

"At last," she muttered, giving the horse's rump a little taste of the reins. Her stomach pitched nervously and her heartbeat quickened. Just another few moments and she'd be face-to-face with the man she'd married. She glanced down at the simple gold band on her left ring finger and remembered the look on Lucas's handsome face when he'd placed it there, giving her his brother's promise.

And a small, very female part of her wondered if her new husband was as handsome as his brother.

She pulled the horse to a stop in front of the cabin and took a good long look at her new home. With the dark and the rain, the place didn't look very welcoming. In fact, she might have thought the place abandoned but for the light in the window and the laundry still hanging on a line and twisting in the wind. The scent of wood smoke reached her and just the thought of warming herself in front of a fire was enough to propel her off the bench seat. Clumsily lifting her wet dress out of her way, she stepped down from the wagon and squished through the mud to the front steps.

Not a sound from inside the cabin. Either her new husband was stone deaf and hadn't heard her approach, or the man couldn't even be bothered to open his door to greet her. Of course, she told herself as she reached for the brass latch, there was another option, too. He just might be too sick to move. Hoping she wasn't going to be a widow before she was a wife, in the truest sense of the word, Molly opened the door and stepped into a warm, completely disheveled room.

In the light of a single oil lamp, she saw clothes scattered about the floor and across the few pieces of furniture. Dirty dishes lay on the rough plank table, and shadows thrown from the fire and the lamp danced across the walls.

Water dripped off Molly's coat and dress and hair, plopping against the wooden floor until she was standing dead center in a puddle. Stunned, she kept looking at the room as if expecting it to change suddenly and become a cozy little cottage. But of course nothing of the sort happened and, after a long minute or two, she gave up waiting and moved farther into the room.

"Rocky shores," Captain Blood screeched. *"Rocky shores. Abandon ship!"*

Not paying attention to the bird, Molly took him from her shoulder and set him on a chair back where he paced to and fro like a short, feathered sentry.

Well, she'd found her new home, but there was still the matter of her missing husband. Turning toward the door on the far side of the room, Molly crossed the floor, kicking shirts and heaven knows what else out of her way as she went.

She opened the door and stood on the threshold, staring into the room dominated by a narrow bed—and the huge man stretched out in it.

"Great heaven, he's a giant," Molly muttered. Even taller than his brother, Jackson MacIntyre's broad, muscular, *naked* chest heaved up and down with each labored breath he drew. Drawn closer, Molly walked farther into the room and stared at the man to whom she'd promised her life. Thick black hair fell nearly to his shoulders and a full beard hid his features from sight. "You might be a troll under all that hair," she whispered, then bent down to lay one hand across his brow. Dry heat sizzled up the length of her arm in response and she blew out a long breath as he twisted his head away from her touch.

"Well then," she said, standing up again, "I guess we'll be getting the worse before the better in this marriage, eh?"

Before she'd resigned herself to life as a spinster, Molly had dreamed, as all girls dream, of her wedding night. She'd imagined a husband besotted with her, showering her with kisses and gently leading her into the secrets of wedded bliss.

Now she had the husband all right, but he was darn near unconscious. "There'll be no bliss tonight, I'm thinkin'," she said, and left the room to do what needed doing. "And no secrets," she added, just a bit disappointed.

An hour later, she had the rented horse fed and resting in the small stable alongside her husband's big black animal. She'd dried off in front of the fire and dressed in one of her husband's shirts, since all of her clothes were in the steamer trunk still sitting in the downpour in the back of the wagon. The long-sleeved wool shirt hung to her knees, leaving her legs bare, so Molly found a pair of socks and pulled them on, too.

Taking a good hard look at herself, she chuckled and thought it was a good thing Jackson MacIntyre couldn't see her now after all. She carried a bowl of water into the bedroom and, setting it down on a three-legged table, took a seat on the mattress beside her husband. Molly dipped a cloth into the water, wrung it out, then sponged Jackson's forehead. He muttered something and turned his face into the cool touch of the fabric. She noticed a cut on his right cheek but couldn't tell how deep or long it was, since it disappeared beneath the full beard he wore. Molly promised herself to look at the cut more closely later. But for now the important thing was to get his fever down.

Again and again, she cooled off his heated flesh, swiping the damp cloth across his face, his neck, his chest, until she felt the fire in his body ease back a bit. And while she worked, Molly indulged her curiosity. After all, they were married and she'd likely never have this opportunity to study him unobserved again. Swallowing hard, she ran her palm across the hard, muscled plane of his chest. So strong. So...big. Her hand swept lower, nearing his abdomen. He groaned, from deep in his throat as she caressed his skin, and that sound encouraged her to explore even farther.

Her cheeks flushed slightly, her breath hitching in her chest, Molly fed her curiosity and lifted the covers back to take a peek at the rest of his body. Her green eyes went wide and her jaw dropped open. "Oh, my!" Her heartbeat thundered in her ears and she let the blankets fall back into place as if covering him now would keep the image of what she'd seen from her mind.

Apparently, her new husband was a big man all over. Quickly her mind raced with all the information she'd ever collected about the marriage bed. Women were never eager to tell a virgin what to expect, but she wasn't stupid and she had an idea of exactly what went on.

And with that thought in mind, she rested one hand on his belly and lifted the blanket again for another look. As she studied him, her eyes went round as dinner plates.

"No," she said with a shake of her head. "That couldn't possibly fit."

Then her husband's hands came around her and pulled her down on top of him.

Chapter Two

"Mmm, darlin'..." he muttered, as his hands rubbed up and down her arms, then over and across her breasts.

Tiny explosions of heat scattered through her like a shotgun blast. Her nipples hardened and a jumping sensation took root in the pit of her stomach. Her breath hitched. His big hands cupped her breasts and, even through the fabric of the shirt she wore, she felt the impression of each of his fingers. Damp heat pooled at her center and an ache throbbed deep inside her.

He knew she was here, she thought. Even in his fever, a part of him realized that she, his *wife,* was here with him. She wondered if he knew just what he was doing to her. Molly sucked in a gulp of air and carefully eased back out of his reach. The man was sick. He needed his rest. And she needed a little time to get used to the feeling of a man putting his hands on her body. With another muttered sigh, he drifted back into a fevered sleep, his empty hands fisted at his sides.

"My goodness," she whispered, and fanned herself with one hand. If a simple touch could set off such reactions inside her, how in heaven would she feel when—"Oh, best not to think of that now," she told herself aloud. Instead, she decided to concentrate on cleaning the cut on Jackson's cheek.

Now that his fever was easing back, she could afford a little time spent on caring for his wound. "If, that is, I can reach it," she whispered, turning his face toward her and scowling at the beard covering her husband's jaw. Was it laziness, she wondered, that made a man grow such a bush on his face? Or did he actually *like* the blasted thing?

"Well," she mused aloud, "the reasons don't really matter, do they? Because to treat that cut, there's only one thing to do." Then she got up and left the room to search for what she needed.

A half hour later, she was back at his side with a heated bowl of water, a rusty pair of scissors and a razor that obviously hadn't been used in months. She'd sharpened it as best she could on the leather strop she'd found in a drawer, but now she eyed the edge of the blade and then considered Jackson's beard. A beard the size of that one actually required the use of a cutlass, she thought with a half smile, but she would have to make do.

Taking up the scissors, she hacked away at the length of his beard until it was cut close to the injured side of his face. Then thoughtfully, she eased backward, cocked her head to one side and studied his now lopsided beard. It was foolish, she thought, to shave only *half* of his face. Why, he'd look ridiculous. Better to just do the whole beard, she told herself. No sense in doing half a task. Surely he'd understand her reasoning.

And before she could give it another thought, she set to work. Sometime later, she wiped the last of the shaving soap from his skin and took her first, unhindered look at her new husband. She smiled. Why, he was much more handsome than his brother. His jaw was more square, his brow more proud and his nose, which had obviously been broken at least once, gave his features character. The fresh cut on his cheek lay directly above an old, jagged scar that slashed across his cheek. This, she thought, was the reason for his beard. He'd obviously sought to cover it up. Hide it from the world.

"Foolish man," she whispered, shaking her head. Didn't he know that the scar only made him look more dangerously attractive? Then she cleaned the fresh wound and was glad to see it wouldn't require stitches. "This one won't scar," she told him though he couldn't hear her.

When she'd finished, she took a moment to study him and a swirl of pleasure lit her up from within. Even with the flush of fever still coursing through him, he was a proud, strong-looking man. Who would have guessed that beneath all that hair was such a good face? "You'll do me fine, Jackson MacIntyre," she whispered, and reached out to stroke her fingertips across the ancient scar he'd kept hidden.

Instinctively he turned into her touch, reaching up to capture her hand and hold it to his face. His lips brushed her palm and Molly hissed in a breath. He murmured something, but she couldn't quite catch it. Still, it didn't matter, did it? All that mattered now was that she was home. At last, she'd found a husband who needed her. A place where the two of them together could build a future. A home to love and care for.

And, she added around a wide yawn, "A bed, thank heaven, to sleep in."

The days of travel, the hurried wedding and the long, wet ride up the mountain finally took its toll. Fatigue clawed at her, dragging her down into a darkness she was all too ready for. Gathering up her things, she took them into the other room, then checked on Captain Blood. She found the ornery bird actually snoring. Smiling to herself, Molly went back to the bedroom and slipped into bed beside her husband. In his sleep, he pulled her close, spooning her up against him, her back to his front. She lay stiffly for a moment, then realized that even in his sleep, he'd reached out for his wife and, pleased, she relaxed against him. His hard, warm strength surrounded her. Heat from his body poured into hers. And relishing the simple joy of being held, Molly fell asleep.

In his hazy, fever-driven dream world, Jackson reached for the woman lying beside him. Dixie, he thought with a smile. Damned if she hadn't missed his weekly visit. She must have trudged all the way up the mountain to see him. A fine woman, he told himself. He didn't know what she was up to exactly, but enough teasing already. Not that he didn't appreciate her cool touch or the way her hands felt smoothing across his chest. But he was ready...hungry for more.

Her body curled into his and Jackson swallowed a groan that ripped through him, along with a wave of need that threatened to swamp him. He bent his head to kiss the curve of her neck and the soft sigh she made gave him the encouragement he really didn't need. The fever still raging in his blood glazed his vision. Shifting slightly, he levered himself up on one elbow, leaned over her and couldn't even make out her features in the darkness. But then, he thought, he didn't need to see her. He'd let his hands do the looking for him.

Besides, he'd held her before, had sex with her once a week for the past few months. She was comfort when he needed it. Warmth when he felt cold to his soul. And another heartbeat in the darkness when he couldn't bear to be alone another minute. Most importantly, she never expected more from him than he could give.

He bent his head to kiss her, drowning in the cool feel of her skin against his. She seemed a little less eager than usual, but his fevered brain put that down to her being anxious for his health. A fine woman, he thought again, and smiled against her mouth. Then he got down to business.

Parting her lips with his tongue, he rushed into her warm mouth and felt a gasp shudder through her body. She squirmed against him for a moment or two and every move she made fed the flames licking at his insides. Then tentatively, almost shyly, she stroked her tongue against his. A flicker of something sweet and wild sparkled within him at her purposely clumsy kiss. That touch of innocence, he thought, and gave himself up to new sensations, new wonders to be found.

His hand swept beneath the hem of her nightshirt. Sliding his palm along the length of her body, a part of his befuddled brain noted that she seemed thinner than before. And weren't her breasts smaller than he remembered? No matter. He liked it. He cupped one breast in his palm and loved knowing that his hand could completely cover her. His thumb and forefinger circled the hard, rigid tip of her nipple and she arched into him, a moan slipping from her throat and into his.

She trembled in his arms and Jackson held her tighter, wrapping his arms around her, holding her to him, molding her body to his, and still it wasn't enough. Different, he thought, despite his bleary vision and muddled brain. She felt different. Better.

Her hands slid up his arms to his shoulders and her fingers dug into his flesh, holding on as if the world was rocking around her. Need bubbled inside him and Jackson gave himself into it, surrendering to the flood of feelings coursing through him.

He took her mouth while his hands explored her curves as if for the first time. Soft, smooth. Dragging his fingertips along the inside of her leg, he drifted higher and higher until he found the source of her heat. He cupped her, his thumb gently rubbing the one sensitive spot that had her twisting and writhing in his grasp. Her soft sighs, eager moans and clutching fingers drove him on. His fingers dipped in and out of her warmth until she quaked and shivered beneath him. When she claimed her release, he gave her still more until she tore her mouth from his and bit down hard on his shoulder to keep from shouting.

''Ah, darlin','' he whispered, holding on to her as her world shifted, splintered, feeling her pleasure as keenly as if it were his own.

Her response fired him, feeding the desire inside until it was a blaze that couldn't be stopped. Jackson quickly shifted position, kneeling between her legs, covering her body with his. He slid into her warmth, claiming her body, needing her more than he ever had before. He didn't understand it, but here in the darkness, he'd found something he hadn't been expecting. This woman he'd thought he knew had touched him unexpectedly. And he needed to know if there was more. He *wanted* more.

Her breath hitched and she stiffened slightly. Her body was tight. Tighter than he'd remembered. Jackson moved slowly, accommodating himself to her. And when she lifted her hips into his, he knew she was ready, that she wanted him as badly as he did her. Jackson built a rhythm between them, moving in and out of her like a man searching for something just out of reach. Her breath dusted his shoulder, her sighs sifted into his soul. She held him to her, arms and legs wrapped around his body, cradling him in her softness. A new wave of release swept through her and she trembled as he emptied himself into her then, groaning tightly, collapsed on top of her.

Still tingling, Molly sighed and ran her hands up and down Jackson's back. Her breath raced in and out of her lungs. Her heartbeat thundered in her ears. Her blood felt as if it was boiling. She'd never imagined…never supposed… But how could she have known? Women didn't talk about such things. At least, they didn't discuss them with unmarried women, which didn't seem fair at all. Someone should have warned her. Someone should have prepared her for the soul-shattering wonder of it all.

His body, so big, so powerful, had slipped into hers like the missing piece of a puzzle. And any discomfort she'd felt had dissolved quickly beneath the sheer pleasure of being joined with him. To know he was actually a part of her. To be able to feel him within her. Then to have the added bonus of actually seeing stars…well, it was simply amazing.

"That was," she said softly, wanting to tell him just how touched she'd been, "absolutely wonderful."

He didn't answer.

She smiled into the darkness. Obviously, he'd been as moved as she by the experience. He couldn't even speak. It was a gift, she thought. To marry a man sight unseen and to find such an instant closeness. Pleasure surged inside her as she acknowledged that she'd made the right decision in coming to Defiance. And now that she'd started her new life as a wife, she had to wonder if perhaps she hadn't already conceived the first of their children.

A curl of anticipation unwound in the pit of her stomach. Only a few short weeks ago, she'd been alone in the house where she'd grown up. Alone and wondering about a future that had stretched out long and empty in front of her.

Now, here she was, married, perhaps pregnant, and…being suffocated by the limp, heavy body of her husband.

"Jackson," she said, and squirmed just a bit as his weight pressed down on her. "I want you to know that I think our marriage will be a good partnership. We'll…" Frowning, she pushed at him a little. Really, he was *very* heavy. She cleared her throat and started again. "We'll make this cabin a home." Molly shifted a bit to her right, but his broad chest wasn't that easy to escape. And frankly, if he wanted to maintain their closeness, she was willing to put up with the crushing weight of him. It was comforting, in a way. She hitched in a breath. "You'll see, we'll—"

A deep rumbling sound interrupted her and Molly's eyes went wide. "What was that?" In the silence, that horrible noise brought visions of mountain lions or bears or…what all else lived in the wilds of Colorado, anyway?

Her gaze shot to the small window and the night outside. Sheer blackness hovered just beyond the glass, where rain still slashed at the little house as if demanding entry. Briefly she mourned the loss of the streetlights at home. Their pale glow against a fog-shrouded night had comforted her more than once. But here, in Colorado on a moonless night, the darkness was all encompassing—and crouched to pounce. Her fingers dug into Jackson's shoulders, taking comfort from the fact that he didn't seem worried. Still, she held her breath and waited what seemed an eternity.

Then it came again—low, deep, guttural. *Close.* Scowling, Molly slowly drew her head back, trying to see Jackson's face.

The man who'd just shown her the stars...the man who'd touched her as no other man ever had...was *snoring.*

''Jackson?''

He snorted, mumbled something and nuzzled her neck.

Sparks of something hot and wonderful sizzled through her bloodstream, but she fought past the sensation. ''Jackson!''

''Can't a man get any sleep around here?'' he demanded in a growling mutter, then pushed himself off her, rolled to the side and in seconds was sound asleep again.

Molly sat straight up in bed and looked down at the man beside her. ''For heaven's sake!''

In the darkness, she could just make out his profile. ''How can he sleep?'' she wondered aloud. She'd never felt so awake...so *alive* in her life. She couldn't sleep now if her life depended on it. There was so much to talk about. To plan. To discover about each other.

Another snore rattled the windowpane and she glared at him. How could a man capable of such magic be so...insensitive? Her back teeth ground together as he shifted position, digging his head into the feather pillow.

Then she remembered. Of course. He was sick. That explained everything. Naturally the man would fall asleep after such exertion. Things would be different in the morning, she told herself. He would be so happy to see her. And no doubt he'd apologize for falling asleep and leaving her to lie awake alone on her first night with him.

Feeling better about the whole situation, Molly stretched out in the bed beside him and stared up at the beamed ceiling. He muttered something just under his breath, then rolled over and reached for her. She went willingly, curling into him, laying her head on his chest, enjoying the feel of his strong arms wrapped around her. Listening to the beat of his heart, Molly stared into the darkness and thought about what the morning would bring. How she and her new husband would begin their lives together.

And as she named their children and planned the next fifty years, Molly Malone MacIntyre fell asleep in the arms of her husband.

Chapter Three

Jackson woke up to the sound of rain hammering at the cabin and the unmistakable scent of coffee.

He rolled over in bed and greedily sniffed the air and also picked up the aroma of fresh-baked bread and bacon. His stomach rumbled in anticipation and he clapped one hand to his empty belly. But for the hunger gnawing at him, he felt better than he had in a long time. The fever that had laid him low seemed to have left as quickly as it had come and he'd slept like a dead man. Who would have thought a simple cut on the cheek could produce a fever high enough to send him to bed?

Opening his eyes, he stared up at the beam ceiling and told himself he was a lucky man. He had a nice warm cabin to sit out the rain in and there was bacon and coffee cooking in the other room. And as that thought settled in and took root, he scowled a bit. Just who the hell was cooking?

Then it all started trickling back to him. Sitting up, he shoved one hand through his hair and gave his skull a squeeze as if it would help him think. Dixie. Dixie was here last night. He remembered sleeping with her, the incredible feel of her body, the flash of desire, the rush of heated blood and her eager, untutored response. But even as the notion came to him, he discounted it. Not only was Dixie no innocent...but that woman would sooner march naked down Main Street than make a trip up the mountain. In the rain, no less. Nope. Dixie hadn't been here.

He must have dreamed that encounter in the darkness. Damn good dream, he thought, but that left him with the question, just who the hell was in his house?

Only one way to find out. He swung his legs off the bed, snatched up his trousers from the floor and headed across the room. If some traveler looking to get out of the rain had just helped himself to Jackson's supplies, then he was about to pay for them. The hard way.

With blood in his eye, Jackson stepped into the main room and stopped dead.

"Good morning!" a female voice called. "Well, afternoon, really."

A tall redhead with a wide smile and sea-green eyes turned to greet him as if he was a welcome guest in his own place. She wore a crisp white apron tied around her narrow waist and a blue calico dress that looked worn from too many washings. Even from across the room, he saw a dusting of freckles across her nose and cheeks that looked as if her pale skin had been spattered with gold dust. Her long hair fell to just above her hips in a tangle of curls that shimmered like a fire at night each time she moved.

Memory danced around the edges of his mind. That hair of hers. He knew it. Knew the soft, silky feel of it, the way the curls would twine around his fingers. A pang of foreboding rocked him as he tried to bring back the image of the woman in his dream. But he couldn't see her clearly. Couldn't make out her features. A dream, he told himself. Just a dream.

"I thought you'd never wake up," she said, snapping him back to the moment at hand. That smile of hers got even wider. "I kept checking on you to make sure you were breathin'."

Breathing and apparently still dreaming, he thought. Best-looking squatter he'd ever seen. And it didn't matter a damn how good-looking she was, he told himself firmly even as something inside him sat up and took notice. She didn't belong here and he was getting her out. Now.

"Lady," he said, his voice low and deep, rumbling just below the sound of the rain drumming on the roof, "who are you and what are you doing in my house?"

"I'm cooking," she said in a tone most people used when dealing with a half-wit.

"I can see that," he told her, though why she was cooking in his house was still a mystery.

"And I must say, your supplies aren't what they should be."

Not only was she trespassing, she was insulting him. Hell, his supplies were just fine—for *one* person.

"Is that right?" He scowled at her, knowing full well that grown men had been known to cower when Jackson MacIntyre turned a cold eye on them.

She didn't seem to notice.

"I'm sure they were sufficient for one, but now that I'm here, we'll have to stock up." Tapping one finger against her chin, she kept talking, listing the things she wanted him to buy. "Let's see…we'll need sugar, coffee, bacon, some salt, of course."

"Of course," he agreed, nodding.

Crazy, that's what she was, he told himself. Which

would explain a lot. No sane woman would troop into a man's cabin and make herself at home like this. Damn shame, he told himself. Fine-looking woman like her. Too bad her bucket had a hole in it. But it wasn't his problem. All he had to do was figure out who she belonged to and how she'd ended up in his house.

Now that he knew what he was dealing with, he interrupted her flow of words in a soft, reasonable voice. "Sure. We'll do that. Soon as it stops raining, we'll go to town." He should be able to find her keepers back in town. How in the heck they'd let her escape was beyond him.

Pleased, she gave him a smile that lit the gloomy room up like a fireworks display. A damn shame, he thought again. A woman that good-lookin' shouldn't be let loose to wander on her own. Especially since her bread didn't seem to be quite done.

"Oh good," she said. "Maybe we'll have time to visit with your brother and his wife." Picking up the coffeepot from the stove top, she poured two cups, then spared him a quick look. "There wasn't much time to talk yesterday. Things were so rushed, what with the wedding and all."

Wedding?

Jackson stared at her, a dark curl of suspicion tightening in his gut. "You saw Lucas yesterday?"

She laughed and shook her head as she set the coffeepot back down. "Of course. How else would I have known where to find you?"

How else, indeed? She'd come to this place specifically to find him. And Lucas had sent her. Still, this didn't mean she wasn't crazy. "And there was a wedding."

She nodded, and her features tightened as impatience

settled in. Crazy or not, the redhead clearly had a temper that was right close to a boil. But mad or not, he needed some answers. He had to know just what was going on. And what exactly Lucas had had to do with it.

"Whose wedding?" he asked, though something inside him told him he really didn't want to hear the answer.

"Whose wedding?" she demanded, and planted both hands at her hips. "What is this about, Jackson Mac-Intyre? Are you tryin' to pretend you don't know who I am?"

"Lady," he said, "I don't know you from Adam's great-aunt. So why don't you climb down off that high horse of yours and just spit it out?"

"Spit what out?"

"What's stuck in your craw."

"A lovely sentiment," she told him, one red eyebrow lifting into an arch.

Jackson sighed. Yesterday he'd felt sick as a dog, and today he didn't have the strength to deal with whatever the redhead had in mind. He was tired and hungry and flat out of patience. "*Whose* wedding?" he asked again through gritted teeth.

"Whose do you think?" she snapped, clearly as irritable as he. "'Twas *our* wedding, you great oaf."

She held up her left hand and his gaze flicked to her ring finger. Sure enough, there was a shiny, brand-new gold wedding band glittering at him. Something cold settled in his chest and he told himself there had to be a mistake here. A man couldn't forget his own wedding. Not even if his fever was high enough to fry an egg on his forehead. And damn it, Jackson would *never* have willingly gotten married. Not again.

"Our wedding," he repeated, and heard the frustration

rippling in his own voice. "And just how did we get married when I was here, on the mountain?" Warming to his theme, he took a step forward, cocked his head to one side and added, "Don't you think if I'd gotten married I would have *been* there?"

"Shove off, matey!" a voice from behind him screeched.

Jackson dropped into a crouch and spun around, instinctively looking for an enemy. What he saw had his jaw dropping open. His Winchester rifle, hanging in its rack above the fireplace, had become a perch for the ugliest bird he'd ever seen in his life. And the damn thing was staring at him through beady little eyes that didn't look any too friendly.

"What in the sam hill is *that?*"

"That," the woman told him, "is Captain Blood. My parrot."

"Well, what's it doin' on my gun?"

"Sitting."

"Get it off!" He'd be damned if his prize rifle was used as an open-ended birdcage.

"We've better things to discuss than Captain Blood."

He swung around to glare at her again. This wasn't happening. He wasn't losing control of his life. His house wasn't being invaded by women and birds. And he damn sure wasn't *married*. "You're right," he snapped. "We do. So why don't you start by telling me how I managed to marry you while I was home sick in bed."

Her foot tapped against the floor in a sharp, brisk tattoo of sound that fought with the rain still pounding away on the rooftop. That thin red eyebrow lifted high again as her green eyes narrowed. She was hoppin' mad. And ordinarily, any man with a lick of sense would steer clear of a female on the warpath. But this one was standing in *his* house, so if somebody was leaving, it was going to be her.

"It was a proxy marriage," she said, that foot of hers picking up speed as she glared at him. "Your brother stood in for you."

Lucas.

"He was very helpful," the woman was saying now, implying with her tone that Lucas was the brother with good manners.

"I'll just bet he was," Jackson muttered, already planning exactly how and when he was going to kill his brother. Damn the man anyway. He'd told Lucas that he wasn't going to get married just because of Uncle Simon's will.

"And did he mention why I wasn't at my own wedding?" Jackson asked hotly. "Didn't you *wonder?*"

"Of course," she said, and folded both arms across her chest. "He said you were sick. And you were," she reminded him. "Feverish all night."

So he had been. But how did she know? It had come on him fast early yesterday and laid him out flat. He could remember feeling as though he were on fire. And he remembered cool hands and damp cloths running across his hot skin. Vaguely he recalled the sensation of relief whenever he felt soft fingers trace across his brow, his chest. Mostly he remembered the aftermath, what he'd thought of as a dream, the naked woman in his bed. And how she'd felt in his arms.

But maybe, he thought now, just maybe that *hadn't* been a dream after all. He had to know.

"Lucas wanted me to wait to come up here until today, when he would bring me himself—"

That would have been convenient, Jackson thought.

He could have buried his younger brother somewhere in the woods without having to go all the way to town to kill him.

"But I knew that you were sick," she was saying, "and rented a buggy and came on my own."

That caught his attention. Cocking his head, he stared at her. "Just when exactly did you get here?"

"Last night," she said.

Last night. She'd been here all night. Alone. With him. Well, that tore it. *She* was his dream woman. The cool-handed, soft-voiced female who'd somehow reached him despite the fever racking his body. She…a tall redhead with a temper as pushy as a wounded mountain lion… was his *wife*.

Pushing that notion to the back of his mind, Jackson shoved a hand through his hair, stalked across the room and snatched up one of the cups of coffee. Taking a good, long gulp of the hot, thick brew, he let the coffee work its way through his system. And before it had even hit the pit of his stomach, he was wishing desperately that it was whiskey. Any kind of whiskey. He wasn't picky at the moment. But then liquor wouldn't change anything anyhow. So instead, he took another gulp of that coffee, looked her dead in the eye and said, "I don't want a wife."

"But you sent for me. You advertised for a wife."

"Lucas," he muttered, and even his brother's name conjured a red haze that blurred his vision. "That was his idea. Not mine."

She blinked, opened her mouth, then snapped it shut again.

He took advantage of her silence to add, "We'll get the damn marriage annulled. Today."

"Oh no we won't," she said, lifting her chin defiantly.

This close up, he could count the handful of freckles on her pale skin. Five on her right cheek, six on the left and two across the bridge of her nose. Gold dust in buttermilk. That's what they looked like. And the green of her eyes was as deep as the forest in springtime, and the red of her hair shone like polished copper.

And none of that mattered, he told himself, since she wouldn't be staying.

"I told you, I don't want a wife."

"That's a bloody shame, since you have one," she told him.

"Look, lady—"

"Molly," she interrupted him with her name. "Molly MacIntyre."

He winced. Lucas was a dead man. He didn't care what it took or how long he went to prison for it. His brother was as good as dead.

"There'll be no annulment," she told him, wagging her index finger at him as she might to a schoolboy.

"And why not?"

"Because we've already had the honeymoon."

He gave himself a mental kick in the behind. Of course. If she was the dream woman, then they'd damn well consummated the marriage. Well, this was just fine, wasn't it? Because he'd been sick, out of his head with fever, he'd been roped into a marriage he hadn't wanted. And now, because he'd already bedded her, there might be a child on the way. Damn it, a man shouldn't be held responsible for what he does when he's insensible with fever.

But that excuse was no good at all and he knew it. Jackson MacIntyre was a man who always did the right thing, no matter the cost to him personally.

Little brother, he thought grimly, say your prayers.

Molly looked at the man she'd married sight unseen and felt the warm curl of last night's welcome dissolve inside her. He didn't want her here, clearly didn't remember the passion that had leaped up between them, and was obviously already planning how best to get rid of her.

Well, he had another think coming.

"This wasn't my doing," he told her, and reached out for one of the chairs in front of him. Curling his fingers around the ladder-back, he held on tight and squeezed. "I never wanted a wife."

She sniffed and let her gaze sweep the cabin dismissively. "That's a pity, since you so obviously *need* one."

"What I *need*," he nearly shouted, "is peace and quiet and to be left the hell alone!"

"Keelhaul the bastard," Captain Blood screamed, his voice scratching the air like nails on a blackboard.

Jackson sent the bird a look that should have dropped him from his perch. "You keep out of this, stew-meat," he threatened.

"Don't you be thinkin' you'll harm that bird."

"You keep him quiet or I swear I'll be seeing him stuffed before supper."

Molly had put up with a lot so far. But she'd been raised around seamen—Irish ones at that, and she was no stranger to a temper. Besides, she did have a bit of temper herself…sometimes. And she was willing to admit that there would have to be a lot of compromising in a new marriage. But now her husband had gone too far. And as her uncle was wont to say, "Set your course at the beginning of your journey." So with that thought in mind, she let him know in no uncertain terms just what he could expect from her.

"Now you listen to me, Jackson MacIntyre," she said,

coming around the edge of the table to stand directly in front of him. "Whether you wanted a wife or no, the deed is done. So, I'll take care of you and *our* home. I'll bear your children and be the helpmate you so obviously need."

"I told you—"

"But," she interrupted him, poking him in the chest with her index finger, "what I won't do, is stand still to be insulted or shouted at."

"I didn't mean to insult—"

She cut him off again and he gritted his teeth in frustration. "Shout at me, and you can expect to be getting some of your own back. You'll be met temper for temper, shout for shout."

"All right," Jackson growled, glaring down at her. "Now you listen."

"I haven't finished," Molly told him, whipping her hair back behind her shoulder and meeting that flinty gaze of his with a cold, determined stare of her own.

"Fine," he said, throwing his hands wide. "Finish."

"You think on this, *husband*," she said, the music of Ireland in her threat, "you lay one hand on that parrot and, by Saint Patrick's staff, I'll shave the rest of your body as bald as I did your cheeks."

Blue eyes wide, he lifted both hands to his jaws and, when he felt nothing but smooth skin and sandpapery stubble, he loomed over her and shouted, "What did you *do* to me, woman?"

"*Abandon ship!*" Captain Blood screeched.

Chapter Four

"Damn it, woman," he growled, clapping one hand to the scarred side of his face, "I've had that beard for ten years."

"Aye," she said, "and it looked as though rats and birds had been nesting in it."

He hadn't cared what it looked like. It was what the beard had been hiding that bothered him. For ten years, he'd managed to avoid looking at the scar he'd picked up on a battlefield in what seemed like another lifetime.

That rebel saber blade had sliced more than his cheek. It had cut him down to the soul. It was as if all the misery of the years spent fighting the war had been wrapped up in that one vicious swipe. But the jagged mark on his face was just the memory now, the echo of what had once been, and he was no more interested in looking at it today than he had been yesterday.

"You had no right," he told her flatly. Damn it, he felt almost naked. No one had seen that mark on his face since the surgeon who'd botched the stitching of it.

"I had every right," she said, and he noticed that the madder she got, the more musical her voice became. It was as though when she was talking without thinking, the Irish in her came through. He was guessing that's where she got her hot temper, too. "You'd a fresh cut on your cheek that needed tending. However did you get it?"

"Rockfall," he said, then shook his head. "Doesn't matter."

"Well, it won't scar if it's cared for," she said. "'Twasn't as deep as the other."

"No," he said tightly, "it wouldn't be." This had been just a glancing blow from a chip of rock, not a swinging, razor-sharp sword being wielded by a desperate man in a losing battle.

Outside, the storm raged and a clap of thunder made his memories all that more real. The skies shook and sounded like the roar of cannon fire. He closed his eyes briefly and pushed those old images back as he had so many times before.

"You're a handsome man, Jackson," she was saying, and he looked at her as if she was as crazy as he'd first thought her.

"Yeah," he said with a snort, "I win prizes at county fairs all the time."

She shook her head. "You've no need to hide beneath that scraggly beard."

"That's my business," he told her, fully intending to grow the damn thing back as soon as he was able.

Oh, Lucas is going to regret this, he thought. Not only sneaking a wife in on him, but one with a head as hard as the rocks he mined.

"You've a hard head, haven't you?" she mused aloud, tipping her head to one side to study him.

"*I* have a hard head?" he said, and choked out a laugh. "Lady, I've seen mules with easier temperaments."

She inhaled sharply and blew the breath out in a rush. "So, it's not going to be an easy first day for us, is it then?"

Now maybe some men wouldn't mind waking up to find themselves married to a woman like this. But he wasn't one of 'em. The last thing Jackson wanted—or needed—was a wife. No point in pretending otherwise.

"Doesn't look like it," he admitted. "No."

"Well then," she told him, "if we're going to go on arguing, you'll need your strength."

"What?" he asked, a reluctant laugh shooting from his throat.

"It's not an easy business, arguing with me," she said, and added, "or so I've been told."

"Is that right?"

"Aye, 'tis." She waved one hand at the table and said, "You must be starved. Sit down and have something to eat. We can continue the fight when you're feeling better."

"Continue the fight?" Most women he knew would have gone all weepy by now, turning to tears to either win or end the argument. Figured that *this* woman would be different. What do you say to a female who's willing to stop arguing long enough to feed you?

"It's no fun arguing with a man who's not at his best."

"*Fun?* You think arguing's fun?"

"And why not? Two people getting to know each other with a spirited exchange of opinions." She picked up a skillet and Jackson kept a wary eye on her, not sure whether he should be looking forward to a meal or getting ready to duck.

She must have read his expression.

"Tryin' to understand me, are you?" she asked, her

lips quirking into that wide, gorgeous smile again. "Well, don't worry if you can't. Uncle Michael always said I was the eighth wonder of the world."

"You and the Gardens of Babylon, huh?"

She gave him a look of pleased surprise.

"Folks west of St. Louis *do* read occasionally," he said wryly.

Molly dipped her head briefly, then nodded. "Yes, well, Uncle Michael liked to say that I was as mysterious as the pyramids and twice as deep as the sea."

He'd go along with that. "Uncle Michael?"

"The man who raised me," she said, and that smile slipped a bit as her green eyes softened in memory. "He died several months ago."

Jackson experienced a pang of sympathy he really didn't want to feel. He knew the pain he saw glimmering in her eyes. He'd gone through it himself. Odd, wasn't it, that both of them had been raised by uncles and they'd both lost those men just recently. Something in common, he thought, and knew that slender thread of connection wasn't nearly enough.

She was a beautiful woman, married to a man who'd spent most of the past ten years hiding his scarred face from everyone. She had a spark of something warm and vital in her eyes and that spark had been wrung out of him too long ago.

Shaking off the trail his mind was taking, he said gruffly, "Lucas and me, we were raised by our Uncle Simon. He died too. Not long ago."

"I'm sorry," she said, and reached out one hand to touch his arm.

Heat skittered up the length of his bare arm and ricocheted around his chest like a spent bullet looking for somewhere to land. He pulled back, mostly because he enjoyed that warmth too damn much.

Silence stretched out between them and, for a long minute, he wasn't sure what to do. What to say. Hell, it wasn't every day a man woke up from a fever to find he'd acquired a wife.

"Man overboard!" the parrot shouted, splintering the moment, and Jackson was almost grateful for the distraction.

Wincing, he looked over his shoulder at the stupid bird and mentally had it plucked, cleaned and simmering.

"Captain Blood belonged to Uncle Michael," she said. "He's really all the family I have left."

Jackson scowled and put aside thoughts of frying that bird. For the moment. "Could you get him down off my rifle?" he asked tightly.

"Surely," she said, smiling, and tapped the tips of her fingers against a chair back. "Come down, Captain."

The parrot craned its neck, ruffled its feathers and then in a blur of colored motion swooped from its perch to take up a stand on the chair beside Jackson. It walked back and forth on the top rail, its clawed feet scraping against the wood and Jackson's last nerve at the same time.

This cabin wasn't nearly big enough for the three of them, he thought, and briefly entertained the notion of being the first to leave. But just as quickly as the idea came, it disappeared. He wasn't a man to cut and run at the first sign of trouble. Besides, he reminded himself, this was *his* house. He wouldn't be run off by a parrot, of all things.

Nope. He'd stay right here until Molly Malone MacIntyre realized just how miserable a thing it was to be married to the likes of him. Hell, he thought, brightening a bit, she'd probably get sick and tired of him in no time. And with any luck, she'd divorce him and then things could get back to normal.

"So," she said, and his gaze darted to her. "Are you hungry or not?"

"Yes, ma'am," he said, figuring that if she was willing to cook, it beat the hell out of him having to do it himself. Pulling out a chair, he sat down and refilled his coffee cup. Taking a long drink, he watched her as she went to work. She moved easily, competently, and he knew she'd done this many times before. A woman at home in the kitchen. Well, he told himself, there at least was one bright spot, if the food tasted as good as she looked cooking it. Within minutes, she had that skillet heating, fresh bacon frying and eggs sizzling alongside.

"Uncle Michael was a hearty appetite on two short legs," she said, and Jackson realized the hardest part of all this was that he was going to miss the silence around here. He didn't think Molly could be quiet for longer than a few seconds at a stretch.

"Most men like to eat," he said.

"Aye, that's the truth of it," she said, and flipped the bacon over to crisp up on the other side. "And Michael would always be bringin' his friends round to the house. So you could say the skillet in our house never cooled off."

"You cooked for all of them?"

She turned, refilled his coffee and gave him a quick flash of that smile. "I did. And they ate anything I put in front of them, but for fish. They never were much for eating the stuff they spent all of their lives catching."

In spite of himself, he was getting caught up in her story. "Your uncle was a fisherman?"

"That he was, and a fine one, too." She flipped the

eggs over in the skillet, nodding when they hissed and popped in the bacon grease. "But he'd a love for the whiskey, as well, and that often kept him off the ships and in the taverns."

She shot him a narrowed look.

"Your brother owns a tavern," she said warily. "Are you a drinkin' man, Jackson?"

"Not so much," he said, understanding why she asked. This couldn't be any easier on her. She'd married a stranger and was now hoping she hadn't made the mistake Jackson thought she had.

"Ah," she said smiling, "that's good."

Then she turned back to her cooking and Jackson's stomach rumbled in anticipation. The scent of the food seemed to surround him and he felt as though he hadn't eaten in years. He helped himself to a thick slice of her fresh bread and nearly groaned aloud when he took a bite. It was almost enough to make a man reconsider this whole wife situation. He'd been eating his own cooking for so long he'd forgotten how good food could taste when prepared by a knowledgeable hand.

"You know," she said, spearing the bacon slices and dropping them onto a plate, "I've been thinking..."

"The most dangerous words a woman can say," he muttered into his coffee cup.

"What was that?"

"Nothin'," he assured her, not willing to start that argument up again until he'd had a sample of her cooking.

"Hmm..." She gave him a curious look as she flipped three eggs onto the plate beside the bacon, then set it down in front of him.

He tucked right in, surprising himself with the hunger scratching at his belly. The first bite nearly made him weep. Bacon crisp, eggs done to a perfect turn. Almost more than a man had a right to hope for. In fact, the meal would have been perfect if not for the screeching parrot and the woman now sitting opposite him.

Damn distracting, trying to enjoy your food while a redhead with fire in her eyes was watching every bite you took.

"Good?" she asked unnecessarily.

"Yes, ma'am," he said, lingering on the taste of that bacon. "Aren't you having any?"

"Oh no," she said, taking a sip of coffee and shaking her head. "I ate while you were asleep."

She'd done plenty while he was asleep, Jackson noted for the first time as his gaze swept the interior of the cabin. He'd been so busy dealing with Molly, he hadn't noticed anything else. Until now.

The floor was swept, his dirty clothes were stacked in a corner, the hearth had been cleaned out and a new fire laid and the stack of dirty dishes had been washed and put away. Gave him an itch between his shoulder blades, thinking of her wandering around his house, rooting through his things while he was flat on his back unable to protest. Besides, he liked his place just like it was.

Wasn't it enough he had a *wife* all of a sudden to put up with?

His gaze slid back to her and he thought she looked plenty satisfied with herself.

"Made yourself right at home, I see."

One red eyebrow shot straight up in a gesture he was coming to be familiar with already.

"If you mean I straightened up a bit, aye, I did."

He set his fork down on the edge of his plate and leaned back in his chair. Studying her, he folded his arms across his chest. Now that his belly was full and his head a bit clearer, he decided now was as good a time as any to set her straight as to how things were going to be around here.

"Well, don't," he said flatly.

"Don't what? Clean my home?"

"*My* home."

"*Our* home."

Jackson sucked in a breath through gritted teeth. "I guess we're about to continue that argument, huh?"

"So it seems," she told him. "And if you're thinkin' to frighten me with that fish-eyed stare of yours, you can think again."

He squirmed a bit in his chair at the accusation, despite the fact that there might have been a thread of truth in what she'd said. "I don't frighten women."

"Not this one any road." She crossed her arms over her chest, mimicking his posture.

"Any road?" Her Irish was definitely up again.

"Fine then. Any *way*." She sniffed. "And don't change the subject."

"And that is?" he asked, losing his patience again as she seemed to talk in circles.

Molly leaned forward, placing both hands flat on the table. She gave him a smile that didn't quite reach her eyes yet somehow managed to steal his breath anyway. Then she looked him dead in the eye and said, "You may not have wanted a wife, Jackson MacIntyre, but you by heaven have got one now. And I'm not goin' anywhere, so you may as well get used to it."

He slapped the palms of his hands onto the tabletop just opposite hers and leaned forward to meet her glare head-on. "There're a few things you'll have to get used to also," he said, "such as, I do as I please, when I please, and that's not going to change."

Her eyes narrowed. "And I don't take orders well."

"When I want to go huntin', I go huntin'."

"I cook one meal at a time. If you're not here to eat it when it's hot, you'll eat it cold."

Jackson stood up, still leaning toward her. "I like peace and quiet."

Molly stood up, too, put her hands at her hips and leaned in at him. "I like to talk. And to sing sometimes."

"I don't want a harpy for a wife."

"And I don't much care to be married to a growlin' bear of a husband."

"I won't love you," he said, and surprised himself with the words. He'd been thinking them, but he hadn't expected to say them out loud.

It was the simple truth, though. He wouldn't love anyone again. Would never let anyone that close to him again. He'd learned that lesson years ago and learned it well enough to last him the rest of his life. That was part of the reason he'd separated himself from the rest of the world.

It wasn't just the scar on his face that had him hiding from people. It was the scar on his soul and that one still felt fresh.

Now, looking into Molly's sea-green eyes, and seeing the flash of hurt there, he almost wished things were different. Wished *he* was different. But like Uncle Simon used to say, "If wishes were horses, beggars would ride."

Molly straightened up and nodded at him. "Fair enough, then," she said. "I won't expect your love, though I think perhaps one day you'll regret sayin' that."

"No, I—"

She held up one hand to quiet him, then went on. "Doesn't matter for now," she said quietly. "Like I said, I won't expect your love, but I *do* expect your respect. After all, I am your wife.''

That last sentence cost her some pride, Jackson thought, and said what he could to ease her on that score. ''You're my wife,'' he agreed, ''and I'll treat you as such.''

''Then we've a truce?'' she asked, sticking out her right hand toward him.

He looked at her small hand for a long minute and considered just what taking it would mean. A truce. And how long could that last, he wondered, when the two people involved both had heads as hard as stone? Still, he'd never been one to walk away from a fight.

Slapping his hand into hers, his fingers curled around her hand and squeezed gently. If he felt a quick burst of warmth shoot up his arm and dart into the dark block of ice that was his heart, Jackson ignored it.

''A truce,'' he said, and was glad she smiled at him again.

Chapter Five

The woman never sat still.

Jackson glanced up from the table where his rifle lay scattered in pieces for cleaning. Three days he'd been...*married,* and just watching his new wife damn near wore him out. Molly had cleaned his cabin until he hardly recognized the place.

The wood floor gleamed damply from her constant scrubbing. The inside of the windows shone, reflecting the firelight, and the only thing that had kept her from finishing the job by washing the outside of the glass panes was the fact that the rain hadn't stopped long enough for her to manage. She'd sanded the tabletop and now the damn thing was as smooth as a baby's bottom. She'd even somehow scraped years' worth of smoke and dirt off the walls. Now the rough-hewn logs were almost white from her attentions.

This wasn't a cabin anymore, he told himself in silent disgust. It was fast becoming a *cottage.* And there didn't seem to be any way of stopping her. Pulling the reins in on Molly would be like trying to lasso a tornado as it sped across the plains.

Though, he told himself as he watched her open that trunk of hers again, it might be worth the effort.

For three days, when he hadn't been off at the mine looking for a little peace and quiet, he'd watched her delve into that steamer trunk and come up with more junk than he would have believed possible. Dishes and rugs and oil lamps and books—all right, he didn't mind the addition of a few new books to the pitifully small library he kept on one low shelf near the hearth. In fact, he was looking forward to reading her stories about the sea and the one by that fella Dickens.

But a few books didn't come near to making up for what she was doing to his life.

"Won't these look nice?"

Jackson came out of his thoughts like a hibernating bear waking up in springtime. He shook his head and lifted his gaze to hers. She held up a pair of white lace curtains and smiled at him.

"Look nice where?" he asked, his voice a low growl of disapproval.

"At the windows," she said, and bent over the edge of the trunk again. "Where else?" she asked, her voice muffled by the contents of what Jackson had come to think of as almost a magical trunk.

There seemed to be no bottom to the damn thing. No matter how much stuff she pulled out of it, there was always more. A part of him wouldn't have been surprised to see her drag a horse and buggy from the depths of the trunk he'd come to hate.

"I've enough for all the windows in here somewhere," she said, and his gaze locked on her behind, jutting up from the trunk.

She shifted and wriggled as she rummaged through the trunk's contents and Jackson swallowed hard. Her skirt hitched up until the backs of her calves were exposed and her behind swayed with her every movement.

Memory stirred inside him and he fought hard to keep it at bay. If he hadn't consummated the marriage, he might right now be a free man. But he had, and that one night with her had sealed his fate.

The fact that he hadn't slept with her since didn't change a damn thing. Hell of a marriage this was going to be, he thought, disgusted. Him walking around frustrated as hell and her sailing through the years, blissfully happy and hanging curtains.

Oh yeah. First chance he got, he was headed to town to take this up with Lucas. The man was going to pay for what he'd started here.

"There," she said, and came up out of the trunk holding her prize high. More curtains. Perfect.

Turning her head, she swung that long fall of red hair back over her shoulders and flashed him a smile that shook him to his toes.

"All they need is ironing and they'll be ready to hang."

"Don't have an iron," he said quickly, hoping to postpone the hanging of lace at his windows.

"I do," she told him, dashing that pitifully small hope.

"Naturally," he muttered, and snatched up the rifle's trigger housing and snapped it into place.

"What?"

He shook his head, then answered her question with one of his own. "Just how much junk do you have in that damn thing?"

"Junk is it?"

He noted the narrowing of her eyes, but he didn't care.

Hell, maybe a fight would take the edge off the hunger she aroused in him just by being here.

Waving one hand at the still overflowing trunk, he said, "I've never seen so much…*stuff*. What good is it?"

Pushing herself to her feet, Molly clutched the curtains in her fists and planted those fists on her hips in a position he'd already come to know as her battle stance. "It's made your *shack* into a home," she told him.

"It is—or it *was* a cabin. Not a shack." He looked around him, letting his gaze slide across a room that should have been familiar and wasn't. "Now I'm not sure *what* it is."

"So you don't like what I've done," she said.

"I liked it fine before."

"Oh aye, I'll bet you did," she countered, shaking one fist at him and sending the lace fabric waving in the air. "Living here like some great beast, tucked away in your dank hole."

"Dank?"

"Dank I said and dank I meant," she snapped. "There was so much grime on the windows, they might as well have not been there in the first place."

"I could see fine."

"For a blind man."

That did it. Jackson stood up and faced her down, not even knowing why he bothered. She'd already made it clear to him that his size didn't intimidate her in the least. But as it was all he had in the war to hold on to his sanity, he clung to it like a drowning man grabbing at a plank of wood.

"I was getting along pretty well on my own, you know."

"Is that right?"

"It is."

She sniffed at him, then turned and stalked across the room to a small cupboard that held his supplies. Flinging open the door, she waved one hand at the contents. "Beans," she said flatly. "Can after can of beans. *This* is how you were getting along before me. Eating your meals out of a tin, for pity's sake."

"There are other things there besides beans," he told her, though he silently admitted, not much more.

"A cupful of flour and a shake of sugar don't really mean much in the grand scheme of things, now do they?"

He scowled at her. There was more than that and he knew it as well as she did. But she and that tart tongue of hers were determined to make a point.

"Do I look like I'm starving to you?" he demanded.

Her gaze moved up and down his body slowly and damned if he didn't feel a quick, lightninglike bolt of pure desire in response. How the hell was a man supposed to keep his hands off his wife if just looking at her set him on fire?

"No," she admitted with a shake of her head, "you don't at that. Though you haven't seemed to mind my cooking."

True enough, the woman was an artist with a skillet. Over the past few days, she'd used his meager supplies and somehow come up with real *meals*. He hadn't eaten so well in years. But that hardly made up for the rest of it. He was a man used to time to himself. He was a man who *needed* to be alone. Hell, there'd been more noise in this cabin in the past three days then there had been in the past ten years.

"Trouble amidships!" Captain Blood screeched and added fuel to the fire.

Jackson snarled at the damn bird. "Stay out of this, Stew Pot!"

"You leave him alone, you great bully."

"Bully?" he repeated, astonished. "You're the one who marched into *my* house like Grant storming through Richmond. Hell, woman, you should have been in the army!"

"If I *had* been," she told him hotly, "there'd have been no bloody war, I can tell you that."

Like air rushing out of a child's balloon, anger rushed from him, leaving him empty inside. He stared at her for a long minute, before saying, "Then it's a damn shame you weren't in charge."

Molly's shoulders slumped as her temper slid from her. Staring at him, the old hurts glimmering in his eyes, she felt a twinge of regret for bringing up bad memories, no matter how unwittingly. But the war'd been over for ten long years. Wasn't it past time for him to put aside the old wounds and pick up the threads of his life again?

Three days she'd spent trying to reach the man she'd married and pledged her life to. But he was as much a stranger to her now as he'd been that first night.

Instantly memories raced through her mind as she watched him. She remembered it all. Every touch. Every caress. Every new sensation that he'd stirred into life inside her. And she wanted to feel it all again.

But the blasted man seemed determined to keep his distance. Every night, she lay alone in the bed while Jackson slept on the floor. She'd tried to argue with him about it. Pointed out that they were married and therefore *supposed* to share a bed. But he hadn't listened. The man had a head like a rock. Still, he couldn't hold out against her forever. Any man who could do such things to a woman's body wouldn't be able to remain celibate forever.

Especially, she thought now with a smile, if a woman made it impossible for him to do so.

"I'm goin' down to the creek," Jackson said, snatching her from her thoughts. "See if the water's gone down enough to be passable."

So he was going to just put their argument aside, she told herself. *Again.* In three short days, Molly had learned that whenever her husband was pushed beyond his temper, he tended to take off. Even the pouring rain that hadn't stopped until the night before hadn't prevented his treks to the mine or the woods or wherever else he went when he left the cabin. Of course, she was in no position to throw stones at his solution to an argument. After all, when her Irish was up, instead of walking her anger off, she worked it off, cleaning and cooking.

"And when we can cross the creek safely," she asked, "we'll be able to go to town for supplies?"

Grabbing up his hat off the peg near the door, he tugged it on, pulling the brim down low over his eyes. Glancing at her, he nodded. "Oh yeah. We'll be going to town all right. There's one or two things I have to talk to Lucas about."

Jackson stretched out on the floor in front of the fireplace, his head resting on a rolled-up blanket. Closing his eyes, he tried not to think about the woman in the other room, lying in his bed. Instead, he entertained himself with visions of punching his brother dead in the face. Which is just what he planned to do tomorrow when he took Molly to town.

And thinking her name only brought his mind right

back to where it'd started. With the image of her, lying alone in that bed.

Grumbling to himself, he threw one arm across his eyes and told himself to forget about her and try to sleep.

It didn't matter that they were married. Or even that they'd already slept together. He had to keep his distance, because he had a feeling that the minute he let Molly under his skin, she'd be able to worm her way into his heart.

And that he wouldn't risk.

So he'd best get used to the feel of hard, wood planks beneath him.

When the bedroom door opened with a creak of sound, he went perfectly still, keeping his eyes closed to feign sleep. What was she up to now? he wondered and lowered his arm to his side. He heard her soft footfalls as she crossed the room and his breath caught when she stopped alongside him. Her scent drifted to him and, though he knew it was no more than soap and vanilla, it twisted his insides and he knew he was in deep trouble.

Jackson felt her gaze on him as distinctly as he would have her touch and he wished to hell she'd go back where she belonged. But he couldn't say so, else she'd know he was awake and then no doubt start in on one of her long, rambling conversations that usually ended in an argument. And he was just too damned tired to go stalking off into the night.

Besides, if he looked at her in that threadbare white nightgown she wore, he might be tempted to slide it off her body and treat them both to a repeat performance of their wedding night. He concentrated on breathing deeply, evenly, and hoped to high heaven she'd go away.

Naturally, she didn't.

He stiffened slightly as she sank to her knees and then

stretched out alongside him on the floor. Gritting his teeth, Jackson tried to inch away from her, but she just followed him, aligning her body with his. She eased his arm back and slipped beneath it to lay her head on his chest. Draping her arm across his middle, she cuddled in close, nestled her head on his body as if he was a feather pillow and settled in to get some sleep.

His heartbeat thundered in his ears. Parts of him came gloriously alive as she snuggled in. Then she sighed, letting him know that at least *one* of them was comfortable. Damn it, why hadn't she stayed in bed? And what kind of woman was it who gave up a perfectly good bed to sleep on the floor beside a man who was doing everything he could to avoid her?

Her breath dusted warm and soft across his chest. Her hair smelled clean and sweet, as if she'd added vanilla to the soap she washed with. Her breasts pressed against his side and, even through the thin fabric of her nightgown, he felt the heat of her flesh as he would a branding iron.

Oh, he was never going to get any sleep like this. Inhaling sharply, he told himself he'd just have to wait until she fell asleep. Then he'd move again. To the other side of the room. As far away from his wife as he could manage.

The dying fire sent soft shadows around the room and hissed and chuckled at him as he lay there, wide-awake, trying to keep his mind off the lush, warm body tucked against him.

Defiance, Colorado, steamed in the morning sun. Patches of mud attracted children and dogs like moths to a flame. The merchants lined the boardwalk rolling up and down the length of Main Street, sweeping the dried-up mud from in front of their stores. From the far end of the street came the clang of the blacksmith's hammer on his anvil and loaded wagons rumbled along the rutted street, creaking and groaning like old men getting out of a warm bath.

Molly sat alongside her husband on the bench seat of the wagon she'd rented what seemed forever ago. She smoothed the skirt of her faded green dress, then folded her hands in her lap. She smiled and nodded to the people they passed and kept her gaze moving over the town that was now her home. After all, this was her first *real* trip into Defiance. The day she'd been married, she'd rushed from the stage to the saloon, where she'd spent the night with her new family.

They passed the bank, a restaurant, a dressmaker's shop and a gunsmith before she quit reading the signs in front of the buildings and concentrated instead on the people. They seemed to be as interested in her as she was in them.

"Do I look all right?" she asked from the corner of her mouth.

"What?" Jackson said, then, "Yeah. Fine."

"Then what are they starin' at?" she asked, smiling at a woman who stood as if lightning struck, her mouth open, eyes wide as she watched them pass.

"Who's staring?"

"All of them," she told him, and tried to sit up even straighter. She wanted to make a good impression on his friends.

He shifted uncomfortably on the seat, flicked the reins against the horse's back and muttered, "Nothing better to do, I guess."

Molly thought about that for a moment or two, then decided he was probably right. In a small town, a stranger would create a stir. But she wouldn't be a stranger for long, she told herself and deliberately lifted one hand to wave at a man shaking his head as if coming up from under water.

Jackson pulled the horse to a stop directly outside his brother's saloon, climbed down and tossed the reins across the hitching post. Then he looked up at her and said, "Well, come on then. You wanted to do some shopping, right?"

"I do," she said, and stood up, holding her arms out to him. She watched his jaw clench, but he put his hands at her waist and effortlessly swung her down from the wagon and set her on her feet with a thud that shook her teeth. "Are you comin' with me?"

Jackson tugged the brim of his hat down low onto his forehead and slanted a glance at the saloon behind him. "No. I've got to see Lucas about something."

"Right then," she said, and something in her expression told him she was disappointed, which left him feeling vaguely uneasy. Rubbing his jaw, he was reminded once again that his beard was gone and, instantly, he stiffened. Here he was, parading through town with nothing to hide his scars, thanks to her. He supposed she'd be fine going to the store on her own.

His gaze drifted over her quickly, from her shining red curls to the slightly frayed hem of that shapeless green dress she wore. Frowning to himself, Jackson realized that all of her clothes looked to be a little worse for wear.

"What is it?" she asked, staring at him as if he'd lost his mind.

"Nothing," he said, shaking his head. "It's just... when you go to the mercantile, why don't you pick yourself up some new dresses?"

She stiffened and he spotted the flush of pride staining her cheeks. For the love of God, this was a touchy woman.

"So you're sayin' you're ashamed of me."

Unbelievable. "I didn't say that."

"You might as well have."

"All I said was you could buy a few new dresses." He threw his hands wide and let them fall to his sides again in exasperation. "Hell, most women'd jump up and kiss a man for sayin' that."

"So you're *not* ashamed of me," she said, cocking her head and looking up at him.

"Didn't I just say so?" This was turning out to be a chore and a half. Just see how long it'd be before he tried to say something nice again.

"But you want me to buy new clothes."

"Yes, ma'am," he said, "I surely do."

"Well then." She jumped up and kissed him flat on the mouth and, before he could think better of it, his body answered for him. His arms snaked around her, holding her close, pressing her to him while his mouth meshed with hers, taking, giving, searing them both to the bone with the heat that erupted between them.

And then she broke the kiss, pulling her head back to grin at him. "Now," she said, "that wasn't so hard, was it?"

"Molly…" He dropped her to her feet and took a step back for good measure. He felt as though that fever was back, boiling his blood, making his heart pound and his skin flush.

"I'm your *wife*, Jackson," she said, "and you'd best get used to that." She lifted one hand and poked him dead center in the chest with her index finger. Pausing, she glanced over her shoulder to make sure no one could overhear them before adding, "And I'll be your wife still, tonight. At bedtime."

That word made him tired just thinking about it. He'd spent half of last night moving all over the cabin trying to get away from her only to wake up and find she'd followed after him. Stubborn, hardheaded, viper-tongued, forest-eyed, creamy-skinned female.

"I'll be at the store when you've finished your business with your brother," she told him with a smile, then hitched up the hem of her skirt and stepped off the boardwalk onto the still muddy street. Hopping from dry patch to dry patch, she made her way in between rolling wagons and riders on horseback. He watched her until the door to the mercantile had swung shut behind her.

At turns, that female stirred him, infuriated him and frustrated him. But whatever else happened between him and Molly, there was one thing he had to do right now.

Spinning around, Jackson turned, folded his right hand into a fist and went in search of his brother.

Chapter Six

It was too early in the day for customers in the saloon, so Jackson wasn't the least bit surprised to find the place damn near empty. He looked around the room slowly though, just in case Lucas had caught wind of his visit and was hiding somewhere.

The sound of footsteps coming down the stairs leading to the second story caught his attention and he moved forward. His fist tightened, then relaxed suddenly as Emily hurried around the doorway and came to a stop. Her always perfect hair was stringing down on either side of her flushed face and, even from a distance, Jackson spotted the smear of yellow paint on her right cheek.

But his sister-in-law looked happy.

"Jackson," she said, pleased surprise in her voice, "I'm so glad to see you." Crossing the floor in several hurried strides that sent the skirt of her dress snapping like a whip, she wiped her hands on a paint-stained apron before reaching for him. She gave him a brief hug that touched him with a breath of family and stepped back. "Why, you've shaved off your beard."

Grinding his back teeth together, Jackson rubbed his

jaw uncomfortably. He'd almost forgotten about his naked face.

"You know," she said with a half smile, "without all of that hair, you're a very handsome man."

Well, he'd thought Emily was a nice woman. Nice enough to tell a lie to ease a man's discomfort.

Then she looked past him and asked, "Is Molly with you?"

"Yes, ma'am, she is," he said, nodding and reaching up to pull his hat off. "She's over at the mercantile, picking up some supplies and such."

"Oh good," she said, and lifted one hand to try to fix her hair. "I was so worried when she insisted on going up the mountain in the rain. But she wouldn't hear of us taking her and refused to wait for the rain to stop."

"That sounds like Molly," he said on a sigh.

"But Lucas told me not to worry," Emily was saying.

"Did he now?" Jackson wondered aloud and kept his gaze shifting over the empty room as if half expecting his brother to pop up out of nowhere.

"Oh yes," Emily said. She reached behind her back to untie her apron and gave the ribbons a few tugs while she talked. "We actually went up the mountain after her but found no sign that she'd had trouble. So he told me that since she was with you, she'd be safe."

A hell of a lot safer than Lucas was going to be when Jackson found him.

"For heaven's sake," she muttered, and tried to look over her own shoulder at her apron strings. "I can't seem to…" She flicked him a glance. "Would you mind? I'd like to go to the store to see Molly, but I'm covered in paint and—"

"Sure thing." As she turned around, Jackson bent to the task of untying damp, paint-stained strings. "If you don't mind my askin'," he said, pulling the knots free, "what's all the paint for?"

Emily turned around, shrugged out of the apron, balled the fabric up in her hands and tossed it onto a table. Giving him a smile bright enough to light up the gloom of the darkened saloon, she said, "I'm fixing up the rooms upstairs for my hotel."

"Hotel?" he repeated, giving the dark, smoke-stained room another look. "Here?"

Women. Molly was running amok at his place and Emily was turning a perfectly good saloon into a hotel. But thankfully, this wasn't his problem. He had enough to deal with at the cabin. Jackson only hoped that Emily was giving his little brother the kind of fits Molly was giving him.

And on that pleasing notion, he heard himself ask, "I'm lookin' for Lucas, Emily. Do you know where he is?"

She paused, tapped her index finger against her chin, unknowingly depositing a drop of yellow paint there, as well, and said, "You know, he was right here a few minutes ago."

Jackson practically growled. The bastard had probably seen him riding into town and decided to run for cover. "Do you know where he went?"

"No, but he did say something earlier about getting his horse shod." She shrugged. "You might try the blacksmith."

"I'll do that," Jackson assured her, plopping his hat back onto his head and turning for the door. He held it open for the blonde already sailing past him toward the mercantile.

While the women shopped, Jackson stalked off down the boardwalk, looking for his brother.

* * *

The short, round woman behind the counter had graying blond hair, soft blue eyes and a nose that practically wiggled in her eagerness to sniff out new gossip. But she stuck out her right hand toward Molly and said, ''Welcome to Defiance. I'm Martha Sutton. Me and my husband own this place.''

''Molly MacIntyre,'' she said, and took the offered hand in a brief, firm shake.

''Good to meet you,'' the other woman said, smoothing her hands down the front of her crisply starched apron. ''I was thinking you'd be by sooner or later.''

''Really?''

''Oh yes, that husband of yours never stocks up on more than flour and beans.''

Molly smiled to herself. ''We do need just about everything,'' she said, her gaze sweeping across the store as Martha reached for a pad of paper and the pencil tucked behind her right ear.

Shelf upon shelf was stacked high with every kind of merchandise anyone could possibly want. One whole wall was covered in leather goods, everything from holsters to saddles, to bridles and reins. Piles of Levi's towered alongside what looked like a mountain of shirts. Shining glass jars lined the gleaming wooden countertop, proudly displaying a wide assortment of penny candy. There were barrels marked Pickles, Crackers, Flour, Sugar and Coffee.

And back along the far wall were dresses and bolts of fabric and every kind of sewing notion. A purely female curl of desire pulled at her, but she fought it. She had business to take care of first.

''Not surprised at all,'' Martha was saying as she poised her pen over the paper and waited.

"There's flour and sugar and coffee, of course," Molly said, wandering around the room. "And bacon, if you've got it and—oh!" She whirled around and asked, "Dried fruit? Do you have it?"

"Sure thing, honey," she said. Martha paused before adding, "You know, you don't seem the type to marry a man like Jackson MacIntyre, if you'll forgive me."

"The type?" Molly asked. She felt a quick flicker of anger sputter into life in the pit of her stomach. She didn't want to make an enemy her first day in town, but she wouldn't stand by and let someone insult her husband, either. "Just what do you mean by that?" she asked quietly.

Martha must have heard the ring of steel in her tone, because she straightened up and held out both hands in mock surrender. "Now, now, don't take offense. It's just that you seem a pretty little thing and he's..."

"Yes?" Molly prodded, and lifted one eyebrow, waiting.

The other woman smiled briefly and said, "No reason to load your guns and come hunting. All I'm saying is the man's a hermit."

"A hermit?"

"Folks say it's because he killed a man once and doesn't trust himself around people," Martha went blithely on, bending her head to her task again. "But I don't believe that one little bit."

"You don't," Molly said, and added silently, *You only repeat the rumors.*

"Oh my no," the other woman continued. "I figure what a man does is his own business." She sighed, added up a column of figures and said, "Hardly see him more than once a week. And when he does come to town, he goes straight to Miss Cherry's and—" Her voice faded off and a bright pink flush swept up her neck and blossomed on her round cheeks as her guilt-riddled gaze locked on Molly.

Miss Cherry. The embarrassed blush on Martha's face explained exactly who a woman named *Cherry* was and what kind of business she ran. She curled her fingers into her palms until her nails dug small half-moons into her skin. Her throat felt tight as she recalled following her husband around the room all night, trying to *force* him to sleep beside her. She'd thought he was being stubborn and proud and—but he wasn't being any of those things. He was simply waiting for an opportunity to come to town so he could visit a more experienced…and no doubt *prettier* woman.

At that thought, the tiny burst of anger within her sputtered into a boiling brew that turned her stomach. Only the anger wasn't for the talkative woman in front of her who'd unknowingly spilled the beans. It was all for the man she'd married.

Was he there now? she wondered. Had he dropped her off to buy food and new dresses and then run right off to the floozies? Were they laughing together about his silly wife who slept on the floor and chased him around the cabin? Was he telling his lady friend that his new wife was a sorry little thing in shabby clothes? Was he holding this faceless woman? Kissing her? Touching her, as he refused to touch his wife?

Fury hummed through her body, drowning shame and embarrassment in a rising flood of anger so rich, so pure, she shook with it. Those questions deserved answers, she told herself firmly and, the moment she'd filled her order, that's just what she'd get. And God help him, Molly told herself, if she found him where a married man had no right to be.

Martha looked as though she wanted to bite off her

tongue. But it was better, Molly thought, to know the truth.

"Molly, honey," the woman began, "I'm sure that—"

Whatever she might have said was lost as the front door swung open, sending the bell hanging above it into a jangling dance.

Emily MacIntyre strode in and paused on the threshold, letting her eyes become adjusted to the dimmer light within the store. And Molly looked at her sister-in-law as she would have the cavalry riding to the rescue.

Horace Baker slammed his hammer down onto the anvil and the red-hot horseshoe atop it. Sparks flew into the air, twinkling in the air briefly before dying. Again and again, the hammer rang out in a steady rhythm, like some ironclad heartbeat. When he finished his task, he used a pair of tongs to drop the finished shoe into a bath of water. The red-hot metal hissed and steamed, sending a cloud of vapor rushing into the air.

Jackson marched into the forge, tore off his hat and wiped his forehead with his sleeve. Damn, it was always hotter in here. He didn't know how Horace stood it, this close to the roaring fire that looked and sounded like the doorway to hell.

"Morning, Jackson," the blacksmith said, picking up another horseshoe and tossing it onto a glowing coal bed. He pumped the bellows with one hand while stoking the coals with a poker.

"Horace," he said with a nod. "You seen Lucas?"

"Sure did." The man's broad face split into a grin. "Stopped by here a few minutes ago. Wanted his horse shod." His brow furrowed as he stared for a long minute. "I don't believe I ever saw you without that beard."

Inhaling sharply, Jackson blew the air out in a disgusted rush. He wanted to clap a hand to his face, to hide the scar that was now out in the open for God and everybody to look at. But he'd need both hands to beat the hell out of Lucas, so that wouldn't work.

"Nasty scar," Horace commented.

Everything inside him tightened, preparing for the questions that were bound to follow. But Horace surprised him.

"Got a few myself," the man said simply before turning his attention back to the fire.

Relief pulsed through him. The man hadn't stared for long. Hadn't been repulsed by the jagged wound that sliced along Jackson's cheek. But how many people would react as this man had? Not many, he'd wager. Most would be curious. Most would gawk and whisper. And he'd just have to put up with it until he'd had time to grow his beard back. But for now...

"Where is Lucas?" Jackson asked, his gaze darting around the enclosure and the stable beyond.

"Left," he said, and lifted the shoe out of the fire, draping it across the narrow end of the anvil.

"Left for where?"

"Wouldn't know." Wide shoulders shrugged.

"Perfect," Jackson muttered. He half turned to shoot a glare down the middle of Main Street like a bullet.

"Your wife make it to the cabin all right?" Horace asked.

"Hmm? Yeah." Turning back to face the man, Jackson said, "I brought your wagon down, but I'm gonna need to rent it again to take all the supplies she's buying back to the cabin."

"Probably be cheaper just to buy it," Horace said thoughtfully.

Maybe so, Jackson thought. But if he went and bought the damn wagon, then it'd be permanent. It'd be admitting that Molly was staying. And though he knew he wouldn't be the one to walk away from a legal marriage...from his responsibilities...he still had a fond hope that Molly might up and quit.

So he'd rent the blasted wagon by the week if he had to and cling to the illusion that soon he'd be alone again.

"No thanks," he said, and dug into his pocket for the rent money. Then he stalked off, still hunting Lucas.

In the next half hour, he covered the whole damn town. The barber, the gunsmith, the restaurant, *everywhere*. And everywhere he went, he was just a minute or two behind Lucas. He had to give his younger brother credit. Defiance was so small, he wouldn't have thought it possible for anyone to hide for long. But Lucas was managing it just fine.

And Jackson's temper bubbled furiously, building each time he was told he'd "just missed" his brother. Folks were beginning to get caught up in the search. He spotted one or two people taking up positions in easy chairs where they could watch him stride up and down the street. Merchants came out of their stores and leaned against the porch posts. Shoppers gathered in tight knots, debating on just what would happen once Jackson caught up to Lucas. And others simply stared at him, as he'd known they would. Their gazes locked on his cheek, he could almost hear their thoughts. *What in the hell happened to him? Isn't that awful? Must have been mighty deep. Think he got it in the war?*

The spot between his shoulder blades itched and he twitched uncomfortably beneath the stares directed at him. This was Lucas's fault, too, he told himself. He was here, in town, making a spectacle of himself because his younger brother had gone out and hunted him down a wife. A wife who'd shaved him clean in his sleep. A wife who drove him to distraction with her constant talking and humming. A wife who filled his dreams and tortured his waking moments. A wife he wanted to touch, caress, kiss. A *wife,* for God's sake!

On his second pass through town, the door to the Western Union office swung open and Lucas stepped out.

Jackson stopped dead, fists clenched at his side, mind racing. He almost *heard* the onlookers' quick intake of breath. Expectation rattled the air. Anticipation simmered through the gathered crowd. There was nothing people liked better than a good fight. Everyone in Defiance was watching as Lucas strolled across the boardwalk and stepped off into the dirt.

"Morning, Jackson," he said warily. "I heard you were looking for me."

"Lucas," Jackson said through gritted teeth. He'd been waiting for this. Planning this since the moment Molly had told him Lucas was behind her being at the cabin. He'd itched to smash his brother's pretty face in. But now, facing the man who was his only family, the man he trusted above everyone else, he was torn. This was his *brother*. Blood of his blood. They shared ties that no one else could even touch.

"How's Molly?" Lucas asked.

And Jackson plowed his right fist into his younger brother's face.

The roar of the crowd drew them from the store. Martha darted out from behind the counter, raced to the door, flung it open and disappeared down the boardwalk. Molly and Emily were only a step or two behind her.

People were gathered in a loose circle in the middle of the street. Dust and mud flew into the air and Molly caught a quick, brief glimpse of two bodies rolling around on the ground at the feet of the crowd.

"What in heaven?" Emily muttered.

"It's a fight," Molly said, and grabbed up the hem of her new dress before jumping off the boardwalk and racing toward the battle.

"Molly, wait!" Emily cried.

But she didn't stop. Something pulled her onward. She'd seen plenty of fights on the docks near where she'd grown up and had long ago ceased to be amazed at how people would throng together to watch two men beat each other to a pulp. Ordinarily Molly wouldn't have bothered. She would have shown her disapproval by staying clear of the whole mess.

But somehow, this was different. She tossed her hair back behind her shoulders and hitched the hem of her deep blue skirt even higher to avoid the patches of mud. Her feet slipped and skidded for purchase as she pushed her way through the crowd. She heard Emily right behind her, but she didn't slow down. Didn't wait.

"Watch his right," someone shouted.

"Hey, no hittin' below the belt!" another man called, clearly offended.

"Git 'im, Lucas!"

"Lucas?" Emily echoed from behind her.

She'd known it, Molly thought. Somehow she'd known it was her husband and his brother rolling around on the ground like a couple of dockside brawlers. And these people, she told herself, with a wicked glare at the excited faces of the crowd around her, were egging them on.

Relief and disgust warred within her, each of them

vying to be recognized. On the one hand, her husband wasn't with some nameless floozy. But on the other, he was beating his own brother with his fists. A flash of anger shot through her, sending Molly into the fray. Gone was the notion of stunning her husband with how beautiful she looked in her new dress. Of making him forget that trollop of his by seducing him with her own beauty. Now all she could think about was stopping this fight.

She launched through the edges of the crowd into the middle of the fight like an arrow from a bow. Lucas sat astride Jackson's chest and as she watched, drew his fist back to deliver a blow. Outraged, she gasped, grabbed that fist and held on.

Lucas never looked back at her, just shook her off, like a minor annoyance, flinging her into the mud where she landed on her backside, legs sprawled. The crowd laughed and cheered in appreciation, but she heard Emily's shocked voice through the babble of sound, shouting, "Lucas, stop that this instant!"

Thick, black mud oozed into the fabric of her new dress, soaking through to her skin. Molly shivered before pushing herself to her feet and staggering over to the two men still fighting fiercely. Every blow landed with a solid smack and, though a part of her wanted to deliver a few sharp blows herself, Molly resisted temptation. By this time, Emily too had joined the fray and her pale face was dotted with splotches of mud that contrasted nicely with the yellow paint streaks.

The two women stared at each other for a long moment, then together, took deep breaths and shouted their husband's name.

"Lucas!"

"Jackson!"

Instantly both men froze. Quiet dropped over the crowd like a thick, uncomfortable blanket. The mud-covered men slowly turned to face their wives as the bystanders, sensing *real* trouble about to start, began drifting away.

Chapter Seven

The fight was over and a *new* fight was just beginning.

"So let me understand this," Molly said, pacing back and forth in front of her husband and his brother. The sodden, mud-soaked skirt of her new dress clung to her legs, making her kick the fabric out of her way as she walked. "You," she said, stabbing her index finger at Lucas, who drew his head back as if that finger was loaded, "advertised for a bride in Jackson's name, *knowing* he didn't want one."

Lucas shifted uncomfortably, shot a look at his wife, found no sympathy in that quarter, then turned back to Molly. "Yes, but—"

She cut him off. He'd already had his say when he'd explained how he'd come to advertise for a mail-order bride without bothering to let Jackson in on his plan. "You lied to me, tricked your brother—your *family*—never caring one way or the other how this might affect us."

Oh, he didn't like that and his stormy expression proved it. One of his eyes was swollen—like Jackson's—but he narrowed the other at her. "Of course I cared," he said in his own defense, "but—"

"Oh aye, I know," she interrupted him again with a wave of her hand, dismissing his argument. "You had reasons." And *such* reasons, she thought, mind racing between sheer fury and righteous indignation. She'd been a pawn. A joke. She'd left her life behind, left all that was familiar and traveled halfway across the country to be married to a man who had never wanted her. Which, she admitted, she already knew. Hadn't Jackson himself told her he didn't want a wife?

"You bartered my life so you could gain ownership of a mine and a *saloon,* for pity's sake!" Humiliation stung, but she fought to hide it.

"They're all we have," Lucas said, offering what she thought was a pitiful defense. "Well, and the ranch."

"You had no right," she snapped.

"But he did it and it's done," Jackson told her.

She looked at him, trying to read the one eye that wasn't swollen shut. "Aye, it's done and look at how well it's all turned out," she said, facing the man who was her husband, but not.

He winced at her words, but she didn't stop. "You and your brother beating each other to dust in the street."

"Oh," Lucas said, "that happens all the time."

"And that makes it all right, does it? Just like it's all right for you to toy with other people's lives?"

"It wasn't all his fault," Jackson said, standing up for the brother he'd been pounding his fist into only moments before.

"Really?" she asked, hands at her hips, "So you told him to send for a wife, then, eh?"

"No, but—"

"No, you didn't."

"No, he didn't," Lucas interrupted. "But he didn't turn you away once you were here, did he?"

Molly swung her head to look at him. She'd liked him when she first met him, and one day she might like him again. Not, however, today. "Jackson," she said slowly, "is a gentleman."

Lucas snorted and her eyes narrowed.

Jackson stepped between them, laying one huge hand on her shoulder. And that warm, steady hand was like oil poured on churning water. It soothed, calmed, even as the heat of his touch sank deeply into her bones.

Molly took a breath, glanced at Emily and felt a momentary sense of comfort swish through her. Here was someone who understood what she was feeling, thinking. And though Emily had married Lucas for the same reason—at least she'd *known* she was entering into a business contract. She hadn't lain awake at night dreaming of love. Of finding the one man who would want her, need her. Someone to whom she could be the most important thing in the world.

Her stomach trembled and tears burned the backs of her eyes. But she wouldn't cry, by heaven. She would not give them the satisfaction.

Them. The MacIntyre brothers. Her gaze slipped from one muddy man to the other, both of them watching her through wary, blackened eyes. They looked worried, as well they should, she thought. She'd half a mind to "whale" into them, as her uncle used to say. But there'd been enough brawling this day already.

Moments of silence drifted into minutes and the tension was strung tautly across the saloon. There was more she wanted to say. But she was suddenly so tired she felt as though she were standing ankle deep in the ocean with the tide rushing out, dragging her in, pulling her down.

Jackson cleared his throat and it sounded like a gunshot. Her gaze shifted to him as he tightened his grip on her shoulder.

"What Lucas did is between him and me," he said. "And that's been settled."

"You're wrong," she said flatly, and watched him wince. Couldn't he see what this had done to her? Didn't he know that to her, marriage was forever? And what kind of life could they have in a marriage that was based on a lie?

"None of this matters, Molly. It's done," he snapped. "Over and done."

"Is it?" she asked, watching him.

"You're my wife," he answered in a low rumble of sound, his voice scraping along her spine, sending shivers throughout her body. "I'm your husband. It's finished."

"*I* think…" Lucas began, and they both turned steely-eyed glares on him. Shaking his head, he closed his mouth and folded his arms across his chest.

"It doesn't matter anymore how this got started, Molly," Jackson said quietly.

"It'll work out, you'll see," Lucas said, standing up but keeping a safe distance between himself and his sister-in-law.

She practically snarled at him.

"Molly," Emily offered, giving her husband a look that should have withered him on the spot, "why don't you come upstairs with me and get cleaned up? We can wash your dress and you can borrow one of mine for the ride home."

Molly glanced down at what had been a lovely blue dress with a white collar and cuffs. Rubbing one hand across the front of it, she watched as dried mud flaked off to land on the floor at her feet. Sighing, she told herself this dress was just like her life. Shining new but splattered with mud.

"New dress?" Jackson asked.

"It was," she admitted, lifting her head to meet his gaze. She stared into her husband's one good eye and tried to read what he was thinking. Feeling.

He hadn't wanted her here, that was plain. But he'd accepted their marriage and maybe for now that was enough. A ripple of determination coursed through her and Molly told herself that her life would be a mess only if she allowed it. After all, just because her marriage had started out badly wasn't to say it would continue badly.

Love grew out of arranged marriages all the time. Two strangers coming together and somehow becoming *one*. Jackson's features tightened as the silence lengthened and she continued to look at him. But she wasn't seeing him as he was now, covered in mud, one eye swollen shut and a split lip. Instead, she was remembering that first night at the cabin. When he'd turned to her, touched her, made love to her. There had been *magic* between them, however briefly it had lasted.

There in the darkness, they'd each found something in the other. The fact that the very next day Jackson had tried to deny it didn't change a thing. His denials, his promise not to love her, these were things that could change. What would *not* change was what happened when they touched. And wasn't that a good place to start? To build the future she wanted so badly?

He was right about one thing, anyway. The deed was done. There was no changing the past. There was only tomorrow to deal with and all of the tomorrows to come.

Molly pulled in a deep breath and silently accepted the challenge in front of her. She would make her husband love her. She would have the family she'd always wanted. And they would be happy, blast it.

Tearing her gaze from Jackson's, she glanced to where Emily stood, waiting. "Thank you for the offer, but I think we'll just be going home."

When she turned back to look at him, Jackson felt a rush of pride. Damned if she wasn't something. A temper like a fire-and-brimstone preacher with hands as soft as heaven, he remembered. He'd almost enjoyed watching her rip into Lucas, a man too used to women falling at his feet.

Wounded pride glittered in her eyes along with a sheen of tears, but she stood there like some mud-covered queen, facing them all down. God help him, he wanted to snatch her up and squeeze her so hard she wouldn't be able to breathe. And that silent admission scared hell out of him. So instead of doing what his heart demanded, Jackson said tightly, "She's right. We're goin' home."

But when he took Molly's arm, she pulled free of his grasp. His hand fisted on emptiness as he watched her march out the door, hips swaying, heels clicking on the shining wood floor. He followed after her, cheered just a bit to hear Emily start chewing on Lucas's hide even before the bat-wing doors swung shut behind him.

Outside, as he helped his wife into the wagon, Jackson's hands lingered a bit longer than necessary on her waist. She lifted the hem of her muddy skirt and he caught himself noticing the curve of her leg and her milk-white skin. Something stirred inside him and he gritted his teeth against it. How long could a man stand it? he wondered. How long could a man remain celibate while faced with a woman like Molly day in and day out?

"Guess I'll find out," he muttered under his breath.

"What was that?" she asked.

He glanced up, squinting into the sun, met her gaze briefly, then looked away as he pulled himself up onto the bench seat beside her. "Nothin'," he said, grabbing up the reins.

She squirmed a bit to get comfortable on the unpadded seat and he wished to hell she'd sit still. Didn't do him the slightest bit of good to have her rubbing her thigh against his that way. He scowled to himself and pain shot through his split lip. Lifting one finger to it, he then drew it away, sneering at the drop of blood.

A lucky punch, he thought, and took comfort in the fact that Lucas looked a sight worse than he did. It had been quite a while since he and his brother had had a knock-down-drag-out, root-hog-or-die fistfight. And damned if it hadn't felt good to release all the fury that had been riding him for days. And *real* good to plant his fist into his interfering brother's face.

He flexed his hands, each in turn, to keep his fingers from stiffening up. The fight hadn't changed anything. Hadn't fixed anything. But that was how it had always been between him and Lucas. Things built to a head, they had a fight, and it was over, each of them retreating to cool off.

Except this time, he wasn't storming off alone. Now he had a wife. A wife he couldn't afford to care about.

Jackson slanted a sidelong glance at the woman sitting beside him. Even covered in mud, she looked too damned good. She had that stubborn chin of hers tilted at a defiant angle and her green eyes were fixed on a point straight ahead. One corner of his mouth lifted into a reluctant quirk of a smile. Bound and determined to ignore him, he thought, and couldn't really find it in him to blame her.

He'd been acting as if it was only *his* life that had been turned upside down, while she hadn't exactly won a prize by getting stuck with him as a husband.

Jackson grumbled to himself as the familiar landscape rolled by. It just wasn't like Molly to be so blasted quiet. He was half tempted to push her into yelling at him. But he kept his own silence and concentrated instead on the images flashing through his mind. He saw her in the cabin, humming as she cleaned. He saw her with that bird of hers. And halfway up the mountain, he remembered how she'd jumped into the middle of the fight. A stir of admiration washed over him. By damn, he'd been so proud of her. She'd looked wild and furious and downright terrifying in a raw, passionate way. Like one of those ancient warrior women Uncle Simon had told them about in his stories. Jackson's heart twisted painfully as he realized there weren't many women who'd dare something like that. Most he'd known wouldn't have done more than stand by and look on disapprovingly. But not his Molly, he thought with an inward chuckle. No sir, she jumped in and grabbed hold of Lucas's fist just before it could connect with Jackson's nose.

The half smile on his face faded as he realized what he'd just been thinking. *His* Molly? Squirming on the bench seat, he guided the horse into the clearing in front of the cabin. She was his wife, yes, he told himself. But she wouldn't be his love. He wouldn't let her be.

It had been a hell of a day, he thought, glad it was close to over. His fingers tightened on the leather straps as he pulled back on the reins, then set the brake and tied it off. He glanced at Molly to find her staring at him.

And that's when his day got worse.

"Did you spend all morning brawling with your brother?" Molly asked. "Or were you able to find a little time for your floozy?"

"What?" he damn near shouted and split his lip a little further. Wincing, he gave her a look that had been known to send pretty tough men running for the hills. He should have known that it wouldn't affect Molly in the slightest.

She sniffed, cocked her head to one side and fidgeted with her skirt. Propping the soles of her feet against the kickboard, she looked up at him. "You heard me," she said. "I want to know if you've been visiting…your lady friend."

Jackson just stared at her. How in tarnation had she heard about Miss Cherry's place? Then the answer came to him. Of course. Martha Sutton. A one-woman telegraph station. Damn interfering females.

Hell, he shouldn't be put in the position of apologizing for visiting a cathouse. He was a man. Men had rights. Needs. And up until a few days ago, he'd been a single man with no claims on him at all. So why was he suddenly feeling so blasted guilty?

Staring down into the face of his *wife,* a trickle of shame drifted through his bloodstream and made him want to look away from her. But he didn't. He'd done nothing to be ashamed of, despite the unexpected discomfort he felt now. And he wouldn't be made to feel like a schoolboy caught with his hand in the cookie jar.

The leather reins woven through his fingers dug into his flesh as he squeezed tight. Jackson looked hard at her, noting the spray of dirt on the side of her face and the hurt suspicion in her eyes. Her skin looked a bit paler than usual, making that handful of freckles stand out in contrast. But it was her eyes that grabbed him, held him, and he met her accusing stare squarely.

Grinding the words out through clenched teeth, he said quietly, "No. I didn't visit anyone but Lucas."

Molly watched him for a long moment and he knew she was weighing his words, his expression, the truth in his eyes. He waited, not sure what she'd say next.

"Not today, but other times," she said, and it wasn't a question.

He blew out a breath, scrubbed his jaw with one hand and muttered thickly, "Damn it, Molly, this isn't the kind of thing a decent woman talks about."

"A decent woman can't talk about it, but a decent man can *do* it?" she countered, and he noted with some regret that the Irish in her voice had thickened. Meaning no doubt that her temper was once again on the rise.

"I can't speak for all men, Molly."

"I'm not askin' you to," she countered and laid one hand atop his. "I'm askin' my *husband* if he's avoiding my bed to visit someone else's."

Her touch skittered through him like a white-hot bolt of jagged lightning and, to keep from relishing it, he pulled away. "And if I answer you, will you believe me?"

She thought about it for a long moment, then nodded. "Yes. Your eyes don't lie, Jackson MacIntyre. You've been honest with me up from the start. Even telling me that you didn't want me here."

Regret poked at him, but he ignored it. He'd only told her the simple truth. He hadn't wanted her here. Hadn't wanted *any* woman in his life, beyond the temporary comfort he'd found in the arms of Dixie. But now that he had a wife, he wouldn't be seeing the prostitute again and he needed to make sure Molly understood that, in addition to the fact that it wasn't *her* in particular he didn't want. "I didn't want to hurt you, Molly," he said.

"I believe that, too," she said, her gaze never leaving his. "But you still haven't answered the question. Are you visiting the floozy?"

A soft wind sighed down off the mountain, lifting her hair into a riot of red-gold curls that danced about her head and Jackson could only think that she deserved better than him. A worn-out man with little heart left for life or anything else. The least she deserved from him was the truth.

"No, Molly," he said, willing her to see the truth in his eyes. "I haven't been back to Miss Cherry's since you got here. And now that we're married, I won't be going back. Ever." Which would, he figured, make him more frustrated and edgy than he'd been since he was fifteen.

She studied him thoughtfully and for the first time in his life, Jackson wished he could read minds. He wanted to know what she was thinking. Feeling. And the fact that he cared worried him more than he would admit, even to himself.

Finally she nodded and gave him a half smile. "That's all I needed to know. We'll put this aside now and not speak of it again."

Thank God, he thought, glad to be done with the subject. He climbed down off the wagon and reached up to help her down as well. She set her hands at his shoulders as he grasped her about the waist and swung her to the ground. And when she was standing on her own two feet, she didn't move away, not even when he released her and shoved his hands into his pockets to keep from reaching for her again.

Instead, looking up into his eyes, she warned, "But you should know one thing."

Wary, he asked, "What's that?"

"I'm not goin' away, Jackson. And you won't be able to ignore me forever." She leaned into him, her gaze boring straight into his. "I'll see to it."

Chapter Eight

~~~~~~~~~~~~

True to her word, Molly spent the next two weeks driving Jackson out of his mind. With surprisingly little effort. "Hell, just lookin' at her is enough to drive a man to distraction," he muttered, and his voice was swallowed by the deep forest.

The cabin seemed to be shrinking. Or at least, that's how it felt to Jackson. Every time he turned around, there she was. Between her and that bird, he hardly got a moment's peace. Molly talked and talked and talked, refusing to be ignored, not letting go of a thing until she got *him* talking. He told her things he'd never told a living soul.

Things like how he'd felt when his folks died. About how worried he'd been because he was the older brother and should have been able to take care of him and Lucas. But how relieved he'd been when Uncle Simon showed up and became their family. He told her about moving west and how he and Lucas had always stood together on everything. What it meant to him to have a brother to count on and to fight with. How lonely the mountain sometimes was. And it felt good to say it all out loud. To have someone—*her,*—listen and care.

He'd told her so much and, yet, still held back. There were some things he couldn't bring himself to talk about. Like the war and what it had cost him. Like the other life he'd lived before coming to this mountain to hide. Those things were buried too deep to bring out now. Digging them from his soul would start him bleeding all over again and he didn't think he could bear that.

So he kept quiet about those memories, despite a part of him knowing she had a right to hear about them. She had a right to know why he wouldn't…*couldn't* love her.

Stalking up to the cabin in twilight, Jackson took a tight grip on the rifle in his hand and stopped at the edge of the clearing. Shaded by the overhang of trees, he stared at the cabin and tried to remember how it used to look. But it was getting harder to recall the days before Molly came.

She'd attacked the place, a paintbrush her weapon of choice, and now he lived in a sunshine yellow cabin with what Molly called, "springtime green trim." A stray spear of dying sunlight fought its way through the trees and lay across the cabin like a blessing. If he'd been a more fanciful man, Jackson might have considered it a sign. Like someone, somewhere, was trying to tell him that in this house lay his redemption…if he had the guts to claim it.

He shrugged his shoulders as though unburdening himself of that uncomfortable notion and thought instead that he somehow didn't belong in that cabin anymore. Molly'd made it a home, not a refuge. And what did he know of homes?

Flowers she'd transplanted from all over the mountain blossomed along the front porch, looking far more at ease here than he felt. Smoke curled from the chimney, carrying the scent of beef stew to a hungry man who'd become too used to eating well lately. And through the front window, he saw her as she lit a lamp and that feeble flame of welcome drew him closer.

He pushed open the door and was greeted by a screeching order that was all too familiar.

"Put some wood in that hole!"

Jackson shot the parrot a glare that should have knocked it off its perch. Every damn day when he opened the door, the bird told him to close it. He shut the blasted door and he could have sworn the parrot smirked at him.

"Howdy, Jackson," a deep voice called, and he turned toward the table where Hardy Phillips and Black Mike Galloway were sitting.

Hardy, a short, barrel-chested man with a bald head and a full beard grinned around a mouthful of beef stew and said, "Your woman surely does set a fine table, Jackson."

"That she does," agreed Black Mike, a tall, thin man with pale skin pockmarked by coal dust, and he reached for another slice of fresh bread.

It wasn't the first time Jackson had come home to find folks pulled up to his table. Hell, he supposed by now his wife had fed most of the prospectors, drifters and cowhands that passed over the mountain. Whenever he said anything to her about it, she only smiled and said, "I'll see no one goes hungry."

He glanced at Molly now as she came to his side, smiling the wide smile that never ceased to hit him hard enough to steal his breath. Her hair was pulled back from her face and tied with a piece of rawhide at the nape of her neck. That bothered him for some reason. He felt as though he should be giving her the ribbons and whatnots that most women set such store by.

But at the same time, he had to wonder if she'd wear frills and furbelows. After all, he'd told her to buy some new clothes and, instead of going hog-wild with shopping, the darn woman had just bought three dresses and a new nightgown that tempted him every time she put it on.

His gaze locked on the red shower of curls that fell along her spine and his fingers itched to touch it, to catch the mass in his hand and feel the silky softness of it against his skin. Then he scowled as he watched Mike noticing her hair and how it dipped and swayed with her every step.

"Your friends stopped by a while ago," she said, and went up on her toes to kiss his cheek as she did every evening. And that simple touch of her lips sent a ribbon of appreciation tumbling through him. He'd become accustomed to it, had stopped trying to avoid her kiss. Had, if truth be told, come to look forward to that greeting when he stepped in from the darkness.

He saw the sharp gleam of envy in the other men's eyes at Molly's greeting and was jolted by a stab of pure pleasure. Mostly, his life hadn't been one that anyone with half a brain would envy. But now Molly had changed that, too.

She kept surrounding him with people, forcing him out of the silence and into life again. These men she called his "friends" were never more than passing acquaintances. But with Molly's warmth, they and others like them were drawn back to this cabin—much as he was, he realized with an inward sigh.

"Are you hungry?" she asked. When he nodded, she turned to the stove to dish up another bowl of stew.

He took his seat at the end of the table and halfheartedly listened to the conversation going on around him.

Their voices were nothing more than a buzz in his ears, a backdrop for the thoughts racing through his mind.

She'd done it again, he thought. Invited people into his world. Dragging him into the middle of it. Expecting him to take part. To appreciate friends and good food and the sound of laughter.

And damned if he wasn't responding. He hadn't meant to. Told himself repeatedly to pull back, keep his distance. But Molly was a force to be reckoned with and she didn't take no for an answer.

Just like at night, when she had continued to follow him all around the cabin, insisting on sleeping with him. Until he'd finally given up and joined her on the too-narrow bed. He'd thought that by giving in on that score he'd be able to get some sleep. But Molly wasn't satisfied with lying beside him. She continually moved into him, curling her body into his until it was all he could do to keep from grabbing her, kissing her, claiming her.

Still he resisted, and usually spent most of the night desperately clinging to the edge of the bed. But that couldn't go on forever. A man needed more than one or two hours sleep a night. He just didn't know how he'd manage it. But then, a man needed other things too, he thought, his gaze sliding toward Molly.

"So, how's the mine coming along then?" Mike asked, splintering Jackson's thoughts and drawing him into the conversation.

"Good," he answered, pleased to have his mind off Molly and onto safer ground. The mine he'd been working for three years was finally starting to pay off. Soon he and Lucas would be able to fund the horse ranch they'd always dreamed of. "Found what might be a vein," he said, unwilling to give them too much information. Greed could turn people mean. He'd seen it too often in the past to not be wary of it now. Besides, he didn't know Hardy or Mike very well. "Looks promising."

"A vein, is it?" Mike repeated with a grin and a wink for Molly. "You've landed yourself a rich husband then, ma'am."

Hardy said nothing, just looked thoughtfully at Jackson before lowering his gaze back to his plate.

"Really?" Molly asked, looking at Jackson. "When can I see the mine?"

He shifted on the seat, forked up a bite of stew and shoved it into his mouth. "Not much to see yet," he said. "Besides, with rockfalls and all, it's too dangerous for you to go into the mine."

"Dangerous?" She picked right up on that word and fired it back at him. "Are you safe in there?"

"Ah, don't you be worryin' about your husband on that score, ma'am," Mike said, laughing. "He's a head as hard as Saint Patrick's Mount. No bit of rock could dent it. Ain't that right, Hardy?"

The other man nodded his bald head, shot Jackson a quick look and said, "Right enough, I reckon."

And as the men laughed together over the foolishness of women, Molly sat quietly thinking.

The very next afternoon, Molly made her way through the forest, following the narrow path her husband took every day to his mine. It was time, she thought, that she found out where he spent his days. She ducked beneath a low-hanging branch and stopped to free her hair when it was snagged by a twig.

"Besides," she told the little dog walking beside her, "I want to let him know he won't be escaping me here, either."

The scrawny pup yapped as if in agreement and Molly chuckled, pausing to toss it another bite of the chicken she carried in the basket on her arm. Gobbling it down, it looked up at her expectantly and Molly shook her head.

"Oh no, you don't, now. Jackson must have *something* for his dinner." She sank down to one knee on the forest floor and held out her right hand toward the poor little thing. It had appeared out of nowhere and attached itself to her, staying close but out of kicking range, which told her someone, at some time, had terrified the poor dog. "You've been hurt and now you're afraid to try again, aren't you?" she asked softly. "But you *want* to try, don't you? You want to be loved, you've just been on your own too long, haven't you?" she asked as it sat down a safe distance from her and cocked its head, watching her. "Don't trust people, eh? Well then, you've something in common with my husband, haven't you?"

Sighing, she stood up and watched as it approached her cautiously, and she had to wonder what Jackson would have to say about her new dog. Judging by how he felt about Captain Blood, she was willing to wager he wouldn't be pleased with this latest addition to their household. But what else could she do other than adopt it? On its own in the woods, it wouldn't live long. And it was such a sweet little pup. Soft brown eyes looked up at her as the dog cocked its head, sending its one crooked ear straight up into a perfect triangle. Its short tail thumped against the earth briefly and Molly smiled.

"Don't you worry about Jackson," she told it. "He'll be too busy being angry at me to even notice you're there at first."

Walking again, she picked her way across the fallen twigs and layers of dead leaves and pine needles that littered the forest floor. Her gaze shifted to either side of the path, and she smiled as she watched the sunlight drift through the thicket of branches to lay dappled patches of gold along the ground. Far above her head, the wind sighed through the treetops and rustled the leaves, sending a few of them floating and twisting through the air.

"It's a lovely place," she murmured, letting her gaze drift across the shadows and light that surrounded her.

Different from what she was used to, of course. But lovely. Growing up in a seaside port, she was accustomed to the ever-present sound of the sea. Like a heartbeat, the waves continuously pounded against the shore and she'd thought she would miss that comforting roar. But here, she thought, was another sort of heartbeat. Quieter, yet no less alive. The wind sifted through the trees, the leaves brushed across one another in a gentle dance and somewhere deep among the trees, wild creatures moved in the shadows.

Here, there were no softly glowing streetlamps. No fog to creep in from the sea with a damp caress. No rattle of wagon wheels on cobblestones. She sighed and told herself that Defiance, Colorado, wasn't much by Eastern standards, but it had a raw, wild appeal that touched something inside her. She smiled to herself as she realized that she must have inherited some of her family's adventurous streak.

Generations of Malones had made their living on the sea. Setting sail in ships that were tossed by waves, run aground on rocks or becalmed on pondlike oceans for weeks at a time, they'd risked their lives for the chance to meet challenging experiences. Now she was finally one of them.

And she'd be keelhauled before she'd let a stubborn bear of a husband ruin the future she planned to claim for herself. It no longer mattered to her that she'd come here under false pretenses. The point was, she was here. And married to the most stubborn man she'd ever come across. Still, if a thing came too easy, who would appreciate it? "You've a wife now, Jackson MacIntyre," she said, liking the sound of the words, "and blast if I won't show you how lucky you are to have me."

The dog yipped and Molly laughed aloud, then quieted again as she rounded a bend in the path and saw the mine. It wasn't much from the outside. Just a raw opening in the side of the mountain. But the path led directly to it and from somewhere inside came the distinct sound of a pickax slamming into solid rock. Jackson. In his cave.

A sudden whirl of nervousness spun in the pit of her stomach. This was different than seeing him at the cabin. This was bearding the lion in his den. Her fingers tightened on the handle of the basket until her knuckles whitened. The puppy whined.

"You're my wife, I'll treat you as such."

He'd said those very words, she recalled, and told herself she had every right to see to it that he started making good on his promise. She was a wife in name only and she meant to change that. *Soon*. Despite the butterflies in her stomach.

"Well," she said to the puppy still watching her, "as Uncle Michael used to say, 'Let's get to the rat killin'.'"

And lifting her chin, she forced a confident smile she didn't quite feel and stepped into the mouth of the mine.

Blinded at first by the deep shadows, she narrowed her gaze and looked around slowly. Dampness stained the rock walls that jutted out in sharp angles, as if the mountain itself was alive, trying to snatch at the unwary. Flickering lamplight caught her eye and Molly moved forward, deeper into darkness. She walked slowly, carefully, moving quietly across the dirt, following the rhythmic smack of the ax into rock.

In the wide opening beyond the entrance, Jackson stood with his back to her. Feet braced wide apart, he swung the pick with almost graceful ease. Sweat streamed down his naked back and Molly watched as his muscles rippled and stretched with every swing of the ax. Her mouth went dry as she watched her husband unnoticed. Broad shoulders, narrow waist and hips, long legs encased in worn Levi's that stacked atop the toes of his scuffed boots.

Chunks of rock fell at his feet and the dog beside her barked furiously. Jackson spun around and dropped into a crouch, ready to attack. When his gaze locked on her though, she saw his eyes light first with pleasure then irritation.

Molly decided to cling to the pleasure and forget the rest. "Hello, husband. I thought it was time I saw the mine."

"Damn it, Molly," he growled, forcing his heart down out of his throat and back into his chest where it belonged. "You shouldn't sneak up on a man."

"I didn't sneak, I walked."

"Well, walk louder." Though if his mind hadn't been filled with thoughts of making love to her, he might have heard her approach. As it was, seeing her in person on the heels of his wild imaginings had his body hard and ready and his heartbeat thundering in his ears.

"Feelin' cranky, are we?" she asked, and sashayed toward him.

Sashay was the only word he could think of to describe the slow sway of her hips and the deliberate tilt of her head and soft, knowing smile. Were women *born* knowing how to do that?

"I'm not cranky." Frustrated as all hell, he thought, but cranky? No.

"Good then." She lifted the basket. "I brought food."

"You shouldn't be here," he started, then sniffed as a mouthwatering scent reached him. "Fried chicken?" he asked, and took a step closer. The dog barked again.

Turning his head toward the sound, he grimaced tightly. Just what he needed. *Another* intruder into his life. "Where'd he come from?"

"I don't know," Molly admitted. "But he followed me here and he's very sweet."

The dog's lips curled back over its teeth as it snarled at him. "Yeah," he muttered, already accepting the fact that the damn dog was now part of the growing crowd occupying the cabin. "Sweet."

While he and the dog sized each other up, Molly handed him the basket and strolled closer to the rock wall where he'd been working. Staring at it, she spotted a glimmer of something shiny and gasped as she reached toward the thin ribbon of glittering rock, asking, "Is that gold?"

He heard the awe in her voice. Setting the basket down, he moved up beside her, knowing instantly it had been the wrong move to make. She smelled even better than that chicken dinner. Kind of flowery and soft. Behind her back, he indulged himself by lifting one of her long, red curls and running it between his fingers. The silky slide of it across his skin had him wanting, hungering for more.

Molly felt the heat of him fill her, surround her and it was even more exciting than what she was looking at.

"Yes, ma'am," he said softly, "it is."

"The vein you were talking about," she said, hardly breathing as she concentrated on his nearness, the hard, warm strength of him—so close.

"It's still pretty thin," he told her, then reached up too, his fingers aligning with hers on the rock face. "But I think she's gonna widen up farther along."

At the moment, she wouldn't have cared if a gold nugget the size of the puppy dropped at her feet. All she could feel, all she could think of was Jackson and how much she wanted him to touch her. And then his fingers closed over hers and heat rushed through her body, setting her on fire from the inside out. Slowly Molly turned her face up to his, hoping she'd see what she'd longed to see in his eyes.

His gaze moved over her features as gently, as thoroughly, as a touch.

"Molly," he whispered, his voice a rough scrape of sound against her soul.

She leaned into him, hardly daring to breathe. Lifting one hand to his bare chest, she felt the trip-hammer beat of his heart beneath her palm. Felt the heat of his skin, the soft, black curls sprinkled across his chest. Her throat tightened and a throbbing ache settled low inside her body. Knees weak, she kept her gaze locked with his, waiting for him to admit that he wanted her too. That he was finished trying to ignore her. She saw it in his eyes. She read the flash of desire that he couldn't hide and *knew* that, at last, she would be the wife she wanted to be.

Then Jackson yelped, broke free and looked down to where the pup had sunk its teeth into his ankle. Blowing out a breath, he lifted his gaze back to Molly and she saw clearly that the moment was over. Disappointment welled inside her as he said tightly, "Go home, Molly. And take your protector with you."

Chapter Nine

Stung to her soul, Molly glanced at the dog, said, "Hush!" then turned back to look at her husband. "What do you mean, 'go home'?"

"I mean I don't want you here," he ground out and took a step back for good measure.

"Oh yes, you do, Jackson MacIntyre," she said, closing the distance between them. "You want me here. You want me at home. You *want* me. And you know it as well as I."

"Damn it, Molly," he said, glaring at her again, "this isn't going to happen."

"Aye, it will, be it here or at the cabin, it *will.*"

His jaw clenched and shifted as though he was grinding his back teeth into powder.

"What, then? Do you plan to be married to me for the rest of our lives and never touch?" she asked, her voice dropping when his gaze shifted to her lips. "Never kiss, never—"

"This isn't helping."

"What will help then, you great oaf?" She planted both hands on his sweaty chest and shoved hard enough to back him up a bit.

"Oaf?" he asked, one dark eyebrow lifting.

"Oaf I said—"

"—and oaf you mean," he finished for her.

Her lips twitched despite the anger simmering within. He already knew her so well. "Aye."

"It's no use getting your Irish up," he told her. "Another argument won't change anything."

Her body still humming, her heart still racing, Molly refused to be put off. Not this time. She was through playing this game of his. They were married and she wasn't about to live the rest of her life like a nun. It was like Uncle Michael always said, *Go after what you want, Molly girl, and don't let anything—or anyone stop you.*

"I don't want to argue," she said. "I want what's mine as your wife."

"You don't know what you're asking for," he muttered.

"I do," she said, and took the last step that put her close enough to him to feel the heat rippling off his body. "And I'm not askin', *husband.* This time, I'm *takin'.*" And with that, she went up on her toes and slanted her mouth over his. To give him his due, he managed to hold out against her for almost two seconds.

Then he surrendered to the fires within, grabbing her close, pulling her into him, running his wide, strong palms up and down her back. Molly groaned, glorying in the feel of his desire pulsing in time with her own.

He clutched at her, grabbing fistfuls of her dress and hanging on as if she meant the difference between life and death.

Molly took all he gave and demanded more. She parted her lips for him and took him inside, meeting his caresses with an eager response. Her breath quickened. She wrapped her arms around his neck and held on as he lifted her off the ground, pressing her tightly to him. Her hands flattened against his bare back and she loved the feel of his skin beneath her palms. She wanted to feel him atop her again. Wanted to know the magic she'd known so briefly what seemed like a lifetime ago.

Again and again, his tongue delved into her mouth, like a dying man looking for the key to heaven. And she felt the gates of heaven swing open as his mouth moved from hers to slide down the length of her neck, stopping only at the trim white collar of her dress.

She sighed, tipped her head back to allow him access and stared blankly at the rocks overhead.

"Molly, sweet Molly," he whispered. His breath dusted across her heated flesh, acting like a match applied to an oil-soaked wick.

And Molly had her answer. She smiled to herself and took a hold on the quivering sensations rattling around inside her. His desire staggered her, ignited her own and told her everything she needed to know. Whether her husband knew it or not, he cared for her. And she loved him. She loved the dark corners of his soul, the kind nature he tried to hide and the slow rumble of his voice. She loved his gentleness, his temper and the heart that refused to let him turn his back on a wife he hadn't wanted.

Now all she had to do was help him see that this was meant. That *they* were meant. And to do that, she had to make him want her so desperately, so completely, he wouldn't be able to turn away from her again.

Molly called on every last ounce of self-control she possessed and used it to push herself free of his grasp. His blue eyes glazed with passion, he reached for her and she stepped back, shaking her head.

"What are you doing?" he asked, his voice tight, harsh.

She pulled in a shaky breath, slapped one hand to the base of her throat and felt her pulse beat pounding like an Irish step dancer's quick feet. This bit of torture she had planned for him was going to be every bit as torturous on her. It was hard, she thought, so hard to keep from stepping back into his arms. But she wanted all of him, not just a bit of wrestling in the bowels of the earth.

"I'm going home," she said as soon as she was sure her voice would work. "Just like you wanted me to."

He reached out one hand toward her, then fisted that hand on nothingness and let it drop back to his side. "Now," he said, breath heaving from his lungs. "Now you're going home?"

"Aye," she said, telling herself to walk, and walk fast, before her body overrode her mind and sent her back to him. "I've supper to tend to, and you're busy here."

And leaving him staring after her, she turned before she could change her mind and quickstepped out of the cave.

Jackson watched her go, the pup chasing behind her, tail waving like a tiny flag. And he was alone.

Which was what he'd wanted.

Right?

Every muscle in his body ached.

Jackson groaned tightly as he walked into the clearing and approached the cabin. He'd worked himself near to death, trying to get rid of the tension rippling through his body. Frustration simmered just beneath the surface and he frankly didn't know how much longer he was going to last, standing against the temptation that was

Molly. And he wasn't at all sure anymore that he *wanted* to resist her.

She'd changed so much in his life. What if she was the only one who could change the rest of it? In the past two weeks, he'd felt more alive than he had in ten long, miserable years.

He never would have believed that a stubborn, mean-tempered, soft-eyed woman could make such a difference in his world. Jackson's gaze swept the tree line at the edge of the clearing, seeing the familiar through brand-new eyes. He'd thought himself content. Living here, apart from a world that held nothing for him, he'd made his own place. Here, in the shadows of the trees and in the dark, cold heart of a mine.

But Molly was one thing he hadn't counted on. He'd thought himself dead to wants and needs beyond the easy comfort of a one-night-a-week woman. Yet now, he wasn't so sure and, though that notion sent a ripple of pure, stark terror running through him, there was something else there, too. Anticipation. Desire. Not just for her body. But a desire to have her heart. Her soul.

"Damn it," he muttered, "you're too tired to be thinking straight." He reached up to rake one hand through his hair.

As he approached the cabin, Jackson heard a long growl from somewhere off to his left. Turning his head, he spotted the dog, lying down among Molly's flowers. Blue, red and yellow blossoms tumbled over the animal but didn't quite hide its snarl or its small row of sharp teeth.

Apparently, she hadn't been able to coax the blasted thing into the cabin yet. Which was good, he thought. At least he wouldn't have to be worried about being attacked in his sleep. Scrawny, pitiful-looking excuse for a dog, he told himself. A man should have a big bear of an animal. Something to help guard his house—and his family—when he was away.

His family.

Molly was his family, he reminded himself. The little dog had already proved itself willing to defend her, and Jackson had the teeth marks on his ankle to prove it.

"Maybe you are a bear at that," he said softly, chuckling to himself when the dog only deepened its growl.

He had a wife he couldn't touch, a parrot he couldn't stand and a dog who hated him. His body was hard as granite and his nerves strung as tight as a hangman's noose. "Well," he told himself, "at least things can't get much worse."

He should have known better.

Throwing open the door, he braced for the damn parrot's call. But when it came, he hardly heard it.

Instead, all he heard was his own blood rushing to a part of his body that already held more than its fair share.

"Damn, Molly!" he roared, slamming the door behind him. "What in the hell do you think you're doing?"

She glanced at him over her shoulder and gave him that wide smile. "I'm taking a bath, though I thought you'd be able to figure that out for yourself, Jackson, you bein' such a clever one an' all."

A long, copper hip bath sat smack in the middle of the room, directly in front of the fire, where yet another kettle of water sat heating. And Molly, every naked inch of her, sat in that tub, with frothy bubbles clinging to her bare shoulders, her hair, and floating into the still air every time she moved.

Jackson's mouth went dry. His vision blurred, darkening at the edges, and he realized he was holding his breath. He emptied his lungs and dragged in another greedy gulp of Molly-scented air, drawing it deep inside him.

As he stood rooted to the floor, Molly shifted, half-turning in the tub toward him. He caught a glimpse of milky-white shoulders, bubbles sliding off her wet skin. The water lapped at the tops of her breasts and he fought to find his voice.

"For God's sake, don't move," he ground out.

She laughed and it sounded as frothy as the bubbles sliding over the lip of the tub. Unbelievable. He was dying and she was laughing.

"What in the hell is so funny?" he demanded, his grip on the rifle in his hand tightening until he was surprised the weapon didn't snap in two.

She shook her head and he noticed a lock of her hair clinging damply to her cheek. "If you could see your face, Jackson."

His view was a lot better than hers, he told himself but didn't think it appropriate to say so at the moment. One thing this wife of his didn't need was encouragement. Damn it, how many more ways of driving him insane would she be able to come up with?

"I've left your supper there on the stove," she said, lifting one arm to point, as if he couldn't have found the stove without her assistance.

But he didn't look toward the food she'd kept hot for him. Instead, his gaze locked on her arm, the graceful sweep of it as she moved, the bubbles sliding down the length of that arm, to her chest, her breasts, the water below.

He growled from the back of his throat and she chuckled again, sliding back down into the water.

"Aren't you hungry?" she asked.

His chest tightened. Oh, he was hungry all right, but

not for the chicken and biscuits she'd prepared. And she well knew it.

She lifted one leg high into the air and slowly, gently rubbed a bar of pale yellow soap along her thigh, her calf and then down again. Her hands made long, sweeping strokes across her skin. She caressed her own body for his benefit and Jackson forgot to breathe again. She dipped that leg back into the water and lifted her other leg and he stared, mesmerized by the soap bubbles sliding along her leg to pool on the water's surface, just above her...Jackson's back teeth ground together as he turned his back to her.

He busied himself with hanging his rifle on the rack, shrugging out of his coat and raking both hands through his hair with enough strength to snatch himself bald. But none of it helped. He'd already seen too much. And his mind was taking care of the rest.

Water sloshed and he closed his eyes, imagining her shifting, moving in the water, bare flesh, soap covered, slick, smooth. His hands fisted as tight as his groin.

Damn, he wanted her more than his next breath.

"Hiding, Jackson?" she asked.

That went against the grain. The fact that it was true only added insult to injury. "I'm not hiding," he lied. "Just tryin' to be polite."

"Polite?" She laughed again. "For pity's sake Jackson, we're *married*."

"I know that," he said, swallowing hard.

"Do you now?" she asked, and stood up.

He knew she was standing up even though he was still looking eyeball-to-eyeball with Stew Pot. He heard the water spill onto the floor and he heard her step out of the tub, noticing the slap of her bare feet against the hardwood floor. In his mind's eye, he saw her lush figurc, full, high breasts, narrow waist and rounded hips. He saw the cluster of red curls at the apex of her thighs and knew he'd go on seeing her this way for the rest of his life.

A man's mind was his own worst enemy.

"You can turn around now, *husband,*" she said.

He gave a quick glance over his shoulder and only relaxed slightly when he saw that she'd wrapped a sheet around her body. With her red hair spilling over her shoulder and her skin flushed from her bath, she looked like a Roman queen, wrapped delectably in her toga.

It took everything in him to keep from crossing to her, and yanking the damned sheet off the body he wanted to lose himself in. But in that way lay madness. He knew it, felt it in every inch of his body. Lying with her wouldn't be enough. He'd need to give her his heart as well, and once he had, he'd never be safe again.

"What game are you playing, Molly?" he asked, hearing the rough scrape of his own voice.

She shook her head and took a step closer. "It's not my game, Jackson," she said. "'Tis yours."

That wouldn't wash. If this was his game, there'd be different rules. "What's that supposed to mean?"

"It means, that as you said, we're married. And from here on, I'll be doing all I can to see to it that this marriage is a real one."

"I can't let it be." Despite what he wanted—no, maybe *because* he wanted what she offered so badly, he wouldn't let it happen.

She blew out a breath that sent a red curl lying across her forehead flying to the back of her head. "Why are you fightin' me so on this?"

"I have my reasons," he snapped, biting off each word as if it came with a bitter taste. Those reasons filled his memory and, though the images were blurred now with time, the pain lingered.

"Well, what are they, man?" she said, stamping her foot and only wincing slightly. "Tell me."

"It doesn't concern you, Molly." He looked into her deep green eyes and saw the hurt there. The wounded pride, the shimmer of defeat, but it couldn't be helped.

"Aye, it does. If whatever it is that's inside your head, your heart, keeps us from finding a way to each other, then it does."

"You can't fix this," he said. "*I* can't fix this. Leave it be."

"How can you ask me to do that?"

"I'm not asking you this time, Molly," he said as ice slid across his heart, chilling him to the bone. "I'm telling you."

"But that's the problem, isn't it, Jackson?" she asked. "You're not tellin' me anything." She came closer still.

Close enough that he could see the beads of water still clinging to her shoulders. He wanted to dip his head and drink her in. "But you want me, Jackson. You proved that today at the mine."

"Wanting and loving are two different things." Or so he kept telling himself.

"But what is one without the other?" she asked, and lifted one hand to trail her fingers down his chest. He felt her touch down to the core of him. "'Tis emptiness," she said, answering her own question.

His eyes closed and he struggled for air that wouldn't come. She filled his vision, his mind, his heart, his soul. She was everything and he knew he didn't deserve her. And God knows she'd done *nothing* to deserve him.

Jackson grabbed her hand, closing his fingers over hers and holding on, keeping her from touching him—

and at the same time, he thought, keeping her from leaving him.

"Be careful, Molly."

"Careful of what?"

He squeezed her hand briefly before releasing her.

"Getting what you want isn't always such a wonderful thing."

Chapter Ten

Two weeks flew past and Molly was no closer to solving the mystery that was the man she married. She had, however, discovered something else. One night in Jackson's bed had sealed their marriage—and created a child.

When her courses hadn't arrived on time, she'd put it down to nervousness. But a day passed, then two, then a week and now it was two weeks late and she'd begun to notice other small changes in her body. Like the swirl of nausea early in the morning and the fact that her breasts ached.

Her hand dropped to her still flat abdomen and she wondered about the child within. Would he grow up with two parents who loved each other...or would he instead live in a silent battleground where neither parent would give an inch?

The way things were going, she would wager on the latter. Her plan to win Jackson over wasn't working. Well, it wasn't working the way she'd planned.

Every night, she lay in bed beside him, and every night, he inched away from her. She dressed and undressed in front of him, felt his gaze on her and ended up torturing herself more than him. He escaped her every chance he got, racing to the mine where he could pretend for a few hours that he was still alone. As he so clearly wanted to be.

"I don't know, Captain Blood," she mused aloud, "but I think perhaps I've overstepped myself this time."

"Abandon ship!"

The familiar screech brought a smile to her face even as a glimmer of tears rose up and filled her eyes, blurring the comfortable cabin around her. "Oh," she said, "I'm not quite ready to do that yet."

In fact, she didn't know if she could ever abandon a man who so clearly *needed* her to love him. She saw the need in him. She saw what it cost him to keep away from her. Why couldn't he admit to it? Why did he have to stay so stalwartly alone? Why couldn't he let her into his heart?

It was all she'd ever wanted. A place to call home. A man to love and be loved by. To know that she'd finally found the one place in the world where she *mattered*. Where she was important.

Snatching up a rag, she walked around the small main room, swiping at dust as though she was smacking some sense into her husband's hard head. Before too long, the small cabin was shining clean. She straightened the quilt she'd brought from home atop the mattress, running one hand along the fragile threads and patchwork fabrics. So many dreams had been sewn into this quilt, she thought, remembering all the nights she'd sat up, stitching by lamplight. During those lonesome months when Uncle Michael's ship was at sea, she'd worked on pieces for her hope chest, planning all the while what her married life would be like.

"And not one of those dreams included a husband who won't touch me," she muttered, and walked back into the main room. Snatching up her knitting, she plopped down into a chair and took up the task of finishing the pair of socks she was making for Jackson.

He was gone again, of course. He'd left early that morning, saying he'd be at the ranch all day and didn't know when he'd be home. Her fingers curled around the knitting needles as her hands dropped into her lap.

"What am I to do?" she whispered to the empty room. She couldn't tell him about the baby. Not with the way things were between them, because Molly couldn't bear to see anything less than joy in his eyes. She didn't want their child to be one more "responsibility" he shouldered. There was cold comfort in being the burden so reluctantly borne.

But whether she told him about the child or not, even Jackson was bound to notice in a few months. So she had only that much time to earn his trust. His love. His heart.

And she knew she'd need every moment of it.

Outside, the little dog, which for some reason Jackson had named Bear, barked and growled.

Her heart lifted as she jumped to her feet and tossed her knitting to one side. The little terror only greeted one person that way. Jackson. Hurrying to the window, she looked out and a spurt of disappointment shot through her. Not her husband.

She watched two men—prospectors by the look of them—approach the house. As they neared, Molly recognized one of them. Hardy Phillips, who'd been at the cabin a couple of weeks ago. With him was a big man, nearly as big as Jackson, with a tobacco-stained beard that stretched to the middle of his dirty shirt.

Bear snarled and circled them, displaying a fine set of teeth, but his size made his threat laughable and the bigger of the men kicked out at the dog, spurring Molly into action.

Marching to the front door, she yanked it open and stepped out onto the porch. "Here now," she said, hands at her hips, "don't you be kicking my dog."

"I didn't kick him," the man muttered, then threw the little animal a glare that clearly said he was sorry he'd missed.

"Not for lack of tryin'," she said, then snapped her gaze to Hardy. A welcoming smile died unborn as she looked at him. He seemed…different today than before. He refused to meet her eyes, shifting his gaze instead in a rapid search of the property. As if looking for something. Or someone.

She'd been only a breath from telling him that her husband would be gone all day, but now for some reason, she didn't want him to know that she was alone here. And would be for hours. Inching backward, into the cabin, she heard herself say, "You've come at a good time for a visit, Hardy. Jackson just walked to the creek. He'll be back in a moment or two."

The man finally looked at her and she didn't like what she saw in his eyes. He didn't believe her. She kept talking.

"As I recall, you had a fondness for my beef stew the last time you were here." There. She'd wanted to remind him that he'd been welcomed into this house as a friend. He hadn't struck her then as a bad man, but he did strike her now as a desperate one.

"Don't be scared," he said, instantly bringing fear into her system.

For the first time since moving into this cabin, Molly truly felt—*alone.* There was no one to hear her cry for help. No one to ride to her rescue. No one at all save a parrot, a dog too small to defend her and a husband determined to stay far away from her. So whatever would be done, would be done by herself. The question was, she thought frantically, *what?*

"Let's get this over with," the other man grumbled, flicking a glance at the still-growling Bear.

"Step aside, Molly," Hardy told her, and walked into the cabin, forcing her backward. Their steps sounded overly loud in the tiny room and, for one stunned moment, she simply watched them as they ransacked her home. Tossing furniture out of their way, they rummaged through drawers and cabinets, tapped on the walls and stomped on the floor. The big man moved into the bedroom, lifted the mattress off the bed and looked beneath it.

"It has to be here," Hardy said, glaring at Molly. "Tell us where it is and we'll get out."

"Where what is?" she asked, backing toward the stove. "What is it you're lookin' for?"

"The gold," the other man said, stomping into the room.

"What gold?"

"Jackson said he found a vein," Hardy reminded her. Molly thought back to that night, when they'd thought they were dining with friends.

"And you're thinkin' to steal from a man who fed you at his own table?" she asked, her gaze boring into his. Anger roared to life alongside the fear and slowly choked it back.

"Keelhaul the bastard!" Captain Blood called out, and Molly was inclined to agree.

"What the hell?" The big man stared at the parrot.

"Run 'im through," the bird yelled, and waved its red and green wings in alarm.

"Shut it up!" the big man shouted.

"Leave him alone," Molly shouted right back at him. *"Lower the dinghy! Abandon ship!"*

"I'll shut it up," the man vowed, reaching for the parrot.

"Keep your bloody hands off my bird!" Molly warned him even as Captain Blood lifted off his favorite perch—Jackson's gun rack—and swooped around the room, shouting curses and swiping at the air with his claws.

Furious now, Molly reached behind her for the first thing she could find and came up with an iron skillet. Brandishing it over her head like a claymore sword, her shriek of outrage rang out with Captain Blood's and Hardy ducked as she came at him.

He wasn't quite quick enough though and she caught him a glancing blow that sent him staggering, one hand clapped to his jaw. She pushed past him, shoving him into the table. The edge clipped the backs of his thighs and he toppled over, smacking the back of his head against the tabletop hard enough to roll his eyes.

"Serves ya right," she snapped, and, with blood in her eye, went after the big man still chasing her parrot. She'd be blasted to hell and back if she'd let two such hooligans enter her home and destroy all she'd worked for.

Captain Blood dipped and swayed about the room, diving at the bigger man, swiping his claws across the top of the man's head and coming away with a hank of hair. The man bellowed his fury and chased the parrot right out the door into the yard, gold apparently forgotten in his anger and pain. Molly was just a step or two behind him when she saw the man pause long enough to kick Bear's side as the little dog jumped at him.

She howled and charged.

Jackson couldn't stay away. Damn it, he'd tried. But the ranch held no interest for him. And he couldn't bear to spend time at the mine anymore. Not since the day Molly'd brought him dinner and then kissed him until he'd forgotten his own name. She'd shattered the peace he'd always found there in the dark quiet. Now, instead of seeing threads of gold in the damp rock, he saw the gleam in her green eyes and her full lips, pursed for a kiss, or stretched into a wide smile that haunted him.

Shaking his head, he came down the path from the mine—he hadn't been to the ranch. He'd only told Molly that in an effort to prevent another surprise visit. But the real surprise was, he missed her.

And as he neared the clearing, he heard her scream.

The sound was like a knife to the heart. Cold rushed into his veins and settled in the blackest pit of his soul. And before that scream could die away, he was running. Racing into the clearing, he spotted the parrot, swooping out the open cabin door in a flurry of green and red feathers. Right behind it came a big man, shouting curses and making futile grabs at the bird. Bear streaked out of the flower bed and the man kicked the little dog, sending it spinning off to one side where it lay still in the dirt. And right behind that man was Molly.

Eyes wide, her cheeks stained with the blush of fury, she chased after the man who was twice her size, swinging a skillet as if she meant to take his head off. And that was good enough for Jackson.

A fierce rush of pure hatred caught him in its grip. Like nothing he'd known since the war, Jackson gave himself over to it, counting on his instincts to save her, to crush what would threaten her. Wild-eyed, a haze of red blurring his vision, Jackson hurled himself at the intruder. Taking him down to the ground. Jackson straddled the big man's chest, took a handful of dirty shirt and plowed one huge fist into the man's face. But even the satisfaction of watching the fella's eyes roll back into his head wasn't enough to smash the fury raging inside. He hit him again and heard the gratifying sound of bone snapping. And with that last blow, the man passed out and Jackson lifted his head like a wild thing scenting the air, searching for another target. His gaze swept the yard, landed on Molly and the frenzied rush of violence left him as quickly as it had come.

He scrambled off his opponent and ran to where she knelt beside the little dog.

Turning her face up to his, she wiped tears off her cheeks with the backs of her hands and asked, "Is he dead, Jackson?"

He shook his head. "No. I broke his nose for him though."

"Not *him,*" she said, her tone conveying how little she cared about the fate of the man lying unconscious not ten feet from them. "I meant Bear. Is he dead? He's not movin' and, Lord help me, I can't look closer."

While she kept her face turned, Jackson ran his hands over the little body and surprised himself with the relief he felt as he noticed the quick breaths heaving in and out of the tiny chest. The little dog had courage, he thought, and he silently vowed Bear would always have a home there on the mountain. When the dog curled its lips back and snarled at him, Jackson chuckled tightly, feeling the last of the rage die away. "He's fine. Winded is all."

"Oh, thank heaven," she muttered, reaching to stroke

the dog's head. "Ah, you're a fine, strong boy, aren't you? Tried to save me, didn't you?"

"You shouldn't have needed saving," Jackson muttered, throwing a quick look at the man lying in the dirt behind them.

She followed his gaze and laid one hand on his forearm, drawing his attention. "Hardy Phillips is out cold in the cabin."

"The son of a bitch," he snarled, pushing himself to his feet. "You stay with Bear," he told her, and ducked as Captain Blood swooped in a low arc in front of him. "And catch that damn bird. I'll take care of these two."

Molly watched him stalk off, and thinking of the wrath glittering in his pale blue eyes, she almost felt sorry for the two men.

Almost.

Jackson stared down at the men stretched out on the stable floor. Bound hand and foot, and then roped to each other, they wouldn't be going anywhere. And they wouldn't be bothering Molly again, either. Just thinking about what might have happened if he hadn't come home was enough to stir his blood into a raging, burning need for vengeance.

Hardy Phillips opened his eyes and looked up at him.

"You came after my *wife*," Jackson said tightly, staring down into the eyes of a man he'd thought he knew.

Hardy worked his jaw, squirmed uncomfortably and said, "I didn't want her. Wanted your gold."

"You're a lucky man, Hardy," he whispered past the knot of emotion clogging his throat. "If she'd been hurt, you'd be dead. Touch her again and I *will* kill you."

As he left the stable, he didn't hear the other man's sigh of relief.

* * *

"Scrape the barnacles off her hull," Captain Blood screeched.

"And that's just to start with," Molly grumbled, while righting a tumbled chair. She'd already cleaned up most of the mess. But wiping away the stink of those men was more difficult. They'd come into her home. And who knows what might have happened if Jackson hadn't—

"Molly…"

She whirled around at the sound of his voice. His features were tight, drawn and his eyes shone with banked fires. He stepped into the room, closing the door behind him.

"The men—"

"Don't matter," he said, walking toward her in long, purposeful strides.

"Jackson…"

"No more talking, Molly." He took her face in his hands, his palms warm against her cheeks. His gaze raked her features as if reassuring himself that she was safe. Unhurt. "For God's sake, Molly, no more talking."

Then he bent his head and took her mouth with a fierce hunger that stole her breath and sent her heart galloping. His fingers speared into her hair, holding her head still, while he plundered her, branding her with his touch, his taste.

Molly reached for him, not caring what had brought him to her, only knowing that at last, she was with him again. That finally, he'd seen they belonged together. She wrapped her arms around his waist and held him to her, as if afraid he might pull away.

But then he scooped her up into his arms and marched for the bedroom, never taking his mouth from hers. His hands moved quickly, feverishly, as if he couldn't wait another moment to feel her skin beneath his.

In seconds, he'd stripped off her clothes, torn off his own and laid her on the bed. His hands were everywhere. Her breasts, her thighs, her...Molly gasped, arching her back, digging her head into the pillow. Eyes wide, she stared up into her husband's face and read the wild passion shining in his eyes. For her, she thought, all for her. She gave herself up to him, running her palms up and down his back, over his chest and up to the face of the man she loved.

He dipped his head, taking first one nipple then the next into his mouth. She sighed and twined her fingers through his thick black hair, holding his head to her. "Oh, Jackson love, that feels..."

"You taste like heaven, Molly," he whispered, his breath dusting across her skin, sending shivers to every inch of her body. "I've wanted you so long. So much."

"I want you too, Jackson, so much it shames me."

He lifted his head and stared down into her eyes. "There's no shame here, Molly. Only need."

And love, she wanted to say, but then he cupped her center, dipping one finger into her depths and her mind emptied. He worked her body, touching, caressing, exploring. His fingers moved in and out of her warmth and Molly rocked her hips with the rhythm he set. She clutched at his shoulders, whispered his name and rode the first crest of pleasure.

Jackson watched her eyes glaze, and the soft moan that escaped her throat set him on fire all over again. While she was still trembling with release, he shifted position, covering her body with his and, in one swift, sure stroke, pushed himself home. Her damp heat surrounded him and he groaned at the simple, wonderful glory in it. Here was home, his mind screamed, and though he couldn't allow himself to admit it, he knew it was true.

His gaze caught hers and, staring down into those forest-green eyes, he gave her all he could. All that was left of the man he once was.

Chapter Eleven

He knew why it had happened. He just wasn't sure what to do about it now.

Jackson stared up at the ceiling and only half listened as Molly talked. She was so happy, he thought, not knowing that any minute now, he was going to ruin it all. Put them right back where they'd been before he'd given in to the rush of emotion driving him since he'd seen her in danger. Pain rippled through him and Jackson clenched his jaw against it. Pain he could deal with. Pain he was used to. It was the other feelings rocking him that he couldn't handle. Easing his arm out from under her head, he sat up and swung his legs off the bed.

"Jackson?" she asked, reaching for him, tracing her fingertips down along the column of his spine.

Desire grabbed at him again and he stood up quickly, before he could give in to it.

"Where are you going?"

He chanced a look at her and was grateful she'd tugged the sheet up high enough to cover her breasts. One more look and he might not be able to do what he had to do.

"I'm taking those two into town."

"Now?" Surprise flickered in her eyes and was quickly replaced by suspicion. "Why now? This minute?"

"Molly—" he started, snatching his pants off the floor.

"You're not." Her voice sounded ominous.

"Not what?"

"You're doin' it again, aren't you?" She came up onto her knees, twisting the sheet free of the mattress and yanking it tight around her body.

Grinding his teeth, he said only, "I'm doing what I have to do."

"Leavin' me," she supplied. "Pretendin' again that you don't want me. Don't need me."

He bent down and stomped into his boots. Straightening up again, he said, "I can't give you what you want, Molly."

She pushed her hair back away from her face and narrowed her green eyes. "You can," she accused. "You just *won't*. And I think I've a right to know why."

Jackson's chin hit his chest. Nodding slowly, he slanted her a look and said, "Yeah, you probably do."

"But you're not goin' to tell me."

"No," he said, grabbing up his shirt and tugging it on. "I'm not."

Stalking across the room, he was almost through the door when her voice stopped him. One hand tightened on the doorjamb. His knuckles whitened as he waited.

"I won't do this time and again, Jackson. I won't be used and then set aside again."

He looked back at her over his shoulder and his heartbeat staggered at the raw, furious beauty of her.

Gripping the sheet in one fist between her breasts, she clambered off the bed, caught her foot in the sheet and stumbled a bit before righting herself. She swung her hair back out of her way, lifted one hand and stabbed the air with her index finger. "I'll not be your floozy, Jackson."

"What?" The word came out small, tight.

But she wasn't finished. "You don't treat me as your wife. I'm your trollop and what's more, you don't even have to pay me for a visit."

"Oh," he told her in a heartfelt groan, as his gaze slipped to the swell of her breasts, "I'm paying."

She saw his gaze slip and folded her arms across her chest in self-defense. "Are you so blind you can't see what I've offered you? Can you not see that I lo—"

"Don't say it," he said quickly, cutting her off before she could finish the word that would tear what was left of his insides out.

Molly sucked in a gulp of air and blew it out again. Her chin quivered and her lower lip trembled, but she didn't cry. And that hit him harder than a flood of tears would have.

"I'm sorry, Molly. God knows I'm sorry." Then he left, while he still could.

After a sleepless night alone in the bed—Jackson slept on the floor in the main room after returning from town and for the first time in their marriage, she didn't follow after him—Molly hitched the horse to the wagon and set out herself for town.

Her husband had left before dawn. "Back to his cave," she murmured, and the horse tossed its head in sympathy. Well, while he was tucked away in the shadows of his mine, Molly was determined to find some answers to the questions plaguing her. And those answers could be found in only two places. Jackson—who wasn't talking.

Or Lucas.

Defiance bustled in the early morning light. Merchants washed windows and swept the boardwalk. Horses, wagons and buggies rattled along the street, oblivious to the shoppers who took their lives in their hands, darting in and out of the crowd.

But Molly hardly noticed. She guided the horse toward the saloon and stopped directly in front of the place. Throwing the brake on, she climbed down off the bench seat, only catching the toe of her shoe in her skirt hem once. Jumping off the wheel onto the boardwalk, she looped the reins over the hitching post and headed for the closed door to the saloon.

Grabbing the latch, she yanked open the door, then pushed the inner bat-wing door out of her way and walked into the shadowy bar. She stopped dead to give her eyes a chance to adjust to the change of light. She didn't want to take a chance on tripping over a chair or crashing into a table. Not in her condition.

"Molly, hello!" Emily's voice came out of the shadows.

She blinked and stared hard at the couple across the room from her. Lucas had stopped swinging his wife around in a circle but still held her, close to his chest, her feet high off the ground. Both of them were looking at her and Emily was the first to react. Laughing, she pushed at her husband's chest and said, "Put me down, Lucas."

"Not likely," he told her, and planted a loud, smacking kiss on her cheek. Then to Molly, he said, "Congratulate me, Molly! I'm a father!"

"Not quite yet," Emily reminded him with a soft smile.

"Close enough," he said, grinning, and set her on her feet as gently as though she were made of glass.

"That's grand," Molly managed to say even as envy stirred inside her. "I'm happy for you both." This is what she wanted from Jackson. Joy. Love. Lucas and Emily had found their way to each other's hearts. A marriage that had started out as a business deal had grown into something wonderful. Was it so wrong to want the same thing for herself?

Her stomach churned unexpectedly and Molly grabbed the back of the closest chair to steady herself. Whether it was the child within, her own fatigue or the welling sadness inside her, she felt suddenly, incredibly weak. Instantly Emily crossed the room, took her arm and ordered, "Sit down, Molly. You don't look well."

She rubbed her forehead directly between her eyes and murmured, "I didn't sleep well, that's all."

Emily's expression clearly said she didn't believe that for a minute. She shot Lucas a quick glance, then said, "I'll get you some tea. You just sit for a moment. Catch your breath."

"Aye, I will. Thank you." She was tired, in body and soul.

Chair legs scraped along the floor and Molly looked at Lucas as he took a seat beside her. So much like her husband and yet so different, she thought. Their eyes were much the same, though it appeared to her that Lucas's clear blue gaze seemed less troubled than in the past. Less shadow-filled. She only wished she could say the same for Jackson's.

"So," he said, his voice low and friendly, assuming rightly that she'd long since forgiven him for his trickery in bringing her to Colorado. After all, if he hadn't, she'd have never met the man she loved so much. "Is my brother to blame for putting that sorrowful gleam in your eyes?''

She swallowed hard, took a breath and then folded her hands on top of the table. Guilt pooled in the pit of her stomach, but she fought it down. This is why she'd come here today, she reminded herself. It was no time to be feeling squeamish about wringing information out of Lucas.

''Why won't he love me?'' she murmured, feeling a hot flush of shame creep up her neck to fill her cheeks.

Lucas sighed. ''That stupid son of a bitch.''

''He's not stupid!''

Chuckling, he asked, ''But son of a bitch fits?''

Now she sighed and shook her head. ''He cares for me. I know he does. But he won't admit it, won't let himself love.''

''He does love you, Molly. I can see it in him. He nearly killed those men for bothering you.'' Lucas shook his head, leaned forward and covered her hands with his. She clung to him. ''It's just—''

''Just what? How can I fight what I don't know? Tell me, Lucas. Help me.''

He looked at her for a long, silent moment. She heard the muted sounds of Defiance filtering through the shuttered windows, but her attention was focused on the man who held the secrets she so needed to know. Indecision flickered across his face and was gone again in an instant.

''He should have told you this himself,'' he said finally, and started talking. As she listened, Molly felt the world slip out from beneath her feet.

Molly was packed and waiting by the door when Jackson came home. She watched him walk up the path toward the cabin, sunlight splashing on his head and shoulders. Outlined against the trees, he stood as tall as the mountain he claimed as his home and Molly knew she would always see him like this. This one moment stolen out of time would live in her mind forever.

And then he crossed the yard, opened the door and stopped dead on the threshold. Snatching his hat off, he looked from her to the stuffed carpetbag at her feet and back again. Scowling, he demanded, ''What's this about?''

''This is about the end of us,'' she said sadly. ''You should have told me about your wife, Jackson. About your *son*.''

He drew his head back as though she'd slapped him. And the hurt in his eyes stabbed at her, reflecting her own. Molly's heart ached and she felt as though there were a crushing weight on her soul. Her hopes and dreams lay shattered around her and all she had left was this one last chance to hear the truth from her husband's own lips.

''Who told you?'' he asked, the tight, harsh words scraping the air like a razor blade.

''Doesn't matter,'' she said with a slow shake of her head. ''It wasn't you and it should have been.''

''Lucas,'' he said to himself. ''Had to be.''

''Will ya leave it alone, man?'' Molly snapped. ''All that counts is that you lied to me.''

''How do you figure that?'' he asked, clearly stunned.

''You let me think—'' She stopped, took a breath and said, ''Tell me about her. Tell me now.''

Jackson looked down at her, into the green eyes that swam with tears she refused to spill. He hadn't meant to hurt her. Hadn't meant to care—or to make *her* care. How in the hell had this all gotten so out of his control?

He tossed his hat onto the table and it landed beside a small canning jar filled with flowers. He sighed to himself, ran one hand through his hair and wished he were anywhere but there.

"You already know the story," he said, and heard the low growl of remembered pain shimmering in his own voice.

"Tell me," she said again. "This much, at least, you owe me."

Did he? he wondered, then acknowledged silently that she was right. If he couldn't allow himself to love her, she at least deserved to know why.

"I was away," he said, before he could change his mind, "fighting on some battlefield...doesn't matter which one. They were all alike. Dark. Bloody." He sighed and scraped his face with both hands. Shooting Molly a quick look, he walked to the window and stared out at the gathering night. "Eliza and me, we had a small place in Missouri. She'd grown up around there. Wanted to move back when we got married." He flashed Molly another slanting look in time to see her wince, and her pain slashed at him.

"Anyway...Eliza got sick. Influenza, they said." The view stretched out the window, shifted, blurred and became another place in another time. He stared down the path of memory and waited for the ghosts to rise. "She died. She'd been dead almost six months by the time I got word. Our boy was only about a year old."

"Jackson..."

He cut her off. He didn't know what she might have said, but he was too caught up in the past now to let it go without looking at all of it. "The Hartsfields, our neighbors, they took Jesse in to care for him until I could get back." His hands curled around the windowsill and squeezed until he thought the wood might snap, and still he didn't let go. "Two years later, the war was over and I went to collect my son." He turned his head to look at her. "Jesse didn't know me," Jackson said, feeling the stab of that ancient pain as if it was freshly given. "No reason why he should, I guess. But he cried, Molly. He cried when I picked him up."

"Ah, Jackson…" Sympathy rang in her voice and he steeled himself against it.

"So I left. The Hartsfields loved him. He was happy there." A shudder passed through him and was gone again. "I haven't seen him since."

"I'm sorry," she said.

"I don't need your pity," Jackson told her stiffly. "It was over and done ten years ago. It's in the past."

"No, it's not." Molly stared up at him and, though her heart broke for the misery and pain he'd suffered so long ago, a part of her wanted to shake him. "You're still there, Jackson. In the past. With Eliza. With your son."

"You don't know what you're talking about." He whirled away from the window, stalked across the room, turned around and came right back again, looming over her like an avenging angel.

She didn't flinch. "I do, to my own regret, I do know. You're so busy living in your past, mourning what you lost, you can't see what you have…or *could* have."

"I didn't *want* a wife, remember?" he shouted, giving in to the age-old rage frothing inside him. "All I wanted was to live out my life. Alone."

Furious, Molly planted both hands on his chest and shoved. But it was like trying to push a mountain. He didn't move an inch, just glared down at her.

"You're *not* living, Jackson!" she yelled at him, trying one last time to reach him. Before it was too late. Before she left him forever and whatever they might have had was lost. "You're existing. You're...taking up space in a world you no longer want and doin' nothin' with it. The sad truth is, you're buried as deep as your past. You just don't know it yet."

His jaw worked, his eyes narrowed and he swallowed hard before saying, "You don't understand. You don't know."

The wind went out of her sails, as Uncle Michael would have said. Her heart reached out to him, but he didn't want it. Or her.

Snatching up her carpetbag, she clutched it and the secret of their child close and looked into his blue eyes for one last time. Lifting one hand, she cupped his cheek and tried not to care that he winced as if her touch burned. "Ah, Jackson," she said softly, tiredly, "until you can put the past where it belongs, you'll never really be alive." Her thumb stroked his cheek. "I know you desire me, I can see it in your eyes. But you don't love me as I'd hoped you would."

"Molly—"

"But I love you, Jackson," she interrupted.

His whole body jerked as if he'd been shot. Air wheezed in and out of his lungs.

"And that's why I'm leaving," she continued, her tone brisk now in an effort to keep the tears at bay. "I can't share a house and a bed with a man who doesn't love me."

She stepped around him, walked to the door and opened it. Captain Blood flew to her shoulder and perched there. Pausing on the threshold, she looked back at him one last time, but he didn't turn. "Take care of yourself, Jackson. For me."

Then she was gone and emptiness crashed down on him.

Chapter Twelve

He'd never known a night to last so long.

Jackson moved through the cabin, restlessly pacing as he had been since Molly had walked out the door yesterday. The damn place felt huge. And empty. Only the day before, he might have said the cabin was too crowded, with Molly's relentlessly cheerful chattering and the goddamned bird's cursing.

But now...he glanced at his gun rack and found himself wishing Captain Blood was sitting there glaring at him out of beady little eyes. "Stupid," he muttered fiercely. "I *hate* that bird." And yet, his brain taunted, wouldn't another voice in this place sound good about now?

"No," he said aloud, and only worried a bit that he seemed to be arguing with himself. A man alone was bound to be a little peculiar from time to time. And alone wasn't an entirely bad thing to be. He'd been alone before she came. And he'd been happy...well, content anyway. He sucked in a gulp of air and said, "I will be again, too." As soon as he could forget the sound of her laughter, the quick spark of temper in her green eyes and the feel of her body wrapped around his during the night.

Shouldn't take more than a hundred years or so.

"Damn it!" he hollered. There was no one to challenge him. She was gone and yet, somehow, she was still here, too. In the flowers on the table. The quilt on the bed. The half-finished sock dangling from the knitting needles she'd left behind.

That's what was making this so hard, he told himself. She'd left so much behind, it was bound to remind him of her. And though that sounded like a good enough argument, he knew it wasn't the truth. Not all of it.

Disgusted, he crossed to the door, opened it and stepped out into the night, looking for the peace he couldn't find in the cabin. The wind sighed through the trees. Sunrise streaked the sky with slices of pink and yellow and a deep, full red that reminded him too closely of Molly's hair. His first day without her, he told himself, and flinched as a black, empty hole opened up inside him at the thought. How would he do it? he wondered. How would he ever survive the rest of his life, knowing he'd never be with her again? He dropped to the porch and sat down, forearms braced on his knees as he stared out blankly at the tree line and the forest beyond.

His mind raced, though, refusing to let him rest. Refusing to let him ignore what was right in front of him. Image after image of Molly rose up in his brain, forcing him to remember. That wide smile of hers, which had taken his breath the first time he saw it. Her laughter. Her off-key singing. Her temper and dogged determination to drag him back into life.

"So much," he whispered, his voice instantly swallowed by the emptiness around him. "She gave me so much and now she's taken it back." Knowing that he'd deserved nothing less didn't make him feel any better.

A rustle of sound from the flower bed had Jackson

scowling more fiercely. The dog. No doubt Bear wanted his shot at chewing on Jackson's hide. Well, perfect. A dog bite would just about complete this miserable night.

Bear slunk out of the flower bed, and stopped, looking up at him. Jackson held his breath, waiting for the up-curled lip. The sharp little teeth. The deep-throated growl of dislike.

But instead, the tiny dog walked slowly forward, keeping its ears cocked as if expecting to be kicked and wanting a good chance at escape just in case. When it reached the steps, it lay down in the dirt and slowly rested its head on the toe of Jackson's worn boot.

Something cold and hard gripped his heart and Jackson stared into two soulful brown eyes that seemed to be asking, *Where is she? Why did you let her go?*

"She saved you, too, didn't she?" he asked, and carefully reached down to stroke the dog's head. "Just like she saved me," he admitted at last. And with that acknowledgement, his heart started beating again—a loud, hard pounding in his chest—and Jackson felt a rush of blood through his veins and drew his first easy breath all night.

"She was right," he said, needing to hear the words aloud. Needing to say them. "Damn it, she was right about *everything*. Hell, I've lived more in the past month than I have in the past ten years."

The dog's ears quirked and Jackson nodded. "You were right, too," he said. "And I'm gonna go get her and bring her back. Where she belongs. With us."

Bear barked once when Jackson stood up, but he paid no attention. There was one last thing to do. Tilting his head back, he stared up at the morning sky and whispered, "Goodbye, Eliza. Look after Jesse for both of us."

Then leaving his past behind, he raced to catch up with his future.

"The stage left early," Lucas said, disgust clear in his tone.

"Early?" Jackson gripped the saddle horn and twisted one way, then the other, checking the street as if still expecting the stage to be there. Somewhere. "Why the hell did it leave early?"

"Does it matter?" Emily asked pointedly. She stared at him with both hands at her hips and a no-nonsense gleam in her eye.

"Yes, it matters," Jackson said. "I've got to talk to Molly."

"Haven't you said enough already?" his sister-in-law demanded. "What could you possibly add?"

"That I'm an idiot," he snapped. Then giving the reins a sharp jerk, he turned the horse toward the road out of town and took off like a shot.

"Well," Emily mused as her grinning husband dropped one arm around her shoulders, "at least he knows what to say."

The stagecoach hit yet another rut in the road and Molly's head snapped back, smacking into the wood and knocking her hat forward, over her eyes. "For pity's sake," she mumbled, pushing the hat up again.

"Yep," the older man opposite her commented, "these roads are a *disgrace* to the stage company. Ought to get someone out here to fix 'em."

The tall, thin bespectacled woman beside her nodded agreement and launched into a detailed explanation of just why the East was so much better than the West.

"Rocky shores, rocky shores," Captain Blood called out from the inside of his rocking cage.

But Molly didn't care about the condition of the road. She didn't care about the blossoming knot on the back of her head. The screaming pain in her heart dominated everything. Turning her head, she stared out the narrow, paneless window and said a silent goodbye to Colorado and the man she loved.

"Hey there!" a voice shouted from somewhere behind the stage. "Hold up! Hold up, damn it!"

"What is that?" the woman beside her whispered, her hand at her throat. "A holdup? Did he say this is a holdup? Are we to be robbed?"

"That's what I heard, too," the man said, and leaned out the window for a look. Drawing back inside the coach, he said, "There's a rider back there. Comin' hell for leather, 'scuse me, ladies, and he looks almighty big and mean."

The driver bellowed suddenly, "Hang on, folks! We'll make a run for it!"

And the stage lurched forward, throwing all three passengers into each other and off their seats. Captain Blood batted his wings against the cage, screeching curses. The ladies struggled back into their seats while the older man rummaged in his carpetbag and came up with a pistol. Spinning the chamber, he smiled to himself and leaned out the window again.

"You damn thief!" he shouted, and fired off a round. "There's ladies present, damn you!"

Molly clutched at the door frame, eyes wide, and listened as that voice called out again, closer this time.

"Damn it, quit shootin' at me! Hold up there!"

"Jackson?" Stunned, she leaned out her side of the coach and, even from a distance, she recognized the big man hunched low over his horse's neck, waving his hat in the air like a madman. He had come after her! Drawing back inside the coach, she noticed her fellow passenger preparing for another shot and dove at him, pushing his arm, ruining—she hoped—his aim.

"Lord love us, lady," the man exclaimed, "you made me drop my gun!"

"That's my husband!" she shouted in her own defense, then reached up to pound on the roof of the coach. "Driver, stop the coach!" She had no idea what Jackson was up to, but a part of her was already quickening with hope.

The stage rolled to a stop, its leather hinges creaking in the suddenly still air. Jackson reined his horse in right beside the blasted thing and shot the driver a venomous glare as he swung down. But he wasn't here to yell at fools. He was here to collect his wife.

Yanking open the stage door, Jackson leaned inside and was met by a chorus of complaints.

"What's the meaning of this?" sputtered the angry man who'd shot at him.

"You can't have my jewelry," shrieked the woman, who looked at him as if he was the devil himself.

And Jackson ignored both of them, locking his gaze on Molly. God, she looked wonderful. Hat askew, hair tumbling around her shoulders from her wild ride, cheeks flushed and those golden freckles of hers damn near sparkling at him. He'd never seen anything more beautiful in his entire life. "I have to talk to you," he said, staring into her forest-green eyes.

She shook her head. "We've said all there is to say."

"Not by a long shot," he muttered, and, despite her protest, reached into the stage, grabbed her around the waist and dragged her outside.

But once she was on her feet again, she pushed away from him, tipped her head back and said, "You've no right to stop me, Jackson. I'm leavin' and that's the end of it."

A half smile tugged at the corner of his mouth. Damn, but he'd missed that temper. What had ever made him think he could live without her? Then shifting his gaze to the driver, sitting hunched on the bench seat, he called out, "Throw me down the lady's bag."

"Don't you do it," Molly ordered the man, who stopped moving when she spoke.

"Throw it down," Jackson called again and, when she would have shouted, he cut her off, saying, "I'm taking you home, Molly."

From inside the coach, Captain Blood yelled, *"Man overboard! Abandon ship!"*

Jackson laughed and reached past her for the birdcage. Hauling it out, he looked at the damn parrot and muttered, "I never would have believed I'd miss you."

"Nothing's changed, Jackson," Molly said quietly, tearing his attention away from the bird. "I won't go back to the way things were. I won't live with a man who doesn't love me."

He sighed and set the birdcage down gently. Looking into her face, he saw the pain in her eyes and cursed himself for ever bringing her a single tear. She'd given him so much and, in return, he'd taken her heart and thrown it away. And silently he made a vow to everything he held dear that never again would he give her cause to grieve.

Cupping her face in his palms, he stared down into the eyes that would haunt him forever and said the words he should have said so long ago. "I *do* love you, Molly."

Her quick intake of breath hit him like a fist in the gut and the sheen of tears filming her eyes finished him off.

He'd been such a fool. Someone upstairs had been looking out for him, had sent him a second chance at happiness. And he'd almost missed it through his own blindness. His gaze moved over her features as he prayed desperately that he wasn't too late. "I think I've always loved you."

More than anything in her life, Molly wanted to believe. But she had to ask, had to know. "What about your past? Your other family?"

Jackson sighed, a fading sorrow briefly flashing across his face. "I'll always regret not being able to know and love my son, Molly. That will probably never go away."

She nodded, understanding that pain and realizing his first child would always be there in his heart. And that was as it should be.

"But I'll love the children we have together, Molly, and I'll treasure each one of them—whether God sends us one...or twelve." His hands moved on her face, his thumbs stroking the tears away from her cheeks, his gaze moving over her features. "As for Eliza," he continued, and she held her breath. "She was my first love. But, Molly," he said, willing her to believe. Willing her to see what was in his heart and hoping she still wanted it. Wanted him. "Molly, *you* are my last love. You're my future. My heart."

Her own heart burst. It was the only explanation for the sweet, full ache in her chest. Molly stared up into his blue eyes and read the truth there. He loved her. He wanted her. And that was more gift than she'd ever dreamed of.

Here at last, she'd found her place. Here, with this man, she'd found her love.

Smiling through her tears, Molly reached up and wrapped her arms around his neck. He inhaled sharply, reeling with the relief of knowing she was still his. That he still had a chance to love her. To revel in the love she had for him.

His arms closed around her, holding on as if she meant his life—and she did. Bending his head to the crook of her neck, he inhaled her scent and felt it warm him down to his bones.

"Well, little lady," the driver called out, clearly impatient to be on his way, "you comin' with me or goin' with him?"

Molly didn't let go of Jackson. She just turned her head and grinned at the driver. "I'm goin' home." She looked back at the man holding her and added, "With my husband."

"Crazy dang females," the man muttered, and grabbed her carpetbag and tossed it onto the ground. Then he snapped the reins and the horses took off, sending a cloud of dust into the air.

"Thank God for crazy dang females," Jackson whispered just before he kissed her, long and hard and deep, showing her without words just how much he cared. How much she meant to him.

And when he finally lifted his head, he smiled down at her slightly dazed expression and asked, "Why'd you leave all your things at the cabin, Molly?"

She blinked at the unexpected question, but the answer was simple. "Because none of it was mine anymore. 'Twas *ours*. It all belongs at the cabin now."

"Like you," he said softly, cupping her face in the palm of his hand.

"Aye," she agreed with a smile and covered his hand with hers. "Like me. Now take me home, husband. I've a surprise for you."

"Molly, as long as I have you, I'll never need anything else."

"Ah," she said, giving him the full force of her wide, beautiful smile, "but our baby will be needin' you."

Jackson just stared at her for a long moment, while the realization of just what she was saying sank in. A child? *Their* child? Oh God, what he'd nearly missed through his own pigheadedness. Humbled and grateful beyond words, he gathered her close, pressing her to his heart, where she would always remain.

"I love you, Molly Malone MacIntyre," he whispered, his voice soft and low and filled with promise. "Forever and then some."

Molly nestled her head on his broad chest and listened to the steady drum of his heart, counting each strong beat as a blessing. He loved her. There were no doubts, now. She felt his love surround her, fill her, and Molly knew the child within would grow strong and proud and loved and, no doubt, as stubborn as his father. She silently thanked her lucky stars and whatever fate had led her to this man. And aloud, she said, "Forever and then some, Jackson MacIntyre."

"Steer for home, matey," Captain Blood screeched. *"Safe harbor!"*

Jackson threw his head back and laughed. Then, one arm still around Molly's shoulders, he said, "Good idea, Stew Pot. Let's go home."

* * *

MONTANA MAVERICKS HISTORICALS

Discover the origins
of Montana's most popular family...

On sale September 2001
THE GUNSLINGER'S BRIDE
by **Cheryl St.John**
Outlaw Brock Kincaid returns home to make peace with his brothers
and finds love in the arms of an old flame with a secret.

On sale October 2001
WHITEFEATHER'S WOMAN
by **Deborah Hale**
Kincaid Ranch foreman John Whitefeather breaks all the rules when
the Native American dares to fall in love with nanny Jane Harris.

On sale November 2001
A CONVENIENT WIFE
by **Carolyn Davidson**
Whitehorn doctor Winston Gray enters into a marriage of
convenience with a pregnant rancher's daughter, only to
discover he's found his heart's desire!

MONTANA MAVERICKS

RETURN TO WHITEHORN—WHERE LEGENDS ARE BEGUN
AND LOVE LASTS FOREVER BENEATH THE BIG SKY...

Harlequin Historicals°
Historical Romantic Adventure!

TRAVEL TO A LAND LONG AGO
AND FAR AWAY WHEN YOU READ
A HARLEQUIN HISTORICAL NOVEL

ON SALE SEPTEMBER 2001
THE MACKINTOSH BRIDE
by **Debra Lee Brown**
A young clan leader must choose between duty and desire
when he falls in love with a woman from a rival clan.

THE SLEEPING BEAUTY
by **Jacqueline Navin**
A fortune hunter enters into a marriage of convenience
to a beautiful heiress with a mysterious secret.

ON SALE OCTOBER 2001
IRONHEART
by **Emily French**
A brave knight returns from the Holy Land and
is mistaken for a noble lady's betrothed.

AUTUMN'S BRIDE
by **Catherine Archer**
FINAL BOOK IN THE SEASONS' BRIDES SERIES.
When a nobleman is wounded by brigands, a young
woman loses her heart while nursing him back to health.

COMING SOON...

AN EXCITING
OPPORTUNITY TO SAVE
ON THE PURCHASE OF
HARLEQUIN AND
SILHOUETTE BOOKS!

*DETAILS TO FOLLOW
IN OCTOBER 2001!*

YOU WON'T WANT TO MISS IT!

PHQ401

HARLEQUIN®
Makes any time special ®

Silhouette®
Where love comes alive ™

*Harlequin invites you
to walk down the aisle . . .*

To honor our year long celebration of weddings, we are offering an exciting opportunity for you to own the Harlequin Bride Doll. Handcrafted in fine bisque porcelain, the wedding doll is dressed for her wedding day in a cream satin gown accented by lace trim. She carries an exquisite traditional bridal bouquet and wears a cathedral-length dotted Swiss veil. Embroidered flowers cascade down her lace overskirt to the scalloped hemline; underneath all is a multi-layered crinoline.

Join us in our celebration of weddings by sending away for your own Harlequin Bride Doll. This doll regularly retails for $74.95 U.S./approx. $108.68 CDN. One doll per household. Requests must be received no later than December 31, 2001. Offer good while quantities of gifts last. Please allow 6-8 weeks for delivery. Offer good in the U.S. and Canada only. Become part of this exciting offer!

**Simply complete the order form and mail to:
"A Walk Down the Aisle"**

IN U.S.A	IN CANADA
P.O. Box 9057	P.O. Box 622
3010 Walden Ave.	Fort Erie, Ontario
Buffalo, NY 14269-9057	L2A 5X3

Enclosed are eight (8) proofs of purchase found in the last pages of every specially marked Harlequin series book and $3.75 check or money order (for postage and handling). Please send my Harlequin Bride Doll to:

Name (PLEASE PRINT)

Address   Apt. #

City   State/Prov.   Zip/Postal Code

Account # (if applicable)   **097 KIK DAEW**

◆ **HARLEQUIN®**
Makes any time special ®

Visit us at www.eHarlequin.com

*A Walk Down the Aisle
Free Bride Doll Offer
One Proof-of-Purchase*

PHWDAPOPR2

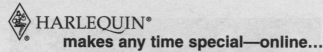

Two very different heroes. Two very different stories.
One gripping and passionate reading experience!

NIGHT AND DAY

A unique 2-in-1 from

HARLEQUIN®
INTRIGUE®

featuring editorially connected stories by:

ANNE STUART

and

GAYLE WILSON

Michael Blackheart and Duncan Cullen are as
different as **NIGHT AND DAY**. Yet they share a goal—
and neither man can imagine the dark world that
such a quest will take them on.

Available in November 2001 at your favorite retail outlet.

HARLEQUIN®
Makes any time special ®